PRAISE FOR ON WAHOO REEF

"*On Wahoo Reef* is entertaining from beginning to end, with effervescent characters, humor, and grit. Five shining stars!" – **Stephanie Elizabeth Long for Reader Views**

"Another gem from Tim W. Jackson. It's obvious he's worked in the dive business in the Caribbean. On Wahoo Reef is a great and fun read!" – **Jerry Beaty, Associate Publisher, Dive Training Magazine**

"A great story with good pace and dialogue, enigmatic characters who are easy to like, and a refreshing feel-good element. Recommended." – **The International Review of Books**

"The latest in the excellent Blacktip Island series. Another great, rollicking tale by Tim Jackson." – **Simon Pridmore, author of the Scuba Series**

"Lighthearted, with interesting characters and funny dialogue. Jackson has done a great job. Once you start reading, you can't stop until the end." – **Manhattan Book Review**

"Captivating and immersive, On *Wahoo Reef Reef* reminds us of the power of friendship and the resilience of the human spirit." – **Jill Heinerth, author, *INTO THE PLANET - My Life as a Cave Diver***

ON WAHOO REEF

A BLACKTIP ISLAND NOVEL

TIM W. JACKSON

Devonshire House

Devonshire House Press
P.O. Box 195682
Dallas, TX 75209

Copyright © by Tim W. Jackson 2024

All rights reserved. No part of this book may be reproduced or distributed in any printed or electronic form without written permission, except in the case of brief quotations embodied in reviews and critical articles. For information about permissions, please contact the publisher.

This is a work of fiction. Names, characters, places, and incidents are either the product of the author's imagination or are used fictitiously. Any resemblance to actual persons, living or dead, business establishments, events or locales is entirely coincidental. The publisher does not have any control over and does not assume any responsibility for third-party websites or their content.

ISBN: 978-1-7351136-4-7

Library of Congress Control Number: 2024901630

Book formatting and cover design by www.ebooklaunch.com

Acknowledgements

Thanks to the many people who helped with this one along the way:

To beta readers extraordinaire:
Debi Belasco
Joe Goellner
Cindy Sullivan

To *The Blacktip Times*' faithful readers for their continued enthusiasm.

To Kay Russo, as ever, for her great editing. I'm still being trained in Oxford commas.

To Dane Lowe, again, for the phenomenal cover art.

To Craig Wiger for somehow making me look not-so-awkward in the author photo.

To Jocelyn Tucker for the timwjackson website updates.

And, of course, special thanks to my wife, Jana, for her support and for always believing.

The Big Chicken is an actual, bright red, 60-foot-high structure, with rolling eyes and an opens-and-closes beak, towering over a KFC on the corner of Cobb Parkway and Roswell Road in Marietta.

Chattahoochee kit foxes are an utter fabrication.

"Repeated encounters with sharks of all species, or hearing of these encounters, may lead the uninitiated to believe the shark is an overgrown bully or coward and easily scared off, but such is not always the case."

> - *The New Science of Skin and Scuba Diving,* Revised Third Edition, Association Press, 1968

1

The Blacktip Haven great room looked like a boat yard had exploded in it, and Wally Breight, his round, cat-like face in its permanent smile, was in heaven. Orange life rings and faded green fish nets and begrimed boat fenders hung from white-painted rafters. The dark-wood-and-brass bar was wrapped with lacquered ropes of varying size, overhung with nautical signal flags and crowned at either end by head-sized channel marker lights—one green and one red. In the room's center was a random assortment of worn, yellow nautical-themed couches, armchairs and a pair of beanbag chairs, filled with post-scuba-dive guests, drinks in hand, all babbling at once about the eagle rays and sharks and triggerfish they had seen on the reefs that day.

At the bar, Wally sipped his bourbon, ran a hand through his shaggy, reddish-brown hair, still unruly from the day's dives. An empty lowball glass sat on the bar beside him, courtesy of happy scuba divers—his happy scuba divers. He had brought them down from Big Chicken Divers in Marietta, Georgia, a small dive shop in the shadow of the fanciful sixty-foot-tall chicken perched atop a fried chicken outlet on U.S. 41, which served as an area landmark, and they were celebrating the end of a great week on Blacktip Island. As the group's leader and organizer, Wally had spent a week herding them around the little Caribbean island's reefs by day and entertaining them around the bar by night. It was a lot of work, but it had its perks, among them free diving, lodging, and food for the week. The next day was their final diving day. The guests would fly back to Atlanta the following morning, giving Wally a day to enjoy the island on his own before heading home, too.

Leading these groups for the dive shop had become second nature, his de facto vacations. As ever, his mind drifted to how he could turn it into a full-time gig, leading dives during the day, shooting the breeze over drinks in the evenings, and never having to go back to an office or traffic or stress. Or shoes. But you didn't just walk away from a career-track job with benefits. No matter how miserable that job got. Was getting. Was. Yes, time on Blacktip was the life. He just needed to figure out how to get more of it.

At the far end of the room, Elena Havens, the resort's owner, was holding court, looming, pale and gaunt, over the seated guests, booming out bits of island gossip and tall tales about her life. She had bought the resort and moved down from Montreal years before. Wally imagined himself in her place, regaling the room every night with stories—true or not. A Jackson Browne song started from speakers behind the bar.

Elena tossed her head twice, pulled her gray-streaked black hair back out of her face so it flowed mane-like down her back. She turned a complete circle, her sleeveless, tie-dyed dress sweeping across the dark wood floor planks, bare feet, with orange-painted toenails flashing. Making sure everyone was watching her. She studied the gathered guests, blue eyes bright, her thin, pale arms waving for emphasis as she launched into her next story.

"I'm the 'warm and tender mystery,' you know." She scanned the guests, waiting for recognition. "Jackson wrote 'Under the Falling Sky' about me."

She said it casually, as if it were an idle thought, though Wally knew it wasn't. She swung her arms wide, taking in the entire lounge and bar area, a queen ensuring all eyes were on her.

"*And* 'Our Lady of the Well.' We were together in Jamaica at the time, so I'm fairly certain I'm 'Jamaica, Say You Will,' too."

Guests' mouths hung open. Several smirked, not buying the tale.

Wally smiled. He heard the story every time he brought Big Chicken groups to Blacktip Haven, and it grew with every telling.

"He's the one who came up with *Calypso Aru* as the name for The Haven's dive boat. I introduced him to J.D. Souther, out in Laurel Canyon. And a doe-eyed, young girl singer named Linda."

The dubious guests rolled their eyes, chuckled. Elena grinned. She knew her audience, and the hook was set. She pointed to one of the chucklers, motioned for him to stand.

"Here, get that photo album down for me."

She pointed to the top shelf next to the bar. Puzzled, the man lifted the thick, spiral-bound notebook down and handed it to Elena. She grinned again, a cat playing with an unsuspecting mouse, and flipped open the yellowed cover. She thumbed through several pages, then set the book on the coffee table in front of the man. He stared for a moment, and then his eyes widened. He stared from the page, to Elena, then back again.

Wally knew the photos the man was looking at. He himself had been the unsuspecting mouse his first time here. The man was standing open-mouthed, eyes scanning four black-and-white photos with lacey white edges, of a twenty-something Elena by the Troubadour club stage beside Jackson Browne and Linda Ronstadt.

"She telling the truth?" Janine, one of Wally's divers, settled onto the bar stool next to him, tucked her curly, dark hair behind her ear, brown eyes on his.

"About *all* of that? I doubt it." Wally laughed. "But she *does* have the photos."

Janine laughed, too. Waved a thin finger at his nearly-empty glass.

"Another?"

Wally paused. A drink with Janine was tempting. He could get used to this attention, too. But he was working and couldn't afford to be hung over. Plus, getting involved with clients usually got messy.

"Thanks, but I have dives to lead in the morning." Wally finished his drink and, slid the glass across the bar.

"Tomorrow, then." Janine smiled, eyes lingering on his. "After diving."

Wally said nothing, slipped out the lounge's back door, careful not to distract from Elena's performance. Above, the stars glowed like a sequined bowl. Among the trees, small yellow lights flashed, fireflies echoing the stars.

The next morning Wally led the twelve Big Chicken divers around The Pinnacle. The thin limestone spire, blackened by weather, rose from the ocean depths at the island's northern point, breaking the surface and extending up 100 feet into the air. Underwater, The Pinnacle's sides were clustered thick with giant barrel sponges, long green strands of wire coral, and clumps of black coral, looking like underwater fern groves. Janine at his side, Wally led the group 100 feet deep, then slowly spiraled his way shallower, pointing out hawksbill turtles, a free-swimming green moray eel, a school of black-and-yellow gobies in a brown barrel sponge cleaning a brown-banded Nassau grouper.

In the shallows Wally found them a nurse shark with its head under a ledge, pairs of black-and-yellow French angelfish, and multiple lionfish, the Indo-Pacific invasive species wreaking havoc on Caribbean reef fish populations.

Back on the boat, several divers told the crew about the lionfish.

"Y'all need to go down there and spear 'em," Brady, a bank manager from Woodstock, said. "That's what they do in Cozymel. And the Keys. Save the reefs from 'em."

"We don't spear *any* fish," Booger the captain said. Tall, thin, with dreadlocks to his shoulders, he towered over the divers.

"Elena's policy. All th' other dive ops do, though. We'll get word out. Somebody'll get 'em."

The second dive was a shallow reef, near the public pier. Wally again led the group along long coral fingers, showing them gray stingrays in the sand, jut-jawed blue-scrawled filefish hovering nose-down beside purple sea fans, a spikey brown burrfish resting motionless in a green coral bowl. And more lionfish.

A sadness washed through Wally. This was the last dive of the trip. His last dive anywhere for a while. After a day off tomorrow, it was back to Atlanta and his public relations job from hell. He pushed that from his mind, and concentrated on enjoying what time he had left on the island. He was almost successful.

At dinner that night the divers were still talking about lionfish.

"Tons of those things on the reef today," Janine said. "I don't understand why y'all won't cull them. You should see the divemasters in the Caymans go to town on them."

"We live and let live here at The Haven." Elena Havens pulled up a chair, joined them at the table "We're a sanctuary of peace and keep negative thoughts to a minimum. That includes killing fish, no matter what kind."

"Seems like that's taking 'eco-friendly' too far," Brady the bBank manager said. "Everybody else just kills 'em. Toot-sweet."

"We don't kill anything here." Elena gave Brady a daggered look. "We run a 100 percent eco-friendly operation and won't tolerate reef crashing or fish harassing or actions of any kind that might have a negative impact on the reef. That's why we require you to use coral-safe sunblock. Here, the fish aren't just friends. They're our family."

Wally smiled at the exchange. He had heard this speech before, too. It was familiar, a well-worn family argument during the holidays.

"Well, what about the fish we eat every meal?" Brady said.

"*That* we ship in from the U.S. There's no killing done *here*. We don't eat family."

Wally wandered to the bar for another glass of wine. Elena followed him.

"You seem down tonight," she said. "Lionfish got you bummed?"

"No, no. It's . . . just I wish I didn't have to leave."

"You say that every time you're here."

"Yeah, but this time I mean it." Wally ran a hand though his too-long hair. Work had kept him so busy he hadn't had a chance to get a haircut for more than a month. "My job . . . I've about had it. I'm *so* tired of running interference for a bunch of yahoos and their damn foxes."

"Foxes? You lost me . . ."

"Chattahoochee kit foxes. Endangered in north Georgia. The Pan-Appalachian Wildlife Society raised money to buy land to save their habitat. I've been taking flak for PAWS for the last nine months, with no days off."

"For saving foxes?"

"For killing fish." Wally took a deep breath, dived in. "Chattahoochees are little mini-foxes. They need open grassland and love rolling hills. PAWS raised enough money to buy either a too-small bit of suitable open land or big swath of forested land totally unsuited to the foxes. Some brain-dead committee opted for the big swath. Then they chopped down all the trees to create open grassland. Environmentalists went ballistic."

"I'll bet." Elena looked horrified.

"Then it rained. A lot. With no forest to retain the rainwater, mud from the runoff flowed downstream, into the 'Hooch, then into the Apalachicola River, clogged it, and wiped out a major Gulf sturgeon breeding ground. The whole southeastern U.S. is out for blood. That's when PAWS hired the company I'm with to . . . ameliorate the situation. I'm good, but how in the world do you spin that positive? I mean, they're paying me well, until the fines and legal fees and lawsuits wipe them out, but I'm exhausted. Leading these groups is one of the few bright spots in my life. There needs to be more of this and less of that. I'd stay here in a heartbeat if I thought it could pay the bills."

"It'd certainly give you a cleaner conscience."

"That, too. You wouldn't happen to need an investor or another dive guide, would you?"

"No to both." Elena laughed. "You'd be surprised how often I get asked that. And life down here, running a resort and a dive operation, is rougher than most people realize. Something's always breaking, or going wrong, and on an island this small, you better be able to handle all that yourself. While you're down looking at the pretty fish, we're running around like chickens with our heads cut off trying to keep everything running smoothly."

Jessie the chef wandered past, long brown hair tucked in a neat bun. She nodded agreement, winked a gray eye at Elena.

"I'd take that over facing the Coastal Conservation Association and the Gulf Fishery Management Council attack dogs."

"Well, it's good to have a daydream." Elena patted his shoulder, and walked back to the guests, shaking her head.

Wally wandered out to the pool and stared at the diamond-bright stars, too depressed to try to mingle with a roomful of gabby divers. Or Janine.

The next morning, he said goodbye to the guests, waved at the Blacktip Haven van rolling down the two-rut track leading to the main road and the airstrip farther up the coast. After he saw the twin-engine Islander bank right over the resort, headed for Tiperon, he borrowed one of the resort's rusty one-speed beach cruisers and headed down the track to explore the island on his own, hoping to lift his spirits. He pedaled north, past the island's other resorts on the west coast, past the island's lone store, and the now-deserted airstrip, then on past the big cement public pier. Farther than he had ever explored on Blacktip, mind already sorting through what he needed to do first back at work.

North of the pier, the road turned west, then north, then back east in a broad sweep, The Pinnacle 100 yards offshore, from this angle looking like an eroded obelisk. He passed a low wooden building at the water's edge, roadside sign declaring it the 'Tail Spinner Restaurant and Bar.' Past that he was surprised to find a ring of weather-worn bungalows, all built in different styles, seemingly at different times, with whatever building materials happened to be available. In their center was a larger building, screen porch along one side, looking as if it had once been the heart of a resort. Crushed-stone pathways lead around the central building and out to each cottage like spokes in a wheel or strands of a giant spider web. 'Noboddie's Inne' was stenciled in flaking red letters on the building's side.

Beyond the bungalows was a small wooden dock, a blue twin-engine boat bobbing beside it, protected from the waves by a fringing reef. Near that was a low, cinderblock building. Peeling teal paint over the building's door read, 'Going Under Divers.' Wally coasted to a stop, leaned the bike against a palm tree, and wandered over for a closer look.

"Lookin' for a room?"

The voice boomed out in the island lilt Wally had grown to love, startling him. In a rolling, bow-legged gait, a man stepped from the central building. He had a dark complexion and closely-cropped, gray-flecked black hair. Torso short and round, with thin arms and legs seemingly too long for his body. Threadbare shorts and a faded blue Spider Man t-shirt.

"No, No. Just exploring." Wally stepped toward the resort buildings to meet him halfway. "Never wandered up here before. Didn't know there was another resort on the island."

"Nearly ain't." The man laughed, setting his belly bouncing. "Business dyin' off. And what guests we do get, they don't stay long." He held out his hand. "Vinson Noboddie."

"Wally Breight." Wally forced himself not to comment on the man's last name. "Why don't they stay?"

"Can't dive." The man pointed to the boat tied to the dock. "Boat needs parts. Parts cost money. Owner can't afford 'em.

Truth be told, he lost the taste for the business. When folks dive somewhere else, they stay somewhere else."

"What's wrong with the boat?" Wally walked to the dock, with its lone palm tree, wondering how anyone could lose the taste for diving. The boat needed a coat of paint and some cleaning, but otherwise looked in good condition. '*J-Valve*' was scrawled in orange cursive script down its side.

"One of those engines broke. Can't run through the reef safe with one engine."

"So . . . the owner'd just need someone to pay for repairs and drive the boat for him . . ."

A plan was forming in Wally's head, a plan so perfect he was almost afraid to say it out loud. Worst case, he would buy an entirely new engine. And he could learn to drive a boat. How hard could that be? He'd watched it done enough. And working outside, he could lose some weight.

"Just." Vinson laughed again. "Yeah, just that."

"And if there were someone who could get the boat operational again . . . and could take out your guests, that person could revive both businesses."

Vinson's eyes narrowed, sizing Wally up. A bemused smile crept across his face.

"A person *could*. Not enough guests come through my place to keep him—or her—in business for long, though."

"Not a problem," Wally said. "The person I'm thinking of is great at public relations. Owns part of a dive shop. Brings divers down all the time. Could even double the number of groups coming down. And *his* partner'd be happy to send them."

Wally had savings. He could sell his car and condo. And his shares of Big Chicken Divers, such as they were. Hank, the other owner, wouldn't mind. The Going Under Divers owner couldn't want too much for this little shack and boat.

"Don't know why anybody'd do that, sight unseen." He squinted at Wally again, scratched at the stubble on his cheek. "Back in the day, though, it *was* a grand life."

"I've seen it. It looks perfect! A little sprucing up, some fresh paint, and it'll be great!"

Vinson grinned at that.

A parrot squawked overhead. Wally looked up to see a pair of them, green with red cheeks, in the palm fronds, and blue sky behind them. Like something from a travel poster.

"Ol' Smackie's two staff'd be happy to have jobs again," Vinson said. "Problem'll be who your Tiperon partner is."

"Why do I need a partner?"

"Law. Any business got to be at least sixty percent owned by a Tiperon citizen."

"So . . . I'd need someone to put up sixty percent of the cost?" Wally raised his eyebrows at Vinson, gave him a knowing smile.

"Oh, I don't got that kind of money," Vinson chuckled.

"The current owner?"

"Done with divin'. He gets a reasonable offer, he'd sell today."

"And there's no way around the partner rule?"

"Usually's just a paper partnership. With the expat shoulderin' all the expense and the local taking a cut of the profits."

"People sign on for things like that?"

"Only folks who wanna have a business here."

"Okay. So, what's the best way to find a partner?" Forty percent of the profits and all the expenses was brutal, but if that was the only way to get the operation running, it would be worth it. The money would come.

"Most folks on Blacktip who wanna be in the dive business're already in it." Vinson stared across the lagoon. Smiled. Made a sound between a snort and a laugh. "Ferris Skerritt's always game for a business venture, but he can be a wily one."

"Wily doesn't matter," Wally said. "I just need that paper partner. Me and the staff'll handle the daily running of the place."

"Ferris may be your huckleberry, then. Just watch the i-dots and t-crosses on anythin' you sign. And don't tell him I sent you. He's a suspicious sort, and we don't always see eye-to-eye."

"And you're good with me running the diving business?"

"Boat needs repairs I don't got money for. Needs staff I don't got money for, either. No dive op to pull folks in, I got to sell my cottages. So, yeah, you, anybody, restartin' the dive op'd be win-win. 'Sides, I run a hotel, not a dive boat."

"Any way to look at the place's books, see what kind of business they did?"

"Oh, sure," Vinson said. "Smackie gave me the keys so I could look after the place."

He went to the central building, came back with a set of keys, and led Wally to the tiny dive shop. Several small brown spiders scuttled across the white tiled floor when the door swooshed open. More hung from high rafters. Wally brushed three off the counter.

"Don't worry 'bout them," Vinson chuckled, "They the security system."

The computer wasn't password protected, and soon Wally was scrolling through the Going Under Divers financial records. 'Smackie' the owner had pulled out most of the funds, but the records showed a steady income and reasonable expenses before he shut the place down.

"This looks like a damn-viable business," Wally said. "Why'd he give it up?"

"Got tired of livin' on this little rock. Less than 200 people, not a lot to do. That, and diving's a rough life. Takes its toll, physically." Vinson winked at Wally. "Makin' more money now on Tiperon, doing less work."

"How do I get in touch with him, see if he wants to sell, what he wants for the place?"

"Oh, he wants to." Vinson chuckled again. "I give him a call right now."

Moments later Wally was talking to Smackie Bottoms. Yes, Smackie wanted to sell the operation, from the boat down to the paperclips. Yes, it had always been a good business, but he was getting too old to run it, and none of his kids wanted anything to do with it. Or Blacktip Island. After some brief haggling, he and Wally had a verbal agreement. He would send papers to Wally in the U.S., and Wally would wire money to Bottoms' account on Tiperon. It happened so fast, so naturally, Wally had to sit, regain his bearings after the man hung up.

"Guess you got you a dive business," Vinson said.

"I guess I do." Wally ran his hand through his mop of hair. Once he had the big stuff settled, the details would fall into place. And he wouldn't need a haircut as urgently as he had thought. "Now, where do I find this Ferris Skerritt?"

A half hour later, Wally was sitting at the Sandy Bottoms Beach Resort bar, pitching his off-the-cuff business plan to a pale, older, potato-faced man with a bulbous nose, pocked, and riddled with crimson spider veins, and eyes that could have come straight from a taxidermist's workshop. His thinning, too-black hair was swirled back across his skull, and his boney shoulders jutted underneath an oversized polo shirt. His hands, on the bar top, were delicate things, long and thin and covered with liver spots, with untrimmed yellow nails like ragged talons.

"Oh, I'm perpetually interested in, ah, little bits of business." Skerritt spoke slowly, jaw barely moving, his words slipping past his teeth in a series of hisses so low Wally had to lean in to hear him. "Such enterprises keep me occupied."

"Well, this would help the island, too," Wally said.

"I do try to . . . reciprocate with the community whenever possible." Skerritt's lips parted in something between a smile and a grimace, revealing uneven teeth as yellow as his nails.

"I have the funds for the purchase. And startup expenses. I just need a Tiperon partner. On paper. You'd get the standard percentage of the profits."

"An arrangement of that nature could be, ah, amenable," Skerritt hissed. With every, 'ah,' he opened his jaw wide, as if he wanted to swallow the bar and everything in it. He picked his nose with a yellowed claw, then wiped his finger on his pink shorts as if Wally wasn't there. "Benefit all concerned. We'll need to draw up papers, make things . . . legal. For the authorities. How long are you here?"

"I leave in the morning. Could you overnight the papers to me in the States?" As frail as Skerritt looked, Wally wondered if he would live long enough for the sale to go through.

"I'll get the, ah, ball rolling this afternoon. We just need to allow time to have them drawn up . . . properly. Boilerplate, but with a few scuba-specific wrinkles. We'll do the standard Blacktip Island handshake deal for now. All that's necessary on this little island. Paper contract's just a, ah, formality. For the authorities."

Skerrit held out his hand. Wally took it. It was cool, sweaty, limp, as if Skerrit had handed him a gutted mackerel. Skerrit smiled his yellow-toothed smile again. Wally let go after a second.

"I'm at Blacktip Haven. And on the 10:15 flight tomorrow, if you can get things finished that soon."

Wally pedaled back up the coast toward Blacktip Haven, smiling. Despite Vinson's warning, Skerrit had seemed fine. Socially awkward, perhaps, and a bit fawning, but nothing like the shark Vinson had made him out to be. With a vocabulary and gift of gab Wally appreciated. And there would be plenty of time to look over any contract before he signed it.

That afternoon at Blacktip Haven, Wally fought to keep his excitement hidden. He was about to own a dive charter company. On Blacktip Island. His dream job. Leading dives all day. Relaxing in a hammock by the sea, book in hand, in the evenings. But he needed to keep it to himself until the deal went through. Until he had a chance to sort things out with Hank at Big Chicken, free up the money he had invested there. He sized up the new guests in the Haven's great room, imagined himself entertaining them the way Elena did.

"You'll break your face, grinning like that."

Elena had sidled up next to him.

"It's been a good week," he said.

Elena studied him, eyes questioning.

He had to tell someone. And he needed to let Elena know before he moved down, since they'd be neighbors now, part of the same small community. Friends who could help each other when needed. He took a deep breath, lowered his voice.

"Look, this has to stay just between the two of us . . ."

"Oh, of course." Elena leaned close, gray hair brushing against Wally's arm. "That's the Blacktip Island motto, you know. Everyone says it; no one abides by it."

"You know that rundown dive shop up by Noboddie's Inne?"

"Going Under? That went under? Sure."

"I'm buying it. With a local partner and everything. It's a dream come true!"

Elena could have been playing poker, her features stayed so blank.

"You sure you know what you're getting into?" she finally said.

"The financials look good, and Vinson seems a good sort. It'll be a rough ride at first, sure, but I'll be doing what I love. Having an adventure. For the love of the game, you know?"

"Oh, it'll be a rough ride. Who's your Tiperon partner?"

"Ferris Skerritt. He's drawing up the papers now."

Elena's expressionless face didn't change.

"You sign anything yet?"

"I'll go over it with a fine-tooth comb." Wally chuckled. "Don't worry about that. I'm not as dumb as I look."

Elena gave him a dubious look.

"Divers are a limited resource on an island this small," she said. "You have a plan to attract more?"

"I have an idea or two percolating in the back of my head. Having Noboddie's Inne'll help draw them."

"You'll get some pushback from other dive ops is what I'm saying."

"Oh, I'll sprinkle rose petals. How much animosity can there be in a place like this?"

Elena grunted and walked to the gathered guests.

The next morning Wally leaned back on the splintered airstrip bench, hands behind his head. He had a Tiperon partner and a contract in the works. Vinson had given him a list of needed boat parts to ship down, and a promise he would talk to someone named 'young Harry' about making the repairs. Things were falling into place nicely. He smiled while watching the twin-engine Islander bounce down the grass landing strip, taxiing to the shack that served as a terminal.

He was about to start a new life in paradise. Despite Elena's warning. Sure, the boat work would be physically demanding, but that was part of the attraction. He had been sitting behind a desk for far too long, nose to the grindstone, and wasn't getting any younger. Besides, he would hire staff to do most of the heavy lifting while he manned the dive shop and led dives.

He would sit down with Hank at Big Chicken Divers as soon as he got back, catch him up on what was happening. If he didn't want Wally's share of the dive shop, he would know someone who did. Yes. This would be perfect. Things would work out. They always did.

2

Wally sat in his study two days later, calculator and a notepad covered in figures in front of him. By selling his stake in the dive shop, his car, and the condo he could buy Going Under Divers without touching his savings, and have a little left over for expenses. And with the numbers he had seen in the company's accounts, he would start making back that investment the first week if he could even half-fill the boat.

He thought about keeping his U.S. savings account open, then swept that idea aside. Keeping the account meant he thought he might have to come back, that the business might fail. He wasn't about to start this venture filled with doubt. This scuba operation would be bursting with optimism from the get-go. He would close out his savings account, get a cashier's check to take to Blacktip Island with him. That would give him a cushion until business started rolling.

He would keep the company name, dubious as it was. Past guests would recognize it, would be loyal to the brand, would flock back to Going Under Divers once they found out it was running again. The boat name would stay the same, too. And he had heard changing a boat's name was bad luck. He didn't necessarily believe that, but he wasn't taking any chances. He wanted all the positive energy he could get.

The first order of business, to see if this plan would work, was to make sure Hank O'Connell would buy him out. Hank had been joking about buying Wally's share of Big Chicken

Divers for years, and the store's dive groups would be critical to Wally's Blacktip Island success. Wally crossed his fingers, drove to the dive shop. He found Hank, small, chubby, with jet-black hair and bushy moustache, ensconced in the back office sorting through regulator parts.

"Hank-O!" Wally beamed at his friend, bouncing slightly on his toes. "Have I got news!"

"You still drunk from your trip, Wally?"

"I might be."

"I've already had calls. Guests're raving about it."

Hank pointed to a chair. Wally waved him off, too excited to sit.

"You know how you've been wanting to find new places in the Caribbean to send our divers? Someplace you know they'll be treated first class?"

"What've you got in mind?" A hint of suspicion crept into Hank's voice.

"How about a new place in the Tiperons? On Blacktip?"

"I thought things went well at Blacktip Haven." The suspicion in Hank's voice turned to worry.

"Things went great. You said it yourself. The guests are happy and Elena's . . . Elena. But I might have an even better operator. One guaranteed to treat our divers the way we'd treat them ourselves."

"There's only a handful of charter companies on Blacktip, and we know them all." The suspicion was still there. "What's this magical company I've never heard of? Rainbow Unicorn Beach Resort?"

"Little dive op called Going Under Divers. One boat, small groups, you'll love the new owner."

"Sounds vaguely familiar . . . Wally, what are you up to?"

"I'm buying the place, Hank. Or am about to. As soon as you buy me out of Big Chicken."

There was silence. Hank sat frozen, eyes locked on Wally. Then one eye twitched.

17

"You thought this through?" he said. "Startups are tough, especially in the dive business. In another country."

"It's a turnkey operation with a ton of loyal past clientele," Wally said. "Add the divers you'll send down, it's a no brainer. I'll be trading I-75 rush hour for a hammock on the beach."

"I'd love to buy your shares, but I need to make sure you're dead set on doing this. That you know what you're doing."

"Never been surer of anything. It's the chance of a lifetime. And it fell into my lap. Like it was meant to be!"

"What if it doesn't work out? You gonna be back up here wanting your piece of the pie back?"

"Nope. I'm all in on this. If not now, when?"

"And your well-paying, career-track job? With health insurance and paid vacations and 401(k)?"

"I'm done with that. I'm just now realizing I stayed there a couple years too long. A simple business like this, with outdoor, physical labor on a beautiful tropical island, it's just the thing to snap me out of my funk."

"Well . . . then, yeah. We'll sort out the brass tacks. And sending divers down'll be an easy sell since most of 'em know you. There's a group going to Blacktip next month. I'll send 'em to you. Elena's okay with all this?"

"She thinks I'm biting off more than I can chew."

"I mean about our divers going to you instead of her."

"We didn't get into details, but I don't see why she'd mind. We've always gotten along great. The Haven's become almost a second home for me. She'll be a great resource. An ally. I get the impression once I'm on the island and mixing with the locals, she'll probably help out a lot."

"All right, then. Let's you and *me* talk financial details."

The next week was a blur of activity for Wally. He quit the public relations firm, passing off the Chattahoochee foxes and dead sturgeon nightmare to some other schmuck dumb enough to take the project. He rolled his 401(k) into an IRA, then set about ordering all the engine parts Smackie said he needed. He scanned the list: heat exchanger, exhaust riser, turbocharger, coolant reservoir. He wasn't sure what some of them were, or exactly what they did, but if they were on Smackie's list, Wally bought them and shipped them off. Vinson had found 'young Harry' the mechanic, and Wally wired money to pay for his time doing repairs. With luck, the *J-Valve* would be operational by the time Wally was back on Blacktip.

Partnership papers From Ferris Skerritt arrived by express courier. Skerritt was as good as his word—everything looked good, exactly as they'd discussed. Wally skimmed over some of the minor points, especially toward the end of the thick document. All was as it should be. Papers arrived from Smackie Bottoms, too, with terms of the sale. That looked good, as well. Wally signed everything and sent it all back, with a note saying he would wire the money to Smackie as soon as Hank's transfer cleared the bank. The deal was falling into place perfectly.

Wally's next call was to his buddy Chuck, the realtor, to list the condo. It was a nice place, in walking distance of the Marietta Square's bars and restaurants, and would go for a good price. He would sell his car, too, but that could wait until right before he left.

"This seems awful sudden," Chuck said when Wally told him about moving to the island. "You sure you want to just up and go like that?"

"Never felt better about anything in my life," Wally said. "Should've done this years ago."

"Seems like you'd want a fallback in case things go belly up. I mean, I'd love to handle the listing, and it'll sell pretty damn quick. But me? I'd wanna have a safety net, some sort of cushion if things don't work out."

"That's exactly the kind of negative thinking that'd hamstring this whole venture from Day One if I gave into it. Nope, I believe in myself. And in Going Under Divers. Don't need a safety net 'cause I'm not gonna fall."

"Well, I wish you'd sleep on it."

"Already have. Tell you what—come on down in a month or two and check the place out, see for yourself what a dream it is. The white sand, the palm trees, the blue water, it's paradise. With parrots! Little green-and-red ones! You'll love it."

Wally spent the next day sorting through what he would take to the island, pushing aside any thoughts of something going wrong, the deal not going through. Most of his things he would leave behind. Some things he threw out. Others he hauled to the Salvation Army in several runs. He would leave the furniture and other big stuff, and Chuck would hire out an estate sale. In the end, he ended up with three medium-sized piles on the spare bedroom floor. One pile was scuba gear, hoses and gauges and fins and neoprene all jumbled together. The next was basic supplies for him and the dive shop for the first week or so. The final and smallest pile was a stack of shorts and t-shirts—how many clothes would he need on a tiny tropical island, anyway? He added two polo shirts for dressy occasions, then added a sweatshirt and a pair of jeans in case Blacktip Island got that chilly in the winter.

What else might he need on a small island? His camera. Binoculars, if he could find them. His e-reader loaded with all the steampunk fiction he could find. A heavy rain jacket. Two towels. The fees for the extra bags would be stiff, but at least he would have everything he needed to get started on the backwater little island.

Two days later an express delivery envelope arrived on his doorstep. Wally tore it open in the hallway, scanned the contents. A note from Smackie Bottoms saying Wally's wire transfer had cleared. A bill of sale for Going Under Divers, with Smackie's signature, *and* Ferris Skerritt's. It was done. He, Wally Breight, owned a dive operation in the heart of the Caribbean. He jumped, whooped, threw his hands in the air, startling his neighbor Mrs. Jameson and her Yorkshire terrier, coming back from a walk. He didn't care. All his dreams were coming true, and this new adventure had started.

He needed to call Melissa, at least let her know he was leaving. They had split up—for good this time—the month before, but he owed her a goodbye, and hoped to leave on good terms. That evening Wally tapped her contact on his phone. Her familiar voice snapped in his ear.

"What, Wally?"

"Hey, I know it's been a while, but I wanted to let you know I'm moving."

"Why would I care about that?"

"No. I quit my job and bought a scuba charter company in the Tiperon Islands. I'm leaving in a few days."

There was a long pause.

"Well, you're crazy, but that's nothing new," she said. "You plan this out, or is it another of your spur-of-the-moment brainstorms?"

"Little of both. Look, we're not together anymore, but I . . . I didn't want to just run off without letting you know. Plus, cleaning out the closet I found a couple of your blouses. I thought you might want them back."

"If I've done without them this long, I don't need 'em. Do whatever you want with them. Anything else?"

"Actually, since you mention it, yeah. Not a big deal, but I set aside everything I might need on the island, and I couldn't find my binoculars. They'd come in handy down there."

"So?"

"They're the compact ones with the great magnification. The ones you liked for bird watching. I wondered if they might have fallen in with your stuff when you moved out."

"*That's* what this is about, isn't it? You want your binoculars!"

"No. I had you on the phone and thought I'd ask. No big deal."

"You think I stole them!" Her voice raised a pitch. "You can't find something and that makes me a *thief?*"

"I *never* said . . ."

"You just did! And wrapped it in nostalgia, hoping I wouldn't notice. Wally, if you think I would *ever* steal anything, even from you, you're a . . ."

"Bye Melissa."

Wally hung up. All the tension in their relationship had surged back full force in seconds. He would miss many things about his life in Marietta, but not those last few months with Melissa. It was good to make a break with this place.

The night before he left, the send-off party was a subdued affair. He and a few friends met at the Two Birds Taphouse on the Marietta square, close enough to his condo he could walk, since he had sold his Mercedes that morning.

"You'll miss the adrenaline rush you got from your job, Dude," Geoff said, red beard bristling. "You'll get all bored and be back inside a month."

"Not a chance," Wally said. "You've seen the photos. How could anyone get too much of that? At the PR agency, I died a little every day I was there."

"You're a city person, though," Maricela, always practical. A flip of her dark hair, her walnut-hued eyes bright. She waved a hand around the crowded bar. "You need the social scene. The excitement. The daily stimulation."

"The past year I've had more stimulation than's good for me. For the first time in my life, I'm doing exactly what I want. The irresponsible thing. Best decision I've ever made."

"That's not a high bar." Wendy, a dark-blonde eyebrow raised, sarcastic as ever.

"It's . . . I'm tired of being that person. It's time I was someone else."

"I get that," Wendy said. "Good luck. You *do* look happier than I've seen you in a while. I'm really kind of envious. Me, all of us, we're on a set course. I know what I'll be doing for the next twenty, thirty years. You, though, are off on a new journey. An exploit. You'll have no idea what you'll be doing from day to day. Or even tomorrow."

"And doing it in a tropical paradise, too, you bastard." Mari grinned up at him.

"We *will* miss you," Geoff laughed. "We'll never admit that again, but we will."

"But that's the beauty of it," Wally said. "I'll only be a few hours away. You can catch the morning flight to Tiperon from here, and the little island hopper'll have you on Blacktip that afternoon. Come down anytime. You're all invited!"

"Well, good luck," Mari said. "You'll need it."

"And good luck with the girls," Wendy said.

Wally said goodbye and walked back to the condo, ready for the adventure to begin. He sat on the balcony, had one last beer looking down at the old downtown. There were good memories, outweighing the bad. But he was stifled here. He had to go.

The next morning, the nostalgia returned when the jet lifted off from Hartsfield. He stared out the window, watched Atlanta dropping away, feeling the finality of completely turning his back on his life in the U.S. and starting from scratch in a foreign country. He was leaving behind all he had ever known. Once again, he wondered if he was doing the right thing. Again, he pushed the thought aside. He had made his decision. He would make new friends and a new life, make the island as much of a home as Marietta had ever been.

At the Tiperon airport, the Immigration officer gave Wally a long, blank stare, then a disgusted grunt when Wally, in his bright red Going Under Divers polo shirt, told him he had just bought the company. So much for a warm welcome to his new home. The airport was packed, making it difficult to wrestle his three big bags through the terminal. Once checked in, he fought his way to the departure lounge. When his flight was called, he waited on the tarmac, made sure all his bags made it onto the little Islander before he boarded.

Waiting had been a mistake. Both forward bench seats were occupied, and Wally had to crouch and half-crawl past them, back to the rear bench seat. He folded himself into place, knees jammed under his chin by the seatback in front of him. Behind his seat, suitcases, dive bags, boxes of bananas and onions and canned beans strained at a mesh netting, the packed cargo compartment's contents pressing against Wally's shoulders, pushing him forward, giving him a tilted view of the wing's underside. A small, elderly woman with two paper shopping bags climbed in behind him, set the bags in what passed for the aisle, blocking any exit he might have had.

The pilot turned around in the cockpit, counted the six passengers, then launched into his safety briefing.

"Welcome to Tiperon Airways and our Britten-Norman BN2 Islander. Emergency exits are located . . ."

Wally burst out laughing before he could stop himself. The pilot stopped talking, glared at him.

"I can't move," Wally managed to wheeze. "If this thing goes down, I'm screwed."

The pilot scowled, finished the briefing.

Wally was surprised when they taxied to the far end of the runway. Every time he had flown from Tiperon to Blacktip, the pilot had taxied the little Islander halfway down the runway and still had plenty of room to take off. Maybe the full seats and extra cargo meant they needed more distance.

Sure enough, the pilot throttled up both engines, but kept the brakes on. The little airplane shuddered. The pilot pushed the throttles farther forward and the engines screamed loud, louder than Wally had ever heard them. Then the pilot popped the brakes, and they lurched forward, bouncing down the tarmac, gradually building speed. The shrieking engines were at odds with the airplane's slow speed. A third of the way down the runway, by the civil aviation center, the plane lifted for a moment, then settled back to the ground. They bounced along, ever faster, but still not as fast as Wally was used to. They drew even with the commercial terminal. The plane lifted again, hung in the air several seconds before dropping back down.

Wally glanced at the woman beside him. She smiled at him, as if nothing was wrong. Wally looked back out the window. They had passed the terminal. Two hundred yards beyond that, the runway ended in Tiperon Lagoon, the tidal lake at the island's center. If the overweighted plane couldn't get airborne, in a few seconds they would be in the water. That was who-knew-how-deep. None of the other passengers seemed bothered.

The plane lifted again, hung in the air, neither rising nor dropping. Wally looked side-eye out the window and down. The tarmac runway was four, maybe five feet below the Islander's still-spinning wheel. Then, in a flash, the tarmac changed to the pale green of lagoon water. White foam flecks, strands of dark turtle grass scudded across the low, wind-blown whitecaps. What could have been a stingray, or a submerged rock, flashed past. The plane held steady, skimming the waves, then gradually gained altitude, a foot at a time.

When they reached the far side of the lagoon, the landing gear cleared the mangrove tops by a few feet, so close Wally could see individual leaves. He leaned back as far as he could, exhaled slow. He had been holding his breath without realizing it. He stared out the window, watching the green island slide past, 100 feet below now. There was a thin strip of black ironshore, then the light blue of water over shallow sand, dark fingers of coral stretching across it. Then the water turned dark blue, sharp as if someone had drawn it with a giant pen. The submerged wall, dropping thousands of feet barely seventy yards offshore. Blacktip Island had the same wall structure. If he survived this flight, Wally would be there soon, taking guests out to dive on it, guiding them along it. The boxes jabbing him in the back and head suddenly didn't seem so bad.

The woman beside him opened a book-sized plastic storage bin. She took out a small square of white-ish cake, then offered the bin to Wally. He thanked her, his voice drowned out by the howl of the propellers, and took a piece for himself. It was light, flaky, tasting of coconut and nutmeg and something else. Ginger, maybe. Wally thanked her again. She smiled in reply, mouthed something that could have been 'cocoa' or 'dodo' or 'toto.' Wally smiled, nodded, as if he understood, waved away a second piece. He needed water, but hadn't brought any.

He leaned his head against the cool window, closed his eyes and tried not to think about how overloaded the little airplane was. If he would actually reach Blacktip Island. What the landing would be like. The pilot seemed to know what he was doing. Or had done this before, anyway. And survived. Wally hoped to do the same.

He imagined the *J-Valve* with reworked engines, gleaming like new in the sun. And once money started rolling in, maybe a second boat to handle all the extra divers. More staff. Divers from other resorts noticing Going Under Divers, switching their dive bookings to him. He would redo the shop. Get a van to haul guests. Watch the awards and rave reviews and accolades pile in.

The only thing that could hold him back was himself. And that wasn't happening.

If only the Islander somehow got him safely to Blacktip.

3

A half hour later, the Islander touched down on Blacktip Island's unpaved landing strip, bounced twice, sending gravel flying and rattling Wally's teeth, then finally settled for good.

Out the window was the same lush greenery he remembered, the same low airstrip check-in shack, the same scudding clouds in the too-blue sky. Only now it was home. Wally smiled. Yes. Home. And he could get out of the flying death trap, if only he could unfold his body.

Vinson Noboddie, looking taller, thinner than before, was leaning against a battered van that may have once been blue, with hand-scrawled 'Noboddie's Inne' and a faded palm tree logo on the side. Wally stepped into the van's shade to wait for the lone baggage handler to unload the Islander's stuffed cargo bay.

"Came back after all!" Vinson laughed.

"Money's changed hands," Wally grinned back. "I'm committed."

"Rock's rollin' down the hill, all right." Vinson nodded. "Let's get you settled."

The baggage handler rolled a cart towering with bags to the dirt parking area. Passengers swarmed around it, snatching bags from the pile, bumping each other out of the way, jostling one another to pull bags free, sending the tower of bags crashing to the dirt. Wally let the frenzy subside before he and Vinson grabbed his three bags and lifted them into the van.

"Got you a room behind Peachy Bottoms," Vinson said.

"Come again?"

"Peachy Bottoms. Owns the store. And the little rooms next to it. Housing's tight on the island, but I scored one for you."

Two minutes later Vinson stopped at a low row of apartments on a dirt track beside the island store. He swung open a weathered door to reveal a narrow room. A musty smell of unwashed dog. Light trickled in through a window to the left, a window beside the door and one at the far end above the kitchen sink. The walls were an even color somewhere between off-white and tan. To the right a single bed was pressed against the wall. Under the side window was a small, round table with a green Formica top and two spindly chairs. A lime-colored stove and refrigerator from the 80s were jammed against the wall between the table and sink, opposite a door to the bathroom.

"She's not much, but it beats sleepin' outside." Vinson grinned, as if proud of securing the apartment. "Got pots and plates and . . . cutlery, too!"

"This . . . might work . . ." It was far cry from Wally's two-bedroom condo on the square, but he was here for an adventure. It would be fine until he could find someplace more suitable. "On the phone you mentioned you found transportation for me, too." Wally imagined a weathered island Jeep of some sort, like Vinson's Van—basic but functional.

"Oh, yeah!" Vinson motioned Wally back out the door and around the corner of the building. He slapped the seat of a mostly rust-free black mountain bike. "Just greased it up this mornin' so it's ready for you. Bobby down at Eagle Ray Cove got fired last week and left 'fore he could sell it, so it cost you nothin'!"

"I . . . haven't ridden a bike since I was fifteen," Wally said.

"So, it'll be nice to get back to!"

"No, I . . . there're no cars available? Or a motorcycle? Something with an engine?"

"The cars for sale now, you don't want 'em." Vinson shook his head. "People'll sell, 'specially to a stranger, but you'd end up walkin' more often than not."

Wally studied the bike. It would be easier to ride the several miles to the dive shop than to walk. And riding would get him in shape. His stomach grumbled. It had been a long day of traveling, and the sun was dropping behind the tree line. Cocktail time at Blacktip Haven.

"What are my food options nearby?"

"Closest restaurant options're Sandy Bottoms a little way south, or the Tail Spinner by me at the north end, 'bout a two-mile ride." Vinson waved a hand toward the store. "Or grab somethin' to cook at Peachy's."

"Peachy's it is, then." Wally wasn't about to bike even 'a little ways' after his long day. "I'll see you in the morning? At the shop? I'll be there at seven."

Vinson raised an eyebrow.

"I'll see you at nine. Ish," he said. "I let Harry and 'Rena know you're comin'. They're on fire to meet you. Wanna get back to work."

Wally watched Vinson and his van rumble off down the dirt road, dust cloud trailing behind it wafting into the roadside trees. He went back inside, grabbed his wallet, and walked to the store. He would need dinner for the night and breakfast for the morning.

Inside, the store looked like a convenience store on steroids, its metal cases jammed with a haphazard collection of food, household goods, and hardware. At the back were refrigerated cases. Wally grabbed two cardboard-boxed hamburgers for dinner, and a carton of eggs and instant coffee for the morning. He glanced at the price on the hamburgers. $8.99 in Tiperon dollars. He mentally calculated the conversion. $11-something in U.S. currency. A misplaced price tag, obviously. He was still eyeing the price when he reached the cashier.

The thin, white-haired woman with a narrow nose behind the counter peered at him through thick, round glasses, looking for all the world like an anorexic barn owl.

"Find what you need?" She smiled, reminding Wally of his grandmother.

"Yes, ma'am . . . a question, though—are these price tags correct?"

"Oh, yes. Everything's a bit more expensive on the island."

"Or, it's a damn-good burger."

"They're all right. Frozen burger's a frozen burger."

"I'm Wally, by the way. Just bought Going Under Divers."

"Oh, yes. I heard Vinson was starting back up. I'm Peachy." She waved backhanded toward the glass door with 'Peachy Bottoms' on it, a quick smirk crossing her face when she said Vinson's name. "I hope you enjoy life on the island. And make a success of the place."

Wally watched the register as she rung up his few groceries, flinched at the final total.

"I'll have to make it a success pretty quick if I want to buy any more groceries."

"Price of paradise," Peachy laughed.

Back in the apartment, Wally put a burger in the microwave. He avoided the rickety chairs and pulled the table to the bed and sat, testing the mattress. The springs creaked, and the mattress sunk more than Wally had expected, but it held. He would see about a new bed soon. The microwave dinged, and Wally stood to fetch his burger. The bed groaned like a gratefully-released animal.

The burger was greasy, hot in spots and cool in others, but it was food. Not worth $11, but it staved off the hunger. Tomorrow he would try one of the restaurants Vinson had mentioned. Wally unpacked his bags, lay back on the grumbling bed, and fell asleep.

The next morning, biking in was more work than Wally expected, and he was sweating when he finally arrived at the shop ten minutes late. A tall, thickset, sun-bleached woman and a shorter, whip-thin, scruffy-haired young man were waiting outside the Going Under Diver shop. Cerena Goby and Harry Blenny, they said—Vinson's 'young Harry,' no doubt—the operation's staff, back from their brief hiatus.

"Great! Good to meet both of you," Wally said. "I'll need all your expertise here to make sure things transition smoothly."

"Good to be working again," Harry said. "Business been down so long, we were 'bout to have to sign on at Eagle Ray Cove."

He gave Wally a knowing look, as if 'Eagle Ray Cove' was synonymous with some mid-range level of hell. Wally nodded, as if Harry's look conveyed all the necessary horror of the competing operation. He made a mental note to ask Vinson about that later. Wally unlocked the office door, swung it open and waved them in, sending a dozen spiders scuttling for cover.

"There'll be plenty of business soon," he said. "When do we have divers next?"

Cerena pulled a yellow legal pad from a file beside the computer, flipped through several pages.

"Got a group starting tomorrow. Six people."

She handed Wally the pad. The page showed the day, the date, and three surnames hand-scribbled in pencil, with 'x2' next to the names. Wally flipped through the pad. Each page was a sequential day and date, with names of divers hand written below.

"This . . . this is your scheduling system?"

"Works pretty good," Harry said. "We can write in or erase names when we need, and at the end of the day we tear off that sheet and put it in the folder with the other old schedules." He pointed to a squat, black filing cabinet. "Got all our divers going back four, five years."

"Why not just make a spreadsheet, in the computer, and update it once instead of writing all the names five or six times?"

"Low tech's good tech on Blacktip," Harry said. "Computer crashes, 'lectricity goes out, we always have this."

"Okay. Well. I'll . . . work up something a little less . . . Neolithic . . . to streamline that process," Wally said. "Maybe show at a glance when a week's going to be busy."

"This's always worked."

"Well, we're going to be too busy to have time for this sort of thing. Divers tomorrow. Right. Were you able to get the boat running?"

"Working on that. Parts sitting in Customs 'til we pay the duty."

"How much is the duty?" Wally pulled out his wallet, counted out multiple $100 bills, handed them to Harry. "I don't have a car. Can you get them? Now?"

"Noddy Bolin, the Customs man, won't be in 'til 10. I'll run down before that, case he gets in early." Harry handed half the bills back to Wally, grinned. "Won't be that much"

"Good. As long as we're running tomorrow."

"Worst case, we keep farming guests out to Eagle Ray Divers, or whoever."

"No! I'll take them shore diving myself before we give our divers away. It's a wonder this place is in the black. Look, get the parts as soon as you can. Tell . . . Noddy Bolin . . . there's a new owner here and can pay extra duty if that'll speed things up. Tell him Ferris Skerritt's our Tiperon partner."

Harry raised his eyebrows at Skerritt's name, then nodded and shuffled out the door.

"I start tearing out that heat exchanger," he said.

Wally turned to Cerena, who was smiling up at him.

"Brave, you buying a company in debt like this." Cerena gave him an admiring look.

"What do you mean in debt?" Wally opened the accounting program. "I looked at the financials when I was here last time. See?"

He pointed to the master spreadsheet showing the operation's modest, but positive account balance.

"Oh, that's not the real one. That's the one Smackie used for investors."

"Investors?"

"Sure. Kept two sets of books. It kept the investors . . . investing."

"These're fake books?"

"Just for emergencies. Here."

She reached across and typed something on the keyboard. A new spreadsheet popped up. Wally scanned the rows and columns of numbers. His eyes stopped on the totals at the bottom.

"But . . . that can't be . . ."

The totals showed Going Under Divers thousands, tens of thousands in debt.

"One of the reasons Smackie bailed," Cerena said. "Great diver, great with the guests, great boat captain. But really bad with business things. Did what we could to soften it, but he was always one step ahead of us. Business mind like yours, though, you'll turn it around in no time."

Wally went cold all over. In an instant he was covered in a chilling sweat.

"So . . . I need to pay what first? Utilities, obviously, but what about the rest of this?"

"Creditors know there's a new owner, they give you some leeway." She paused, dark eyes locked on Wally's. "Smackie was behind on payroll, too."

"I'll take care of that first!" Wally pulled his cashier's check from the folder. "Out of my own account, and I'll sort things out later. Where's the bank?"

"Down by the store. Not open 'til Thursday, though."

"I have to wait four days to open an account?"

"So few people on Blacktip, tellers fly over from Tiperon just once a week."

"Sooo . . . you learn to keep cash on hand on Blacktip. How much are you due?" He had brought emergency cash. He could dip into that.

"'Bout $1,200. Harry's the same."

She clicked on a tab on the computer screen. The pay-owed numbers popped up.

"Crap. Okay. I have some cash..." Cerena's and Harry's back pay would take almost all the cash he had brought. "How much do you need to tide you over 'til Thursday?"

"Rent's due in two days. And the cupboard's pretty bare right now," she said. "Been over a couple weeks."

"So... I have money at my place. I can pay you both this afternoon. Plus maybe a little extra, for your patience." He had to do something—he couldn't lose his entire staff the first day.

"That works." Cerena smiled. "I'll go tell Harry. He's been sweating his 'lectric bill."

"Actually, could you bring him back with you? Before he runs off to Customs, I need to talk to both of you about cross training your work responsibilities."

"Cross training?"

"So you can fill in for each other if need be."

"I do the office work and ordering and whatnot." Her lips tensed into a thin line. "Harry does the boat driving and maintenance and gear repair."

"Well, with a staff so small, we all need to be cross trained as much as possible," Wally said. "And I'll be doing a lot of the ordering and check writing, so that'll free you up for the boat."

"I do office work," she said. "I'm the office girl."

"Well, now you can be the boat girl, too. And Harry can take a turn at office boy. We'll all lend a hand as best we can. You'll get into the groove soon enough."

She gave him a dubious look, then walked out the door and around the corner. A few minutes later Harry walked in, brows furrowed and jaw set.

"I do diving and driving," he said. "Don't even know how to turn on that computer."

"Understood," Wally said. "I'll be doing all the accounting. I'll walk you through the basics of checking people in and out, swiping their credit cards, simple stuff like that."

"'Rena does that. Good at it, too. I'm good at fixing things."

"You, neither of you, are willing to even give this a try?"

"Seems like you're in a rush to fix something's not broken," Cerena said.

"Not broken, no, but it can be . . . improved. You'll see."

Harry scowled, went back outside.

Wally dropped into the desk chair, exhaled slow. The two of them, by Vinson's account, were both good at their jobs. But they were also, by their own accounts, used to managing the owner. He would have to change that, quickly, if Going Under Divers was to thrive. This insubordination might have even contributed to Smackie's throwing up his hands and walking away. With just the three of them, everyone had to be able to do basic tasks on days when one of them had a day off or was sick or hurt.

In the meantime, if he spent most of his cash today on back pay and Customs, that could leave him in a bind if more bills, or some other unexpected expense popped up between now and the bank opening on Thursday. He needed a cash backup. A line of credit. He left Cerena behind the desk and grabbed his bike. Moments later he was pedaling down Blacktip Island's dirt road in search of Ferris Skerritt.

Skerritt's house was in a row of small, traditional Tiperon cottages attached to each other, painted a bright teal, with pink vanes with heart shapes cut out of them running the length of the rooflines, on a low bluff overlooking the sea. Wally found Skerritt on a screen porch at the far end, sipping coffee. An empty breakfast plate was on the small table beside him. He motioned Wally inside.

"First day on the island and you're already on the run." It came out in a wheeze. Skerritt waved a claw at the empty plate. "Have time for breakfast?"

"Thanks. I ate already," Wally said. "That dive op's going to make for early mornings and late evenings."

"Well, good of you to, ah, pay a visit so soon."

"It's not a social call, I'm afraid." Wally settled into the chair facing Skerritt. "Turns out Smackie Bottoms kept two sets of books. The place is in some pretty significant debt."

"Blacktip Island, it does like its surprises." Skerritt gave a wet, gurgling sound that could have been a chuckle. "That's unfortunate for you."

"Thing is, there's utility bills stacked up, and the staff hasn't been paid in weeks. I wanted to let you know, as a partner in all this, I might need to get a brief loan from you until I get a bank account set up Thursday." It came out too fast, but Wally couldn't help it. He hadn't expected this serious of an emergency right off the bat.

"Oh, no. That's not at all possible, you know." Skerritt's voice dropped into a more pronounced Tiperon lilt. "Our contract *and* the law say so."

"It would be temporary. Just a few days. Here's the check I'm going to deposit." Wally unfolded the cashier's check, showed it to Skerritt. "I just need to make sure Cerena and Harry don't bail on me, on us, if I don't get them paid ASAP asap, and that'll take most of my cash. And there's bills overdue."

"All debts and losses, past, present and future, are the responsibility of the expatriate partner." Skerritt raised his hands, as if to show how powerless he was. "Sorry you're in this, ah, predicament, but there's nothing I can do without running afoul of the law."

"If the staff leaves, our company could go out of business before it starts."

"You'd be liable for all that, too."

A sick feeling washed over Wally.

"So . . . you're saying, by Tiperon law, you get a cut of any profits, but are banned from helping with the expenses?"

"Way to protect local entrepreneurs," Skerritt said. "Didn't do that, expats'd buy up all the businesses here, end up controlling the country. Put locals out of work."

"That's robbery!"

"That's the law."

"And you never told me this?" Wally stood, trying to keep his temper in check.

"It's in the contract you signed." Skerritt sipped his coffee. "'Subject to all applicable Tiperon laws' is how it's worded."

"But it's not right."

"No difference if it's right. It's legal." Skerritt studied Wally for a moment. "I imagine Cerena and Harry *are* antsy about getting paid. Technically, ah, *you* don't owe them anything. Smackie Bottoms incurred that debt. Dismiss them, you'd save that money and could hire new staff for cheaper."

"They're our staff! There's no way I'd do that to them!"

"Just a suggestion. Partner to partner."

Wally ran his hand through his hair. This was crazy. Skerritt was a partner in a business, and he didn't care if it failed. Or if its employees walked out.

"What if Going Under goes out of business?" Wally tried a different angle. "That'll have a negative effect on you."

"Oh, I'd keep the business. Find someone else to sell that forty percent to."

"Well, I'm gonna make sure you don't get the chance!"

Wally stomped down the porch steps, grabbed his bike and pedaled hard as he could back down the road toward his apartment. He would make sure Cerena and Harry got their money even if the power company turned off the electricity and he had to take guests shore diving for the next month.

When Wally returned to the dive shop, the sound of clanging, hammering from the dock told Wally that Harry was at work on the boat. Sweating, face red from biking, Wally crossed the sandy lot to the resort. Maybe Vinson could help with Wally's potential money crunch. He found Vinson in The Inne's kitchen in his faded Spider Man t-shirt. A pot on the stove was bubbling with something noxious smelling. Vinson grinned at him.

"Forgot to say—you can take your meals here, if you want."

He held out a spoon filled with a brown, viscous liquid. Wally sniffed the spoon. Definitely the smell's source. Not wanting to be rude, he took a small sip. His throat tightened. Whatever it was, it tasted worse than it smelled, like rotted mushrooms laced with maple syrup.

"That's . . . something else." Wally, eyes watering, managed to swallow the stuff. "Thanks, but I have a . . . special diet I try to stick to, though."

"You out taking exercise early!" Vinson pointed to Wally's sweat-soaked shirt. "Got nervous energy?"

"Look, Vinson, I just came from Ferris Skerritt," Wally said. "Cerena and Harry need to be paid. That's gonna take almost all my cash, and I can't deposit my cashier's check until Thursday. Skerritt says he can't legally advance me any money."

"That does sound like Ferris." Vinson grinned bigger. "But there's plenty of money in that account."

"Fake books. The place is *way* in the red."

"Do tell." Vinson's voice and face told Wally he wasn't surprised.

"There any chance you could make a small loan, if need be, 'til Thursday? I'm good for it."

Wally showed him the cashier's check. Vinson's smile faded.

"Empty resort don't leave much extra cash sitting 'round," he said. "I'm holdin' my breath 'til the next guests get here. And cash out end of the week."

"Right. Thanks anyway."

Wally would give Cerena and Harry what they were owed, eat light, and keep his fingers crossed nothing happened before Thursday. He walked to the dock, where Harry was hunched over the *J-Valve*'s starboard engine. A rectangular metal box with pipes coming out of it was set on a towel. Harry was pulling on a metal tube at the back of the engine, cursing with every tug.

"How's the repair going?" Wally needed good news this morning.

"Not bad, y'know." Harry squinted up at him, grease smudged across his nose and a greasy rag in his hand. "All the parts didn't make it, but Finn, up at CSD, loaned me what we needed. Said you can replace 'em as soon as you get set up."

"Finn. Good. I'll stop by and say 'thanks.' CSD is . . ."

"Club Scuba Doo. 'Bout five miles that way." He waved a wrench south, toward the store.

"I'll check with Elena, up at The Haven, too, see if she has any parts to spare," Wally said. "You need any help with this?"

Harry squinted at Wally again, as if trying to decide whether Wally was serious.

"Know anything about engines?" He sounded doubtful.

"Honestly, no. But if you need an extra set of hands, I'm happy to help."

"Yeah, kind of a one-person job right now, but I'll let y'know."

"Great. Right. Well, Cerena showed me the two of you haven't been paid for a while. I ran home and got what cash I have. I'll split it up, have your pay in an envelope inside when you're done. Plus a little extra for your understanding."

"Money's always good!" Harry grinned. "This engine, she should be running soon. I'll launch the boat, tie her up at the dock."

Harry bent back over the engine, gave a shout of joy when the tube snapped into place.

Wally stepped into the dive shop, divided his cash, gave Cerena her share, then put Harry's in an envelope. Cerena counted her money twice before stuffing it in her dry bag.

"Don't trust the new management?" Wally said.

"On Blacktip, you treat every fish like a shark 'til you see it not attack when there's blood in the water," she said. "Nothin' personal."

Wally laughed, settled in at the computer to start building a new scheduling system. Despite his unexpected cash shortage, and his talk with Skerritt, things were falling into place.

Two hours later he heard a boat engine roar to life, then another. He stepped outside to see the *J-Valve* idling across the lagoon, Harry at the helm. When the boat reached the cut in the reef, Harry pushed the throttles forward and the boat jumped across the low waves, propellers throwing a broad, white wake behind. Harry made several turns, fast and slow, then drove back into the lagoon. Wally met him at the dock.

"She running like new!" Harry said. "Ready for divers."

"Harry, I can't thank you enough. And your back pay's ready for you in the shop."

They walked to the shop together. At a nod from Cerena, Harry pocketed his envelope without counting the cash.

"Hey, with the boat all set, I'm thinking of heading out early," Harry said.

"Oh, sure," Wally said. "You knocked yourself out today. Both of you. I'll see you in the morning."

If both of them were gone, he could build the new scheduling system faster, have it ready for the next day.

Cerena and Harry glanced at each other, as if communicating something, then nodded to Wally and left. Moments later their Jeep grumbled down the road.

Wally leaned back in the office chair, hands behind his head. All this was his, from the shop to the boat to the souvenir shirts and caps and down to all the spiders in the place. He owned a dive company. He couldn't wait to meet his divers in the morning.

A small brown spider dropped from the rafters and onto the computer keyboard, then scuttled off the back of the desk. Wally made a mental note to get bug spray that evening.

4

Wally rose at sunrise the next morning, pedaled down the west coast road, then up the narrow track to the top of the bluff and Blacktip Haven. He wanted to check in with Elena, let her know he was back on the island and was officially a fellow dive-operation owner.

The kitchen staff was putting out the breakfast when he walked into the main room. He waved to Jessie, then headed to the dining room where he could hear Elena finishing one of her stories for the guests.

"… but Helen didn't realize Payne had put the panties in Frank's glove box as a joke. She beat Frank about the head and shoulders, then didn't talk to him for a week! Then, when Payne fessed up, she whacked *him*. And *still* doesn't talk to him."

"It gets better every time I hear it," Wally said.

"So you really did buy that old place." Elena shook her head. "Good luck. You'll need it. How's the boat?"

"Harry Blenny's got it running great, just in time for divers this morning." Wally said nothing about the place's finances. "One reason I'm here—Harry borrowed a few parts from Club Scuba Doo, but I don't want to rely on them too much. In an emergency, could we maybe borrow engine parts from you and replace them later? And vice versa?"

"Our engines are Cats," Elena said. "Yours are what, Cummins? The parts aren't interchangeable, but with anything else, sure, if we can help, let us know."

"Great. Thanks. I won't keep you. Need to get to the shop."

Wally grabbed a tall paper drink cup from next to the coffee urns, filled it with bacon and scrambled eggs on his way past the buffet. Jessie gave him an odd look, but said nothing.

At the dive shop, Wally waited for Harry and Cerena to arrive. And waited. He called their numbers. No answer. A group of dive guests straggled over from the resort, bulging gear bags on their backs or bundled in their arms. Still no Harry or Cerena. Wally glanced at the *J-Valve* tied to the dock. The seas were flat. He felt fairly certain he could drive the boat, but he wasn't sure which dive sites were which. And he couldn't lead dives *and* tend the boat at the same time. He crossed to the resort. Maybe Vinson could help for a few hours.

"Not happenin'," Vinson said. "Got rooms to clean, then lunch to prep."

"I can't run the boat by myself."

"You piss off Harry and Cerena?"

"No! That's just it. I paid them everything they were owed yesterday! In cash. With interest."

"That's what did it." Vinson chuckled to himself. "They been fillin' in at CSD. They prob'ly gone there full time after they got their cash in hand."

"Scuba Doo? But why?"

"That Finn, he does pay better. Their guests tip better." Vinson gazed past Wally to the dock and boat. "And their boats don't need so much work as that old *J-Valve*."

"If that's what happened, I'll track them down and . . . do *something*. But right now I have divers and no dive staff!"

The divers had dropped their bags outside the dive shop. Several were staring at Wally, hands on their hips.

"Vinson, could I borrow your van for the morning?"

"Sure. I'll be busy here."

"And could you help me throw some tanks in the back?"

The guests watched, sour-faced, while Wally and Vinson loaded the van with scuba cylinders and gear bags.

"This's supposed to be boat diving," a man who introduced himself as 'Roger' grumbled. "We paid for boat diving."

"Yes, but there's no one to drive the boat, so we're going shore diving instead." Wally gave him his cheeriest smile. "Just for today."

Still grumbling, the divers climbed into the van. Wally slid into the right-side driver's seat, eyed the stick shift. He could drive stick but had never shifted with his left hand. He pressed each pedal, checking which was the brake and which was the clutch. He started the van, shifted into what he hoped was first gear, and ground his way, herky-jerky, onto the roadway.

Diddley's Landing public pier was just down the coast, with its wide cement steps as an easy exit point. Wally would take the guests diving there, schmooze them, make them happy, then track down Harry and Cerena in the afternoon.

Five minutes later he parked on the broad expanse of cement that was the pier. Wally unloaded the van and had the guests gear up, giant stride off the lowest step, then he followed them in. They dumped air from their vests and descended.

Wally had dived off the dock once before and had a general idea of what to expect. He led the group into deeper water, following a long coral finger, then turned north and wound his way through a maze of coral heads, his six divers following. He pointed out yellow-headed jawfish rising up like miniature ghosts from their holes in the rubble. A pair of white-spotted filefish nipped at a stand of fire coral, their toothy underbites breaking off bite-sized pieces. He guided the group into the shallows then and turned back south along the ironshore wall, jagged as the filefish's teeth and packed with red-lipped blennies and juvenile sergeant-majors. At the pier's steps, a flash of color caught his eye. He pointed up and toward the shore, counted five, six, then eleven hand-sized reef squid flashing a rainbow of colors at the gaggle of divers.

Wally signaled to go up, then led the guests up the algae-coated concrete steps. A woman, in running shoes, shorts, and a sweat-spotted, light-blue tank top leaned against the van, watching the divers climb out of the water, a puzzled look on her round face. Egret-thin, medium height, about Wally's age, pale mocha skin and straight jet-black hair fell to her shoulders and hung forward, partly hiding her face. Head cocked to one side, birdlike, her obsidian eyes studied him.

"Looking to go diving?" Wally said.

She laughed, high and musical.

"You're . . . not Vinson." A light voice, and soft, with a vaguely-Spanish accent. She stepped toward him, slightly pigeon-toed, still looking puzzled.

"Correct. I'm Wally. Vinson loaned me his van for the morning."

"Ah. I wondered why he was out so early. And diving, of all things. I'm Val."

She gave him a crooked, hair-obscured smile, held out a tentative hand. Wally shook it, then slid his scuba gear to the ground, grabbed a towel, and dried his head. Around him, his divers were doing the same, and switching their gear to new cylinders.

"You just moved here." It was a statement. She eyed the concrete next to Wally's feet.

"How can you tell?"

"No tan. Fresh haircut. And the 'dive staff' t-shirt in the front seat means you're not a tourist." Her black eyes scanned him, as if registering every detail, then went back to the concrete. "So Going Under Divers is back in business?"

"Yep. I bought it last week."

"Wow. You're either brave or crazy."

"I've been called both. In the last twelve hours." Wally moved his regulator and buoyancy vest to a fresh cylinder. "You need me to give Vinson a message?"

"I'll catch him at the Inne. I'm headed that way, anyway." She turned to go, stopped, then turned back. "My favorite spot off the pier is the coral head straight out, due west, maybe fifty yards. There's always something phenomenal there. I dive it on my days off."

Wally followed her slender, pointing finger, saw a dark blob lurking beneath the bright turquoise water to the west.

"Fifty yards. Two-eight-five on your compass," Val said. "Your guests'll love it."

She spun away, jogged down the road toward Noboddie's Inne, dark hair flying behind her.

After a break, Wally led the still-unhappy divers back into the water. He followed Val's directions and sure enough, found the coral head she mentioned. 'Coral island' was a better name. From the sand at fifty feet, it rose to within fifteen feet of the surface, and was so wide Wally couldn't see either end of it. At its base was a six-foot-wide tunnel leading to the other side, partially open at the top.

Wally signaled he was going through the tunnel. The divers followed. Part way through, a side tunnel intersected the main one. Wally's light revealed a green moray eel lurking there, its toothy jaw opening and closing to pump water through its gills. He signaled 'eel' to the divers in single file behind him.

Once through the tunnel, Wally made a slow circuit around its base, showing the guests a blue-spotted flounder in the sand, a pipe horse, looking like a mossy twig clinging to a piece of sea grass, then kicked his way shallower, spiraling up the coral head, pointing out more creatures as he went. The worries about money, about the bank, about Harry and Cerena, it all evaporated as he glided around the coral. After forty-five minutes they reached the coral's crest, and he compass-navigated the group back to the pier, swimming at fifteen feet from the surface as their safety stop.

After the dive, Wally drove them all back to the resort in time for lunch. Most were still grumbling about shore diving and hauling gear. Wally pulled Vinson aside.

"Someone named Val was looking for you."

"Oh, yeah," Vinson said. "Sorted out a food order we split between us. She's a sweetie, Valeria. Goin' through a gray patch, but good people."

He eyed Wally, as if about to say more, then held out a serving spoon filled with what could have been meat in a dark broth.

"Got stew for lunch, if you're hungry."

"As good as that sounds, Vinson, I have an errand to run first," Wally said. "Where, exactly, is Club Scuba Doo, and can I borrow the van just a little bit longer?"

A few minutes later he was rolling south down the island's west coast, stomach grumbling and the van clattering around him, dust cloud trailing behind. He passed the airstrip, then Sandy Bottoms Beach Resort. After two miles he pulled into the sand parking area of a collection of pastel bungalows by a 'Club Scuba Doo' sign. The receptionist pointed to a crushed stone walkway leading down to the dive shop by the water. The dock sat empty, the resort's morning dive boats not back for lunch yet. Inside a thin man, younger than Wally, with spikey bleach-blonde hair sat behind the counter, bare feet propped up, computer keyboard in his lap.

"I'm Wally."

Wally held out his hand. The other man looked confused.

"Just bought Going Under Divers."

"Oh! You're here about Harry and Cerena, right?" A faint Australian accent. He stood, shook Wally's hand.

"Yeah." So they *were* working here. "I . . . who are you?"

"Finn. I run the place. Such as it is."

"Finn. Right. Thank you for the loan of the engine parts."

"No worries, Bro. We pull together on this little rock."

"Yeah, that's what I wanted to talk to you about. I have no staff. I had to take my guests shore diving just now."

"Sweet! Great thinking!"

"But I had no warning Harry and Cerena were leaving."

"Huh. They shoulda told you."

"Or you could have talked to me first. You know, pull together on the little rock."

"They said everything was cool. Oh, well. Their choice, Dude."

"But I need them back!"

"Can't have 'em. They're on CSD work permits now—they're mine for a year."

"That's crap! Where the hell am I supposed to get staff on this island?"

"I know, right? I got lucky when Harry and Cerena came on board!"

"I'm scratching and clawing to make a go of this dive op, and you just screwed me over!"

"Hey, they're free-willed beings. Where they work, that's their call. Take it up with them. I can't help you."

"But I can't operate without staff!"

"Can't give you what I don't have, Bro." Finn put his feet back on the counter, went back to typing on the keyboard.

Wally stared at him a moment, unsure what to do. People didn't just poach employees like this. His vision of Blacktip being a tropical Eden where everyone got along took another hit. Clearly, Finn didn't care and wasn't going to help. Wally stalked out, let the dive shop door slam behind him. He would take his time getting replacement engine parts back to Finn. And he would tear into Harry and Cerena the next time he saw them.

On the way back to Noboddie's Inne, Wally turned up the track leading to Blacktip Haven. The staff would be setting out the lunch buffet about now, and he could grab something edible, quick, to take with him. He stepped to the buffet to make a sandwich when Jessie came out of the kitchen carrying a tray of baked fish filets. She gave him a surprised look, then stepped between Wally and the buffet table.

"Wally, you shouldn't be in here."

She set the tray on the table. The smell of spices rising from the fish made his stomach rumble louder.

"I'm just stopping by to say 'hi'." He gave her his most disarming grin. "And grabbing a quick sandwich."

"That's the thing—I don't think you're supposed to."

"It's just a sandwich. Elena won't mind."

"She's . . . we're in cost-cutting mode right now. You really need to clear it with her first."

"And she's where?" Wally looked around the dining room, hoping to see Elena.

"In town. At the store."

"I'll track her down."

Wally grabbed a chicken tender off the end of the buffet as he walked past, grinned over his shoulder at Jessie and was out the door. It was odd, Jessie suddenly being so uptight.

Wally coasted down the hill to the main road, stomach still grumbling. He needed more than a single chicken finger. The Tail Spinner restaurant was near the dive shop. He would grab a quick lunch there, see how the food was, then head back to work. The food couldn't be worse than what Vinson served. He dropped the van at the Inne and biked back to the restaurant.

Where the coastline took a sharp turn and ended in a rocky jumble, the Tail Spinner sat in The Pinnacle's shadow. A low, rough wood-paneled building with a broad wooden deck wrapping around three sides and large windows facing west toward The Pinnacle. 'The Tail Spinner' was painted on the building's side, with a cartoon shark underneath, jaws gaping, and a propeller at the tip of the tail, about where the restaurant would be on a shark-shaped map of the island. Wally wedged his bike in the empty wooden bike rack and stepped inside.

The room was fancier than any Wally had ever seen on Blacktip, with dark walls, and brass railings around a dining area of white-tableclothed tables. The bar at the near end of the room sported a dozen padded bar stools and a zinc bar top. Stuffed reef fish crowded the wall behind the bar.

Wally took a stool at the bar, picked up a menu. A woman stepped from the kitchen alcove. Black hair hanging across a round face, black eyes, now framed by wire-framed glasses, hint of a crooked smile.

"Didn't expect to see you again so soon," Val said.

"You . . . work here?"

"I run the place. How'd the dive go?"

"Good. Thanks for the tip on that big coral head. The divers were . . . less grouchy after that."

"Why were you shore diving at all?" She tucked her hair behind one ear.

"Staff didn't show up. I've never driven the boat." He paused, watched her eyes, wondering how much to share. "That may have to change tomorrow, though. If you know of anyone looking for a job . . ."

"I'll send 'em your way."

"Thanks. Could I get a draft and a chicken sandwich?"

"Not into Vinson's cooking, huh?"

"People really eat that stuff?"

"He serves massive portions. Guests love that."

She filled a glass mug from the tap and set it foaming on the bar.

"And you're from . . .?" Val said.

"Atlanta. Ish. Marietta?"

"Sure. I lived up in Buford for a while. Used to dive Lake Lanier."

"And you called *me* brave?"

"Eh. It's what was available. You run a dive outfit there?"

"No, I did public relations for . . . I did P.R."

Val's eyebrows shot up.

"You've never run . . . Well, welcome to the island of misfit toys. It can take some getting used to." Her gaze dropped to the bar. "Let me know if I can do anything to help. Getting out, like this, meeting people's a good start. And it's island-wide happy hour tonight at Sandy Bottoms. Good place to look for staff."

She looked as if she was going to say something else, but turned and walked down the bar and into the kitchen.

Wally finished his lunch and pedaled back to the dive shop. Searched the internet for how-to-drive-boats videos. There was no way the guests would put up with another day of shore diving, and he didn't know any other shore dive entry points. He spent the afternoon going between the shop computer and the *J-Valve*, identifying switches, gauges, throttles, imagining how the boat would maneuver with him at the wheel. Practiced starting and stopping the engines. He had driven pontoon boats with outboards before. This wouldn't be *that* different. He would drive the *J-Valve* the same way, and everything would be fine.

He thought of Val's suggestion about happy hour. He wasn't eager to hang out with awkward, tomboy Val, but he liked the idea of meeting new people. And finding new staff.

That evening he pedaled down to Sandy Bottoms, just past the airstrip. If Noboddie's Inne was the rustic hotel option on the island, Sandy Bottoms Beach Resort was its polar opposite. Wally stepped through the tiled lobby and out onto a broad limestone verandah with the pool and a covered, outdoor bar at the far end. Multi-colored lights spiraled up multiple palm trees around the verandah's edges. The space was nearly filled with guests and locals there for the Wednesday night happy hour. Wally elbowed his way to the bar and ordered a beer from the bartender sporting a nametag declaring him 'Barry.' Ceiling fans stirred the air, a welcome relief after a day in the sun. He scanned the crowd, looking for any familiar faces, saw none. Someone bumped into him straining to reach the bar.

"Barry! I need shots! Four, no five of 'em." A short, deep-tanned woman in her mid-twenties, with a husky voice, pushed her way to the bar, slopping half of Wally's beer down his shirt front. "Oh, sorry. Don't know my own strength, huh?" She grinned up at him, small and slim as a sixth-grader, but with the curves of an adult and a face as thin as a fox's. Ink-dark lashes over orange-tinted eyes. Long, sun-bleached hair, once dark brown, looking like she combed it with her feet, beads woven into it on the left side. A floral shirt. Short cut-off denim shorts and tanned legs. Dusty flip flops.

"No worries." Wally grabbed a handful of bar napkins and blotted at his shirt.

"Hey, you wanna a shot?" The woman was still staring at Wally. American accent, though he couldn't place where. She held onto her 's'es when she spoke, in a subtle, not-unattractive, sibilance. "You need a shot. Barry! Make it six!"

"No, you don't need to," Wally said.

"That's what makes it such a nice thing to do. And I *did* dump beer all over you. I'm Alison."

She held out a thin, tanned hand, and Wally shook it.

"Wally."

"Staying here?"

"Just moved down. Bought Going Under Divers."

"Oh! You're *that* dude! Man, you got brass balls, taking on that bad boy."

"So I'm learning. You . . . work here?"

"Not here-here. Down at Eagle Ray Divers. Been there?"

"I always stayed at Blacktip Haven."

"Oooo hooo!" Alison angled her nose up, flicked it with her finger. "Came down from Elena's rarified air to slum with the riff-raff, huh? Oh! Here's the shots!"

Barry the bartender slid six shot glasses filled with a yellow liquid across the bar top. Alison handed them into the crowd behind her.

"So. Introductions," she said. "Gang, this's Wally. He's the whackadoo taking on Going Under. Wally, meet the gang: Here's Cal, and Marina, and Hugh, and . . . ha! Jessie."

Wally nodded to Cal, about his height with close-cropped black hair, to Marina, tall, dark-skinned with black hair falling to her shoulders, and to skinny, sun-baked Hugh.

"Jessie I know," he said.

"Right! The Haven connection. Well, welcome to your first Blacktip happy hour."

Alison raised her glass. The others did the same. Wally joined them. As one, they tossed back their glasses, draining them. Wally's throat burned with chilled tequila.

"So how d'you like the island so far?" Hugh ran a hand over his haystack of sun-bleached hair.

"Still settling in," Wally said. "Getting to know how things work and who everyone is."

"That's the trick, isn't it? I've been here two years, and I'm still trying to figure that out."

"We're hanging by the pool. Join us." Alison flashed a quick grin, locked her eyes on his for a second, then sauntered away, shoulders and hips swaying. The others followed.

"So you made it, huh?" Val stood in front of him, hair half-hiding her face again. "Good to see you out."

"You said this was the place to be." Wally watched Alison join the group by the pool. Yes, he needed to join them. Her.

"People from all walks of life gather here Wednesdays. It's like the watering hole in *Jungle Book*." She took a glass of water from Barry. "Everyone from millionaire homeowners to the lowest-paid dive staff."

"Don't mention dive staff." Wally's thoughts about Alison evaporated. "I still have none."

"I may know of someone. I'll get back to you."

"No time to get work permits for them."

"Let me worry about that." She smiled, as if remembering something funny. "Like me to show you around, make introductions?"

"Actually, I was about to join . . . Jessie and her friends." Wally motioned toward the pool.

"Oh. That's right. You were a Haven guest. Well . . . have fun."

Wally nodded, eased his way through the crowd. As pleasant as Val was, he hadn't come to Blacktip to hang out with someone he could have met, or worked with, in Marietta. He was here for an adventure. By the pool, Alison flipped her hair to one side, beads rattling, laughed at something Jessie said. Wally walked faster.

The group grilled Wally—where he was from, how he found out about Going Under Divers, what his plans for the place were. A round of beer arrived, followed by another round of tequila shots. Wally warmed to the subject, joking about the engine repairs, that morning's grumbly guests, the crazy divers Hank-O would be sending down from the U.S. Jessie looked surprised at that. Or possibly impressed.

Hugh slid an arm around Jessie's waist. They were together, then. And Cal and Marina's body language said they were a couple, too. That left Alison unattached. If he happened to pay more attention to her than the others, she didn't seem to mind. He was making friends. And, mentally, was as far removed from Chattahoochee kit foxes as he could be. The drinks were coming fast, though, and he needed to be sharp for the guests in the morning. Wally eyed the resort exit across the verandah. He needed to ease his way out before he was too tipsy to work the next day. And for the bank.

Another round of shots arrived. Another mouthful of chilled tequila coursed down Wally's throat. A swallow of beer eased the sting.

"You're funny after a couple of drinks." Alison peered up at him, face red from the heat, the alcohol, or both. "We're gonna have chicken fights in the pool later. You in?"

"Wally's a good egg, but always so buttoned-down leading those Haven groups." Jessie winked at him. "It's fun seeing him loosen up."

"Sounds like a dare." Alison grinned.

"No. Not tonight. I have my cranky guests to deal with first thing in the morning. Then I have to get a bank account. I've got to be on top of my game."

"Sic Cerena on 'em," Alison said. "She can chill the most P.O.-ed guests with a word."

"Yeah. Cerena works at Club Scuba Doo now. Harry, too. It's just me tomorrow."

"Woah. Trial by fire," Alison said.

"If anybody knows divemasters looking for a job . . ." Wally floated it, hopeful. Received a round of shaking heads.

"You know how to drive a boat?" Concern played across Hugh's face.

"In theory."

The group exchanged glances.

"I'm a quick study."

"Better be," Alison laughed.

"It's that or more shore dives," Wally said.

"Yeah, no." Alison gave him a horrified look. "Shore dives suck. And you're a drink behind now. You got catching up to do."

"No. Seriously." Wally wanted to stay and drink with them, with Alison, but he didn't dare. "I can't afford to not be in top form tomorrow. I really need to run. Rain check?"

Alison's orange eyes scanned his face, appraising.

"I'll let you skate this time, but you owe me a bar crawl."

"I could also use someone to show me around the island."

She gave him a faint smile, eyes narrowed, put her hand on his arm.

"We'll see."

She turned, rejoined the others with a flip of her hair and a clatter of beads.

Wally pedaled back up the coast toward his apartment, head spinning with thoughts of Alison. Whether she was actually attracted to him, or simply flirting, didn't matter. Meeting her was finally something fun, something positive on Blacktip. He would see where that led. This was the kind of evening he dreamed of when he imagined moving here. Being social was as important as finances, if he wanted to stay sane. He needed more of this.

He was sweating by the time he reached the apartment. The bike was fine for getting to the office each day, but for visiting other places on the island, he would need to find some kind of motorized transportation. As soon as he had money coming in. Wally collapsed on the groaning bed, watched the ceiling spin, dreamed of happy dive guests. Of colored lights around palm trunks. Of orange eyes and clattering beads.

5

The dive guests were already milling outside the dive shop the next morning when Wally arrived, still trying to shake his head free of the fog clogging it from the night before.

"We're not doing that shore diving crap again, are we?" Roger said.

"We paid for boat diving, and that's what we're gonna do," another said. "I can shore dive for nothing anytime I want back in Flor'da."

Wally eyed the *J-Valve*, still tied to the dock, weighing his options. The sea was flat. The cut through the reef was plainly marked with red and green posts. Just like the online videos. How hard could it be to take the boat out in such great conditions? Like driving a car. The guests clearly wouldn't stand for another dive at the pier. But he didn't know what any of the nearby dive sites were.

"Can y'all give me *one* minute?" Wally trotted to the resort's main building, where Vinson was still clearing the breakfast tables. Wally tried to ignore the reek of scorched bacon grease.

"Vinson, can you point out a couple of good dive sites nearby? If I don't take my divers out in the boat, I'll have a mutiny, crew or no crew."

"Oh, yeah. Were cranky at breakfast. Know how to run that boat?"

"My dad's boat had an outboard when I was little. This'll just be a bit bigger."

"There you go! Your boat, you drive it." Vinson grinned, pointed at the sea. "Moorin' ball straight out the cut is Hole in the Wall. Then, in from there's Wahoo Reef."

"Good dives?"

"Dunno. Don't dive. But folks seem to like 'em." He grinned. "I'll sit here and watch 'til you clear the cut."

Wally bolted out the door and across to the dive shop.

"Everyone meet me on the dock," he yelled to the divers.

A new diver had joined the group, was standing apart from them, gear bag on his back, smiling. Short-cropped white hair, but still fit, though with the wide shoulders and potbelly of an athlete gone to seed. He stood a head taller than Wally, smiling like a favorite uncle.

"I'm Wally." Wally held out his hand. "Are you part of the group?"

"No, no. Just over from Tiperon for a day or two. Hoping to get a few dives in, if there's room. Chip Pompano."

"Welcome. There's plenty of room. I . . . I'll meet you at the boat."

Wally ran to the dive shop, grabbed his dive gear and the boat key from the desk, then quick-stepped down to the dock. Once the divers were on board, he gave them an abbreviated boat briefing, then scanned the boat's controls—steering wheel, twin throttle levers, tachometers, pre-visualizing how they would all work. He crossed his fingers, turned the key, and pressed the start button on the dash. Harry had done good work—the twin engines fired up. Great. Now to get the boat loose. Wally climbed back onto the dock, uncleated the stern line, and tossed it onboard. He did the same with the bow line, then jumped onto the bow and settled in behind the wheel.

The boat bobbed beside the dock, a slight breeze blowing down its centerline. How to get it away from the dock? Wally turned the wheel all the way to the right and bumped the starboard engine into reverse for a second. Sure enough, the bow swung just enough to the right to catch the wind, away from the dock. With the wheel still hard-right, Wally put both engines in gear. The stern swung to the left, crunched into a dock piling, setting all the scuba tanks on the dock clanging against each other. Wally put the engines back in neutral, smiled at the startled guests.

"All part of the show, folks," he said.

He let the breeze catch the boat, and the bow slid away from the dock. When it sat at a forty-five-degree angle, he straightened the wheel and put the engines in forward again.

Wally idled between the channel markers and out the cut. Soon they were at the nearest mooring ball Vinson had indicated. Wally put the engines in neutral, climbed onto the bow to grab the mooring line, silently cursed when the *J-Valve* glided to a stop several feet short of the yellow line. He crawled back to the helm, put the engines in gear for a moment, climbed back to the bow, and cursed out loud as the boat slid past the line and mooring ball. On his third try, Wally managed to grab the mooring line as the boat passed it, dragged it to the bow and tied off without getting pulled overboard. The guests were now staring narrow-eyed at him, giving each other worried glances.

"OK, folks, here's one of the most popular sites on the island, Hole in the Wall!"

Wally had no idea what the site was like, so he launched into a generic dive briefing—shallow water under the boat, the wall, then the deep water—mentioning the titular hole and warning not to go into it since he didn't know how deep the exit was, if there was one, and hoped his description somehow resembled the actual site. After getting all the divers into the water, he said a silent prayer the mooring line wouldn't break, then jumped in after them.

Fifty feet below him—not the thirty feet he had briefed—a sand and rubble field spread as far as he could see, with coral hills jutting up in irregular patterns. To his right the coral ended, the wall's vertical face dropping thousands of feet into the blue. As the site's name suggested, a hole in the coral led down to who-knew how deep on the wall. Several divers were already making their way toward it. Wally kicked after them, caught them before they could go inside, motioned for them and the other divers to follow him.

He led the group along the sheer wall at eighty feet, sculling past car-sized brown barrel sponges and slabs of plate coral the size of dining tables, Chip at his shoulder. Along the wall he used his dive light to show them spiny lobsters, a black-and-white spotted moray in a crevice, a school of 100 or more silvery horse-eyed jacks circling in the open water off the wall. Wally worked his way back up to sixty feet and reversed his course, bringing the divers back to the hole in the wall in half an hour. A glance upwards showed him the *J-Valve* was still tied to the mooring. He exhaled slow with relief, then signaled he was surfacing, letting the divers finish the dive under the boat.

Once all the divers were back onboard, the mood on the boat was more upbeat than it had been. The guests joked with each other and chattered about the fish they had seen. No one seemed to notice the underwater geography was nothing like Wally had described in his briefing. Wally untied the bow line and idled toward the mooring ball closer to shore Vinson had said was Wahoo Reef. Once again, Wally had no idea what that site was like underwater, but he had dived Blacktip Island's shallow reefs before and could guess close enough. Not that the divers would notice, apparently.

At the mooring he caught the mooring line on his second try. He studied the water around him—bright turquoise over the sand, with long, dark fingers where coral heads rose. Easy enough to navigate, especially if he stayed close to the boat. Wally gathered the divers and gave another seat-of-his pants site briefing, using the coral blobs around the boat as reference points. He helped the divers get geared up and into the water, as before, and spent several minutes helping the last one swap out a leaky o-ring on her tank valve.

With another silent prayer the mooring line wouldn't break, Wally shrugged into his gear and jumped in the water. Below him the coral heads looked like miniature mountain tops poking through a flat layer of snow-white sand. Chip was under the boat and again fell in beside Wally. The other six divers were in their buddy pairs, which was good. But they were heading in three different directions. Wally raced after the closest pair, motioned them to follow him, then headed in the direction the next closest pair had gone.

He wound his way among the coral fingers, heading generally towards shore. He hoped. After five minutes he spied twin white columns of bubbles rising to the surface. The second pair of divers! Wally circled in front of them, stopped them, and signaled them to follow him. He turned to his left, in the direction he thought the final pair had been headed, and led Chip and four divers with puzzled faces off through the coral maze.

Wally weaved through the coral, eyes toward the surface, straining to see the telltale bubble trails, not even pretending to show the divers underwater wildlife. Ten minutes later he found the final two divers, Roger and his buddy, on their stomachs in the sand, taking photos of a feeding stingray. Relieved, Wally looked around for any familiar features to tell him where the *J-Valve* was. He thought it was to his left, but he wasn't sure. All the coral looked the same. He signaled to the divers and swam in the direction he thought the boat was moored. The divers followed. Wally steered a crooked path along the coral, anxious for something familiar looking. Nothing was. He pointed out purple-and-yellow fairy basslets upside-down under ledges, a hawksbill turtle, another stingray, as if nothing was wrong. Ten minutes passed. Then fifteen. Then twenty.

A tug on his fin made him turn. Roger's buddy was making a slashing motion across his throat with one hand and shoving his air gauge at Wally with the other. Out of air? Sure enough, the man's gauge read 100 p.s.i. Wally tapped on his tank to get all the divers' attention and signaled they all needed to surface. The divers looked puzzled but still followed him.

At the surface there was no boat in front of them. Wally looked left, then right. There, forty yards away and slightly behind him, bobbed the *J-Valve*. Vests inflated, the group swam on the surface to the boat. Wally climbed out, then helped the others.

"What the hell kind of outfit is this?" Roger demanded. "I'm down there taking pictures, next thing I know you're making me follow you."

"I was making sure everyone was together before I went back to the boat," Wally said.

"Well, we came up nowhere near the damn boat!"

"We were getting here when your buddy ran low on air."

"We were heading in the wrong direction. You need to get your act together, pronto. I didn't pay good money to get dragged around the reef, either."

"Just bear with me. Today's not the norm." Wally started the engines, worried this was fast *becoming* the norm. Maybe he should stay on the boat next time, let the guests dive without a guide. No, that created more, potentially worse problems. He idled back toward the dock, feeling everyone except Chip glaring at him. Daydreaming about finding even one divemaster to hire.

The wind had picked up, sending small white swells rolling across the fringing reef, making the cut's green water stand out. Wally steered left to line up the white square and triangle range markers on shore to center himself in the cut. He seemed to be too far toward the green-painted channel marker, but so long as the range markers were lined up, one video had said, he was on course.

When the *J-Valve* was nearly in the cut, a frothy wavelet behind him rolled past, foaming over the coral just off the port bow. It was too late to alter course. Wally held his breath as the boat slid past the green marker, so close one of the guests could have touched it. The coral loomed, brown and green, two feet from the boat's hull. Wally exhaled, checked the range markers.

Still lined up. What the hell? Had someone moved the markers as a sick joke? He stared straight ahead, not daring to look at the guests' faces behind him.

At the dock, Wally nosed the boat up to one of the cleats, jumped off, bow line in hand, and cleated it off. He jumped back on the boat, cut the wheel hard left, and reversed one engine until the stern crunched against the dock, then jumped off and cleated the stern line. Not pretty, but it worked. The guests watched him, clearly not impressed with his boat handling. They gathered their dive gear and stomped up the dock towards the gear-drying shed. Roger gave Wally a nasty glare. Chip slapped Wally on the back and flashed an encouraging smile.

Val, on her way down, passed them at the top of the dock. A younger man and woman followed her.

"That was an . . . interesting . . . docking." Val tried to hide a smirk. Failed. The smirk morphed into a slight smile. "How'd it go, running solo?"

"The docking was the best part of it."

"From the faces going up the dock, I figured. But I have a solution for you." She motioned to her two followers. "This is Angela and LB. They're both divemasters and can both dock better than you. Oh, and LB's a mechanic, too."

Angela was short, thin, with dark skin and blue eyes. LB was short, stocky, and looked vaguely piratical with his tattooed arms and shaved head and ear piercings.

"They . . . I mean, you, both of you want to work here?"

"I do know that old boat," LB said.

"Me and LB grew up on these reefs," Angela said "We know these sites blind."

"What about work permits?" Wally looked to Val. This was too good to be true.

"That's the best part. They don't need them. They're Tiperon citizens. Oh, and did I mention they can start tomorrow?"

"Where . . . How . . ."

"You said you needed staff. I knew Angela was just back on island and LB had just quit Eagle Ray Cove."

"Then let me find some staff shirts and . . . Can you really start in the morning?"

"Tomorrow'd be good," LB said.

"Great! Let me show you the shop."

Wally led the way toward the dive shop. This was a bizarre stroke of luck, but he wasn't going to question it. He should interview them before hiring them, but if they were the only staff available, he would hire them and hope for the best.

"I can pay you what I paid . . . no, you know what? I'll pay you *more* than Harry and Cerena got, as a 'thanks' for being available."

"You wanna ignore those range markers, y'know." LB said. "Got set up wrong, way back when. I seen you come in." He stifled a smile.

"Ha! Already proving your worth." Wally said. "That was . . . uncomfortable."

He glanced around the desk at the jumble of scuba parts, first aid supplies, and Going Under Divers shirts and caps.

"I'll get you staff shirts later," he said. "As soon as I find them."

After the three left, Wally found Vinson in the Inne's dining room with the guests and pulled him aside.

"You know anything about two local divemasters named LB and Angela?"

"LB's a good guy. Haven't seen Angela for a while, but she's all right, too. Why?"

"They're my new staff. Fingers crossed they're reliable?"

"As reliable as the next person on Blacktip."

"That's what worries me."

"How'd you track 'em down so fast, you bein' on the boat all mornin'?"

"Val, from the Tail Spinner, brought them. I mentioned I needed staff, and boom, she showed up with LB and Angela."

"That Val, she's quiet, but got her finger on the pulse of everything." Vinson nodded, looking thoughtful. "May be getting' her touch back. That gal's magic. And where there's magic, look for miracles."

"I can certainly use both right now."

"Good one to have on your side. Worth gettin' to know."

"A little plain for my taste, but I'm grateful she felt like helping."

"Ought to buy her a drink as a 'thank you.' Maybe two."

"Yeah, I'll make it up to her . . . somehow. But right now I need to get to the bank, set up an account."

Wally was lost in thought pedaling to the bank, cashier's check, papers, and passport stuffed in a brown envelope, legs aching from several days of the unaccustomed exercise. He needed to find a way to thank Val without it seeming like he was attracted to her. She was nice enough, but she seemed too eager. He needed to shut that down as politely as possible, without offending her. Or telling her Alison was a lot more interesting.

The Blacktip Island bank was a squat, cinderblock building, painted a bright tangerine color, with a wide, glass floor-to-ceiling door. He reached for the handle as a security guard inside was locking the door.

"I need to get in. To open an account!" Wally waved his cashier's check at the man.

"Closed for lunch." The guard waggled a finger at him.

"Closed . . . it's midday. I have business to conduct!"

The guard waggled his finger again, pointed to the hours of operation taped inside the glass. Sure enough, the bank was closed for an hour midday. Wally ground his teeth, headed for home. He would get lunch, calm down, and come back. At least there were no afternoon dives.

He stopped at the store to grab something to microwave, eat in a hurry, then get back to the dive shop. There wasn't much in the frozen case, but Wally grabbed a burrito and went to pay.

Peachy smiled as he approached. The door next to the register swung open. Harry and Cerena walked in. They froze when they saw Wally, eyes widening.

"I knew I'd run into you two, but didn't think it'd be this soon," Wally said. "Where do you get off leaving me in a bind like that with no warning?"

"Hey, we helped you out by staying like we did," Harry said. "Finn offered us jobs the week before."

"It wasn't personal," Cerena said.

"It was to me!" Wally had to force himself not to shout at them. "I had six, seven divers and no crew. You left me standing there looking like an idiot in front of the guests."

"Finn needed us to start straight away," Harry said. "We known him way longer than you."

"The least you could have done was to tell me you weren't coming so I could make other plans. You stayed long enough to collect your money, then left, all the time knowing you weren't coming back!"

"That would have made for a really awkward conversation," Cerena said.

"Like this one?"

Wally was nearly shouting now. He turned to Peachy, held out a stack of cash. If he said any more to Harry or Cerena he would end up cursing.

"Oh, hey. I left a mask in the dive shop," Harry said. "Can I drop by and get it this afternoon?"

"Hell, no! It's mine now!"

Wally snatched the frozen burrito off the counter and pushed past the two divemasters. If he stayed in the store any longer, if Harry asked another stupid question, he might punch the man.

In his apartment, Wally wolfed down the burrito, thinking of all the other things he should have said to Harry and Cerena. He took a deep breath, exhaled, then again. His jaws unclenched.

His shoulders relaxed. Staying angry wouldn't make the situation better. It would just ruin the rest of the day. He had a staff now and could move forward. Harry and Cerena could do whatever they wanted—it no longer mattered.

Wally arrived at the bank as the guard was unlocking the door. He pulled his cashier's check from his big envelope and stepped to the sole teller.

"I'd like to open an account, please." Wally slid the cashier's check across to the teller.

"Why you need a Tiperon bank account?" She gave him, and the check, a suspicious look.

"To deposit my money into and pay bills out of."

"You work here?"

"As of last week, I own Going Under Divers."

"All right, then" She gave him another suspicious look. "Need to see four forms of identification."

"Four?" Wally dug into his envelope, pulled out his passport, his U.S. driver's license, his divemaster card, and a credit card. "That seems extreme."

"It's the law. Got to know who's openin' accounts. Stop money launderin'."

The teller took all the I.D.s, squinted at each in turn, then photocopied them all.

"Need a faxed letter from your U.S. bank confirmin' you got that check from them, too."

"The bank's name and address're on the check! And if I were hiding money, why would I use a check?"

"Got to have confirmation."

"You're making this up."

She slid a paper with bulleted points across the counter to him.

"Got to tick each of those items to get an account."

Sure enough, 'Confirmation from issuing bank' was on the list. Feet shuffled behind him. Impatient customers. If he stepped aside now, it could be a while before he got to the front of the line again. Wally pulled out his cell phone, called the stateside bank's number on the check. He handed to phone to the teller. After a brief conversation she handed the phone back to him.

"They'll fax us a letter."

"Fax?" Wally said. "I thought that was a slip of the tongue."

"Use 'em a lot here."

"Wow. Okay. So, we about set?" He glanced at the list of requirements.

"Need proof of employment, too."

Wally handed her the partnership contract for Going Under Divers.

"No, no," she said. "Need a letter from your employer sayin' you really work here and how much you make per week."

"Seriously?" Wally tapped the partnership agreement. "*I'm* my employer! And how much I make depends on how many divers I have each week!"

"Can't open an account without an employment letter."

She crossed her arms. Wally had an inspiration.

"What if I let you talk to my Tiperon partner?"

Hopefully there was nothing in the contract prohibiting Ferris Skerritt from talking to the bank teller on Wally's behalf. He dialed Skerritt, explained the situation, then handed the phone to the teller one more time. After a brief conversation, she handed the phone back to Wally.

"He'll fax a letter, too. Soon as we get those letters, we can get you set up." She slid a handful of papers to Wally. "Need to fill out these, too." She pointed to a chair across the room, then motioned for the next customer to approach.

Wally sat, leafed through the papers. A statement acknowledging the money was acquired legally. A statement avowing he had no criminal record. Other statements of good character, of financial responsibility. Wally filled them all out and signed each one, then waited for the fax machine to beep. Half an hour later the clerk motioned to him.

"Got both letters now," she said.

"Great! Here's all these forms, completed, and here's my cashier's check!"

"Application still has to be approved." She took the forms from him, slid the check back. "Come back next week."

"Next week? I can't wait that long! I have a business to run! Employees to pay!"

"Rules're rules. I open an account without that approval, I lose my job."

An idea popped into Wally's mind, so obvious he didn't know why it hadn't occurred to him before.

"What if I deposit my check in the Going Under Divers account?" He could access his money from there, then transfer it over whenever he had his own account.

The teller looked dubious, then tapped on her keyboard. She pursed her lips.

"You can deposit it, but you can't get it back out. You're not a signatory."

"But I own the company."

"Still not a signatory. And anyway, the account's frozen."

"Frozen for what? Why?" He needed that account.

"Insufficient funds."

Wally glanced at the wastepaper basket by the door, certain he was going to throw up. There had to be some way to get cash for the coming week. He pulled his gold credit card from the brown envelope.

"Can I get a cash advance with this?"

The teller studied him, her suspicious look returned.

"Got to charge a fee," she said.

"Fine! Fine! I need money!"

After Wally filled out three more forms, the teller scanned his card and counted out a stack of bright-colored pink, blue, and green Tiperon bills. Wally thanked her, stuffed the cash into his envelope. Outside he dialed Smackie Bottoms. If Smackie was a signatory on the G.U.D. account, he could get Wally's name added. No answer. Wally left a message. Then he called Ferris Skerritt. He would need to know what was happening with the company bank account.

"Young Wally, it's good to hear from you again," he hissed through the phone.

"Yeah, thanks for your help earlier. Look, I'm locked out of the Going Under Divers bank account. I've got a call in to Smackie Bottoms . . ."

"Oh, that won't do." The words came out like vapor escaping a vent. "That won't do at all. That account is *needed* for business."

". . . to see if he can add me to the account . . ."

"I'll have a word with Jack Wrasse at the main branch on Tiperon. He and I have a certain, ah, relationship. A bit of quid pro quo might be appropriate in this instance."

"I . . . great!" After their earlier conversation, Wally hadn't expected this one to go so smoothly. "Let me know how that goes and when I can use the . . ."

Skerritt hung up.

Wally stared at his phone. Skerritt was rude, but he was getting Wally the needed account access. He grabbed his bike and pedaled back to the dive shop, thighs aching with every turn of the pedals.

At the shop, his stomach tightened at the sight of the spider-covered pile of past-due bills. With no bank account, there was no way he could get caught up on all that before the next month's bills arrived. He put his cash in a metal strongbox under the desk, then tossed the note to return engine parts to Finn in the trash. Finn could damn-well wait for *that*.

He thumbed through Cerena's convoluted booking sheets. An upside to her leaving was he could throw the damn legal pads out and start from scratch with something better. Something computerized.

By the end of the day, he had finished transferring all the bookings from the notepad to his new scheduling spreadsheet.

Instead of stacks of legal pads, they could now make one entry in 'reservations' and be done with it. He would walk LB and Angela through the process the next day, make sure they were comfortable using it for times Wally wasn't around. In a box under the desk, he found a half-dozen green STAFF shirts in various sizes. He brushed the spiders off the counter with his arm, then set the shirts on the counter for Angela and LB.

Wally leaned back in the desk chair. All in all, it had been a good day. Frustrating, but things had worked out. Or soon would. He glanced around the office, making sure everything was in place. A well-used black dive mask sat on the bottom shelf next to two small dry boxes. Harry's mask, no doubt. Wally scooped it up on his way out the door. He locked the shop, hung the mask on the door handle for Harry to find. He wasn't about to be so petty as to not return a mask.

6

The next week, Wally slipped into the Blacktip Haven dining room through the side door, tried to blend in with the guests. He spotted Jessie at the head of the buffet tables and cut his way across to her.

"Hey, that was a great time the other night," he said. "I've never seen you away from work."

"Yeah, happy hours on Blacktip can be . . . interesting."

Wally grabbed a tall paper cup, dropped in three slices of bacon and a big scoop of scrambled eggs.

"How's it going today?" he asked.

Jessie looked uncomfortable.

"You might not want to do that." She nodded at the cup of food.

"That again? It's just bacon and eggs. Elena doesn't care."

"Yeah, it's just . . ."

"There'll be no more of that, Wally." Elena's voice boomed from behind him. "You're welcome to breakfast, if you pay for it. You have to understand you're no longer a guest here."

"That's fine." A quick, hot breakfast was worth a nominal fee. "How much?"

"Twenty-five dollars."

"For bacon and eggs?"

"That's our price. It's built into the all-inclusive fee."

"But it's just a quick bite."

"And you're no longer a guest."

She took the cup from Wally's hand and tossed it in a trash can. Jessie edged away.

"So you're going to throw it away instead of letting me eat here one last time?"

"I'm making this point as clear as possible." Elena drifted back to the kitchen, shouting at the staff before the swinging door slapped shut.

Jessie gave Wally an 'I-tried-to-warn-you' look and followed her into the kitchen. Resort guests eyed Wally as if he might steal their valuables.

Teeth grinding, he snatched a slice of bacon and left, grabbed his bike and pedaled north as fast as he could. He would get some microwaveable dreck from his apartment and eat it in the dive shop before the guests arrived.

A late model blue Cadillac was parked outside the shop when Wally arrived. He hopped off the bike and stared. It was the first vehicle he had seen on the island without rust and dents and cracked glass. Even the tires looked new. He crept toward it, half expecting it to disappear as he drew closer.

"She's a dandy, isn't she?"

A familiar voice hissed from inside the open dive shop door. Ferris Skerritt stepped into the morning sun.

"It is . . . how'd you get in?" Wally was certain he had locked the shop when he left the day before.

"Had a key made." Skerritt could have been commenting on the weather. "Part owner you know. Need to gain access from time to time, and you're not always around."

"I . . . sure. Something I can help you with?"

"No, no. Just getting acquainted with the place."

Skerritt climbed into his car and drove away. Wally stepped into the shop, wondering what Skerritt could have been looking at. Or for. Before anyone was there. Everything seemed to be how Wally had left it. The computer screen was on, though, so Skerritt had been looking there for . . . something. Wally couldn't imagine what in the computer might interest the man. Or why he had waited until Wally was gone to look. That didn't bode well.

Wally's wondering was cut short by Angela's arrival.

"Great! You're here," he said. "I wanted to go over some new office procedures with you."

"New?" Angela looked skeptical.

"The old way was a bit . . . clunky. Let me show you the way we enter bookings now."

Angela watched Wally walk her through entering names on a master spreadsheet, then their advance deposits in the accounting program, nodding all the while. Wally had her enter several parties and deposits to make sure she was comfortable with it.

"You've got it. Easy, huh? The system before was insane, with a legal pad and a new sheet for each day."

Wally waved Cerena's old dive count pads in the air, then set them on the desk. Angela thumbed through the top legal pad.

"This old way's better," she said. "I know 'Rena's writing. She's a smart cookie."

"Yes, but we live in the 21st Century."

"Simpler than a computer, though. On Blacktip, simpler's better."

"So I've been told. But since we have a computer, we're going to use it and run this shop properly."

"Mister Wally, on Blacktip, a lot of times when you do things the right way, they don't work. And when you do things the wrong way, they *do* work. This schedule . . ." she shook the legal pad at Wally for effect, ". . . it works. I'm gonna do things the wrong way and everything'll work out fine. You'll see."

"Absolutely not! We have modern technology that makes the task more efficient . . ."

Angela was already leafing through the sheets of paper, ticking off names and dates with a pencil as she went.

Wally threw up his hands, walked outside to calm down. He had employees, yes, the only ones to be had. But what was the point if they wouldn't take direction? He walked to the road, then strode across to the resort. He couldn't afford to fire, or cross, Angela. He would throw out the old scheduling pad that evening. Faced with the choice of starting a new one from scratch or simply typing names into Wally's spreadsheet, Angela would take the easy route.

The door to the Inne's central building seemed off, as if it had moved farther down the wall. Wally stopped, confused, staring from the door to where he thought it had been. There was no way the door had been moved, especially not overnight. The faceoffs with Angela and Elena must have rattled him more than he thought.

Inside he found Vinson sweeping the lobby, seeming bigger inside the small room, singing a song with a syncopated beat.

"Ol' Vin-son, he the smartest one . . . Vin-son he got all the fun . . ."

"I'm learning what you meant by 'as reliable as the next person on Blacktip,'" Wally interrupted him.

"More problems, Mr. Livin'-in-Paradise?" Vinson stopped sweeping. Grinned.

"Just Angela won't do scheduling on the computer."

"Oh, she does have her quirks." Vinson chuckled. "Good worker, though. And honest."

"But I'm trying to improve the business. Bring it into modern times."

"Any harm lettin' Angela do things the way she knows and likes?"

"You're saying cave in."

"I'm sayin' you got troubles enough without creating more. Go with what works. This is Blacktip, y'know. Get upset over every minor thing, you go crazy here."

Wally crossed back to the dive shop, defeated. Vinson was right. He had enough on his plate without starting a war with the only staff he had. But he would keep up the scheduling spreadsheet for himself, gradually slide it into the daily routine.

At the shop, Angela handed him a slip of paper.

"Bank on Tiperon called," she said.

The scrap of paper had only a line of a dozen numbers, with no explanation.

"This is . . .?"

"Your account number," Angela said. "Said the tellers'll bring your checkbooks when they come on Thursday."

"And the Going Under Divers account? Can I access that?"

"Didn't say. You can ask . . ."

"On Thursday. I know."

Wally leafed through the stack of past-due bills, sorting out which were the most important to pay. Electricity. Internet. He shuffled through the cash till, making sure he had enough cash to cover LB and Angela's pay for the week.

He left Angela flipping through the legal-pad schedules, humming to herself, and went to find LB, see what sort of insurrection the mechanic harbored. Wally heard a tapping sound from the *J-Valve*. He peered over the gunwales. LB had the engine cover up and was on his knees, rapping a screwdriver on something in the bilge.

"Getting things ready for the morning dives?"

"I wish," LB said. He straightened, gave Wally a pained look. "Stringer's getting soft."

"And the . . . stringer . . . should be hard?" Wally had no idea what a stringer was, but it seemed important to LB.

LB stared at him a moment, then smiled.

"Stringers're those long strips runnin' the length of the boat." He motioned to thin, low fiberglass-over-wood rails parallel with the boat's centerline. "Hold the hull together. Reinforce it so it don't twist and buckle."

A chill shot through Wally.

"Soo . . . If the stringer's soft, the hull's not as strong as it should be?"

LB nodded.

"Bilge water seeped through the gelcoat somewhere. Got in the wood. Rotted it." He shook his head at the hull. "Boat inspection should've caught that. Ought to get your money back."

Wally's chill turned to a greasy knot in his stomach. He didn't dare tell LB he hadn't thought to get a boat inspection. Hadn't *known* to get a boat inspection. And what was worse, he didn't have time, or money, for expensive boat repairs. And what LB described sounded expensive. Plus, they had divers booked every day for the next month. Not many, but Wally couldn't afford to lose any of them by not running.

"Realistically, how bad is this?"

"Not critical right now, but needs to be fixed. Sooner than later. Whenever you can pull the boat, rip out that old stringer and put in a good one."

"So, we can still run the next month or so?"

"Should be able to. Treat her gentle. 'Specially with dockings." LB smothered a smile.

"Right." Wally ignored the ribbing. Relief washed through him. This wouldn't put him out of business. Not immediately. "What does something like that cost to fix?"

"Depends." LB shrugged. "Best option's take her to a boat yard on Tiperon. Don't have that kind of time, you could fly somebody over to do it here. Got to pay for their lodging and food, though."

"Something you could do?" If LB made the repairs, that could save a ton of money.

"Gelcoat and all, sure. But that stringer needs somebody who knows what he's doing, if you want it to hold up."

"You suggest anyone?"

"Got a buddy on Tiperon. Lemuel could do it."

"Lemuel?"

"Lemuel Chromis, I got his number. Tell him I sent you."

LB pulled out his phone, showed Wally the contact screen. Wally punched the number into his own phone.

"I'll give him a call as soon as you and the guests are off the dock."

LB ducked back into the bilge.

Wally walked up the dock, mind racing about money, about the damaged boat, about being persona non grata in the Blacktip Haven dining room, then stopped. He did a slow 360-degree turn, taking in everything. The turquoise water. The waves breaking white across the reef. Cumulus clouds high in the bright blue sky. The rocky beach. And behind that, the palms shading the dive shop, their fronds quivering with the faint onshore breeze. Parrots chattered high in the fronds. This was his office now. Despite the money woes, the difficulties with the boat, butting heads with Ferris Skerritt, and getting shooed out of Blacktip Haven, he was lucky to be living here. And wouldn't trade it for anything. He inhaled deeply, absorbing the scent of sea and sand and the building tropical heat. Things would work out.

At the dive shop, he sent a quick note to Hank-O, checking on when the promised Big Chicken Divers group would arrive. He mentally tallied the money he had in cash and with the cashier's check. Money would be tight, and he had no idea how much fixing the boat's hull would be. The income from this week's divers would make a huge difference.

Voices, shuffling feet outside told Wally this week's divers had arrived. He went out, greeted them and started down to the dock. From the Inne, Chip Pompano fell into step beside him.

"Got room for me today?" he said.

"Sure. I . . ." Wally studied Chip for a moment. "I want your job, whatever it is, that lets you hop over to dive for a day or two whenever."

"I'm just a boring finance guy," Chip laughed. "Over on Tiperon. Work for myself, so the boss lets me set my own schedule."

They were at the dock then, where Angela and LB were prepping the *J-Valve*.

"Folks, welcome to Going Under Divers and the *J-Valve*," Wally said to the guests. "Today you'll have the honor of diving with Captain LB and Divemaster Angela. They grew up on these reefs and'll take you to the primo spots."

Chip gave him a grin and a thumbs-up. At a nod from LB, the guests all clambered aboard, fins and masks and wetsuits going a dozen different directions. Wally pulled LB aside.

"You think you could teach me to drive this boat?" he muttered so only LB could hear. "There's gonna be days you're off, and, well, if I'm gonna make a go of island life, I need to be able to take a turn at the wheel."

"Oh, sure," LB said. "Did all right before. We just need to tweak your docking."

Wally cast off their lines, stayed on the dock, and watched the *J-Valve* idle through the cut, then throttle up, leaving a broad white wake behind.

In the shop Wally glanced at his bank account number on the scrap of paper. Now that he had an account, he could start budgeting money for bills. And boat repairs. He grabbed the stack of bills from the back of the desk, shook three small, brown spiders off of them and went through them one by one, writing the amounts due on a legal pad. The total was more than Wally had expected and would eat up more of his cash than he had hoped. It couldn't be helped, though. He just needed more divers. More than the reservation sheets showed. He glanced at his phone. Still no reply from Hank-O. Wally put the high priority bills on top of the stack and slid the less important ones to the bottom. If he had known the company had so much debt, he wouldn't have been so eager to buy it.

Movement by the door caught his attention. Vinson stood in the doorway, grinning again.

"Boss man hard at work, I see."

"Yeah. Vinson, did you know how much money Smackie owed his creditors?"

"I knew he didn't like messin' with numbers. And was eager to sell. Your good fortune."

"At this point I *need* a fortune. You knew this place was in the red?"

"Now, there's knowin', and there's *knowin'*. Can't say I *knew* anything."

"You let me buy the place. You encouraged me to buy it."

"Struck me as somebody lookin' to make a change. Any change. You were more than halfway there."

"You could have told me."

"Where's the fun in that?" Vinson erupted in a deep, rolling belly laugh. "You'll do fine. You'll see."

"You put me behind the eight ball for fun?"

"Put yourself there. I just agreed it'd be a interestin' place to be."

Vinson turned and was gone, trailing laughter behind him, leaving Wally sitting at the desk, mouth hanging open. Vinson had suckered him. Pranked him. For laughs? That made no sense. He needed Wally's divers to fill his rooms. But at no cost to himself. That had to be it. And Wally had jumped at it. There was no undoing it. And Vinson was right: he *would* be fine. The beginning was just turning out to be bumpier than expected. Another spider dropped on his desk. He swept it into the trash can and reminded himself again to get bug spray at Peachy's store.

Wally scrolled through Angela's reservations sheets. There was a three-day gap in bookings next month. He could block those days out, maybe get the *J-Valve*'s stringer replaced then. He called the phone number LB had given him for Lemuel Chromis.

"This Lemuel." A nasal, high-pitched voice answered.

"Hey . . . Lemuel . . . This's Wally at Going Under Divers on Blacktip. I need a boat stringer replaced, and LB said you're the one to call."

"Oh, I can do that, Mr. Wally. It'd be next month or so, though."

"Perfect! We have a break in guests then and can make do in the meantime. How long would it take you to replace a stringer on a twenty-six-foot boat?"

"Depend on the boat. And the stringer. Maybe two days. Maybe three. Need all the supplies, though."

"LB and I'll get everything."

"Tools, too. Be doing it on the side, and boss won't let me use his."

"No problem. When can you get here?"

"Say . . . three weeks from Tuesday?"

"Great." That coincided with the gap in bookings. "I'll fly you over and put you up in Noboddie's Inne."

"Food, too?"

"Of course."

"And drink?"

"Absolutely." Whatever it took to get the guy over. Lemuel would need something to wash down his food with. And if he had a beer at the end of the day, that was worth the minor expense.

"I see you then, then."

A scratching sound came from behind him. Wally spun his chair. A brown rat the size of his hand was doing its best to scramble up the wooden post and into the 'As GUD As It Gets' t-shirts for sale on the shelves above it. Wally yelled, snatched the stapler from the desk and flung it at the rat. He missed by a foot, but it had the desired effect. The rat dropped to the floor and scampered behind the big supply cabinet in the corner. Wally pushed against the cabinet, trying to move it, chase the rat outside, but it wouldn't budge with all the office and boat supplies inside.

Wally locked the shop, grabbed his bike, and pedaled south. In ten minutes he was in Peachy's store, buying bug spray and rat traps. He scanned the shelves for something to use as bait. Raisins! Perfect. He added a box of those to his stack and went to pay for it all. At the register, Peachy was talking to a big-bellied man with gray, three-day stubble and a faded red Eagle Ray Cove polo shirt.

"I hope those are for your dive shop, not the apartment," Peachy said.

"Shop. Definitely the shop," Wally said. "You wouldn't believe the spiders out there. And a giant rat just introduced itself."

"That Vinson, he won't like you spraying his spiders," the fat man said. He eyed Wally, as if looking through him. "Them spiders're part of that place. Why you'll make a go of it."

"Wally, this's Antonio," Peachy said. "General handyman and island seer."

"Seer? Like a fortune teller?" These two were pulling the island newbie's leg.

"See what's gonna happen," Antonio looked past Wally, eyes unfocused. "What could happen. *Sometimes* there's a fortune. But most times not. Truth be told . . . never."

Antonio nodded slowly. He could have been talking to someone behind Wally.

"Well, if Vinson's spiders don't stay off my desk, they're gonna get sprayed. He protective of the rats, too?"

"Ol' Vinson don't care 'bout rats." Antonio chuckled. "He took a interest in you, though."

"He maneuvered me into buying the place. For laughs."

"That *does* sound like Vinson" Antonio said. "You got an adventure ahead of you. Ready or not."

"Vinson's an odd duck, and not one to cross lightly, but he's taken a shine to you," Peachy said. "You'll be fine. You doing karaoke Tuesday?"

"On Blacktip?"

"Sure. Down at Eagle Ray Cove. On-and-off tradition. And Tuesday it's on."

"Oh, I don't do karaoke," Wally said.

"One of the island major social events," Antonio said.

"Not if I sang. I'd clear the bar before I finished one verse."

"Good way to meet folks, too." Antonio flashed a half-smile. "Or see 'em again."

Wally smiled, too. He had been working too much lately. He had moved to Blacktip to embrace new things, improve his quality of life. And it would be great to meet up with Alison. But how had Antonio known? Had he been at happy hour that one night?

"So, Eagle Ray Cove," he said. "Where would I find that?"

"Down the coast road, past Sandy Bottoms and Club Scuba Doo," Peachy said.

Wally paid and pedaled back to the dive shop, wondering what to make of Antonio. And what Antonio and Peachy meant by their comments about Vinson. Vinson was odd, but so was everyone else Wally had met on the island. 'The island of misfit toys,' Val had called it. He may have encouraged Wally to buy a less-than-viable business, but he was providing guests to make the business work. That counted for something. And Antonio had been right about one thing—Going Under Divers *would* be successful.

Ferris Skerritt's car was sitting at the shop again when Wally arrived. Wally pushed open the unlocked door and found Skerritt in the middle of the dive shop, eying the walls and ceiling.

"Something wrong with the place?" Wally said.

"No. Just imagining where you could put some more shelves, have more shirts and caps and other, . . . haberdashery. We need to squeeze as much, ah, juice out of this orange as we can."

"Well, I have boat repair expenses coming up, so that'll have to wait. Unless you want to pay for it."

"Oh, no." Skerritt waggled a boney claw at Wally. "The expenses are all yours."

"But the more money I make, the more you make. You won't bend the rules to help with that?"

"I'm making sound, business-like suggestions." Skerritt smiled, as if explaining something simple to a child. "And I gained access to the shop's bank account."

"Seriously? That's great! How do I access it?"

"Oh, *you* don't." The condescending smile didn't waver. "As the principle owner, I'll be the one using it."

"So how do I pay bills, and payroll?"

"I understand you now have a personal account?"

"Use my personal account for business expenses . . . not the business account?" There was something he was missing, not understanding.

"You *can* use the business account. That's where you'll deposit my share of profits each month. From *your* account."

"So why not use *your* personal account for that?"

"Because it concerns my business. It's how I'll keep the income from here separate from my other . . . income streams."

"It's my business, too. My account." Wally's stomach did a slow roll.

"I *did* pay off the overdue funds, so I'm actually out of pocket on the deal," Skerritt said. "But I'm willing to overlook that, keep it just between us, as a benevolence."

Wally slumped into the office chair, defeated.

Both men looked up at the sound of feet scuffling. Vinson ambled through the doorway, stomach bulging and mouth grinning.

"Not interruptin' an executive meeting, I hope," he said.

Skerrit stiffened, turned to face Vinson and eased toward the door, keeping the distance between them.

"A simple discussion among associates." It was a sharper hiss than usual. "We were just concluding."

"Good to see you takin' a interest in the place," Vinson said. "Wally here, he's workin' night and day to make things work out."

He clapped an arm around Wally's shoulders, shook him as if they were long lost friends. Skerrit continued his slow shuffle toward the door, circling past Vinson like a wrestler squaring off.

"We all want Wally to succeed. But I do have pressing affairs elsewhere."

Skerritt backed outside. Moments later the sound of a car starting, then pulling away came through the open door.

"What was that about?" Wally said. 'Not one to cross' echoed in his head.

"Ol' Ferris, he does get jumpy sometimes. He's a flighty little feller."

"He's a rapacious little fellow. Who seems uncomfortable around you."

"Ferris does blame other folks for things goin' wrong in his life." Vinson chuckled, setting his belly jiggling.

"Is he right to? With you?" Fear shot through Wally, wondering what kind of lunatic he had fallen in with.

"Everybody responsible for what happens in their own life. Folks who make bad choices, well, some of 'em do like to blame other folks."

"And why's he blame you?"

"Families never cottoned, I reckon. I live and let live. Friend to everybody."

Vinson spread his arms wide, palms up, as if questioning how anyone could think badly of him.

Wally let it pass. Vinson had seemed harmless so far, and if he kept Skerrit away, that was a plus.

"Came to tell you Val did stop by while you were out," Vinson said. "Said she got some ideas for g'tting' you more divers."

"That I could use. But how'd she know?"

"Val, she knows. That Tail Spinner's fertile ground for talk and rumor. And problem solvin'. Kind of neutral ground on the island, with her in the middle of it."

Vinson looked like he wanted to say more, but paused.

"What's the deal with Val?" Wally said.

"Deal?"

"She stays in the Tail Spinner, doesn't hang out with anyone, doesn't go to parties, doesn't drink . . ."

"Once upon a time she did all that," Vinson said. "Used to be right in the mix. Everybody's favorite. In a good way."

"And now?"

Vinson studied Wally, as if gauging how much to say.

"Her story to tell . . . but Val, she had some rough luck. May be you the one to pull her out of that."

"You want me to ask her out?"

"No, nothin' like that." Vinson paused, took a deep breath. "Val had her heart broke and her cash stole in one fell swoop a while back. Had saved up, dreamed of buyin' a sailboat, explorin' the world. Ran into a guy down at Scuba Doo, had the same dream. Found a boat on Tiperon, the boyfriend flew off to bring the boat here, and that's the last she saw of him."

"Lost at sea?" Wally's mind raced through all the ways someone could die on a sailboat.

"Nope. Lit out with the boat. And the money. Her old job was filled, so she took to runnin' The Spinner. Dump when she took over. Built it up nice, but buried herself there. Good to see her back out, mixin' a little."

"That's . . . I wouldn't have handled that as well as she did."

"Oh, she's a tough one, that Val. Made of sterner stuff than she looks. Her takin' an interest in your business's a good thing. In the day, she had a way of bringin' folks luck."

"We'll see."

"You'll see, all right. You'll see."

Vinson strolled out the door, chuckling.

7

Eagle Ray Cove was as Peachy had described it, a dozen wooden bungalows on three-foot stilts, strewn across an expanse of sand and palm trees south of the Blacktip Haven turnoff. At the center of the complex, music was blasting from a thatched tiki bar surrounded by a wooden deck and pool.

Wally made his way to the deck, looking for familiar faces. He found Angela at the bar, talking to Jessie. Jessie gave him a thin smile.

"Hey, I'm sorry about the other morning," she said. "At the Haven. I was trying to warn you."

"I caught Elena at a bad time is all," Wally said. "I certainly know how important cost cutting is. And I'm still waiting for my buddy in Atlanta to send the divers he promised to send."

"Well, that was really more of the norm, is the thing. Elena's great to work for, but she's not always the laid-back, eccentric groupie she shows to her guests."

"Not a worry," Wally said. "We'll patch things up. I'm not gonna let it get me down."

"You gonna sing tonight?" Angela said.

"Not a chance. My voice sounds like someone's skinning a cat."

"Oh, we get a lot of that here. You'll fit right in."

Val crossed the deck, greeting people as she went. A smile here. A hand on a shoulder there.

"I was wondering if you'd be here." She smiled at Wally, nodded a greeting to Jessie and Angela.

"Time to get out of my bubble," he said. "I've been letting work stress me out way too much. There's been too much of that."

"Still having a rough time?"

"Well, you helped, bringing me Angela and LB. Can I buy you a drink as a thank you?" This was the perfect time to share one drink with her, then fade into the crowd.

"Oh, I don't drink at these things." Val gave him a half smile. "When I first got here, sure. But the novelty wore off. And once you've been here a while, you realize it's all the same drama and arguments and stories, the faces just change. Now, I sit back and enjoy the show."

"So, at this point you know everyone on the island," Wally said.

"Pretty much. The Spinner's a popular spot, too. You should stop by more often."

"Yeah, I probably should." Wally didn't want to tell her his main motivation for being here was to run into Alison. And he liked the crazy Caribbean vacation vibe at Eagle Ray Cove. The Tail Spinner was a bit stodgy for his taste. He scanned the bar, looking for Alison.

"If you're stressed, take an afternoon off, do a shore dive," Val said. "For me, that's the perfect relaxant."

"You should've been a divemaster."

"Nah. I don't like the early hours. And it takes its toll on your body—you don't see many older dive staff. Plus, I don't want to ruin something I love by turning it into a job."

Across the deck, Cal, Alison, and a short, stocky man, with a coyote's face and dark hair trying to be a flattop, were making their way to the bar. Wally excused himself and went to join them. Hopefully Alison would be drinking lightly tonight so he could spend time with her without getting rat-faced drunk, let her see the real Wally, not the idiot drunk who ran off early last time.

"Wally! You're just in time!"

She grinned, handed him a beer, passed others to Cal and the other man.

"This's Lee," she said. "He's a DM here, too."

"Didn't think we'd see you out." Lee said, accent nasal and thick and British. "Or if you even existed. Not the most sociable chap on the island, are you then?"

"Work's been busy. Doing all the things your boss does for you."

Wally didn't know why Lee was being snarky and didn't much care. He wouldn't let it ruin the evening. Alison appeared with another round of beer.

"C'mon, Wally! Let's have a proper piss-up!" She said in an exaggerated British accent. She clinked their glasses together, switched back to her normal voice. "You're behind, loser!"

She nodded at the half-finished beer in front of him. Wally forced down what was left of it, then reached for the basket of popcorn on the bar. He should have eaten more before he went out.

"Nah, Mate. You don't need that." Lee pushed the popcorn away. "If you're eatin', you're cheatin'!"

"Didn't know it was a contest." Wally wondered if it would be bad if he punched Alison's friend.

"Not a contest, but you want to get the full effect don't you?"

Wally accepted a fresh mug, watched Alison and Lee down half of theirs. Cal sipped his. Antonio appeared at Wally's side, seemingly out of nowhere, pulled him aside.

"Don't worry 'bout young Lee," he whispered. "Alison eyein' you got his dander up."

"He and Alison are together?" That seemed an odd pairing.

"No, but Lee, there, needs to be the center of things, even if it's for bad reasons." Antonio slapped Wally's shoulder, spoke louder. "You fittin' in nicely, Warren. Meetin' folks. Makin' friends. And vice versa. You chasing the light, though, when you should be chasing the dark."

"It's Wally. And I'm chasing . . . I should be drinking dark beer?"

"Oh, not about that, y'know. The dark's for you. I *seen* it." He put a forefinger under one eye, pulled the eyelid down slightly. There was something about the way he said 'seen.' Wally started to ask more, but Antonio disappeared into the crowd. Wally turned to Alison.

"What was that about?"

"'Tonio and his Second Sight." She rolled her eyes. "His predictions don't usually work out, but when they do, it's hella-spooky."

"Or lucky." Wally laughed. "What was that about dark and light?"

"Not a clue. And neither does he. He loves to drop stuff like that into conversations, though. You ready for another?"

Wally shook his head. How could someone so small, so thin, put away that much beer so quickly? Alison pushed another full mug toward him.

"Drink up, lightweight. The party's about to rock." She finished off her latest beer and headed into the crowd.

A driving, pounding drum beat started. An electric keyboard kicked in. Something that sounded like wind chimes in the background.

"Welcome, everyone to Eagle Ray Cove's karaoke night!" A short, thin man with a shock of white hair boomed into a microphone. "Kicking things off tonight is our very own Gage Hoase!"

A tall man with a mop of sun-bleached hair, looking like an animated Q-Tip in an Eagle Ray Divers staff shirt took the mic and belted out a rough-but-listenable "Gin and Juice." Heads in the crowd bobbed, enjoying the performance. Wally burped, tried to quell the rumbling in his stomach. Four beers in quick succession had been a mistake, but he wanted to impress Alison. She grinned up at him, head bouncing in time with Gage's singing.

"It's his signature tune," she yelled to Wally above the music. "Always knocks it out sometime during the night."

Wally nodded, not trusting himself to speak without belching. Alison waved toward the bar. The bartender nodded.

"So what's *your* tune?" she shouted at Wally.

"Nothing. I have a voice that turns any song into a Gregorian chant."

"No, no. You've *got* to sing *something*."

"Be careful what you ask for." There was no way he was going to sing, especially in public. And in front of Alison.

"We'll see."

Alison patted him on the shoulder, then fought her way to the bar. She came back with orange drinks in tall, clear plastic cups. She handed one each to Wally, Cal, and Lee, and kept one for herself.

"Now we get serious!" She raised her cup. "To new adventures!"

She drained a quarter of her drink. Lee did the same to his. Wally sipped at the cocktail. Orange juice and vodka. Lots of vodka. Great. Alison motioned for him to take another drink, looking hurt.

"You don't like it?" she said.

"No, no. It's not that," Wally said. "I'm just taking it slow, is all."

"I thought you were down with this. You need to loosen up, Dude."

She motioned to him again. Wally took another sip. He didn't want to offend Alison. He was here to do just the opposite.

"That's the spirit!"

Gage finished singing. A woman took the mic, launched into a version of "New York, New York" in a thick Deep South accent. Alabama. Or maybe Mississippi. Alison laughed.

"Sick, right?"

Wally smiled, nodded, guessing from the context that 'sick' was a good thing.

More singers passed the mic around. More drinks arrived. Wally did his best to keep up, not trusting himself to speak more than a syllable at a time.

Lee took the mic. Music came up, oddly familiar. Then Lee launched into "What's New, Pussycat," doing a fair Tom Jones impersonation.

"That's *his* standard," Alison yelled over the music.

Wally gulped what was left of his old drink and took the next from Alison. They were getting along great, but he didn't know how long he could keep this up. Luckily, LB and Angela would be on the boat tomorrow, so he wouldn't have to interact with guests unless something went wrong.

Lee was playing to the crowd now, making eye contact with women around the deck, circling back around to point a finger at some of them, grinning between pauses in the lyrics. A few women laughed. Most looked dubious.

"This how he picks up women?" Wally said.

"I know, right! It's how he *tries*!" Alison laughed. "He's really bad at it, but every once in a while, one'll bite. For a drink or two. In his mind, though, he's Don Juan."

"So why hang out with him?"

"He's fun. And entertaining. On this island, you can be the biggest a-hole and no one cares. For long. But being boring's a cardinal sin."

Lee finished with a bow, made a show of holding the mic out as if he would drop it, then set it on the deck at his feet. Wally nodded a greeting to Hugh, standing with Jessie across the crowd. At the back of the deck, under guttering tiki torches, a group of older residents gathered, men in collared shirts, women in long dresses. They clustered together in a semicircle, watching the singers, but keeping to themselves and apart from the crowd. Alison pressed another drink into Wally's hand.

"Who're the standoffish people at the back?" Wally pointed the drink at the group.

Alison stepped close, pressing against him, eyes following his arm to where he was pointing. A flowery smell wafted up from her hair.

"Oh, that's the island gentry." She laughed, low and throaty. "The got-rocks. Second- and third-homeowners. They show up for the spectacle, but tend to keep their distance. They'll warm up to you in fifteen, twenty years, maybe even lower themselves to have dinner with you."

Wally's stomach rumbled, not pleased with the mixture of beer, vodka, and orange juice. But Alison was smiling at him, still pressing close. That was good. He willed his stomach to behave.

"Picked out a song yet?" She stood on her tip-toes to shout it in his ear.

"Seriously, I can't sing."

"Too bad." She handed him a notebook with songs listed on laminated pages. "You have to. 'Specially since it's your first time."

Behind her, Lee and Cal nodded, solemn-faced.

Wally took the book. Apparently, there would be no getting out of it. He felt sorry for the people listening. He skimmed the song lists. Nothing jumped out at him. But he had to pick something.

Alison wandered away, toward the DJ at the head of the bar. A woman in her twenties started singing a heartfelt, if off-key, rendition of "Strawberry Wine."

Wally kept flipping through the lists. "The Monkees' theme song? No, too cheesy. "American Pie?" No, it had about eight verses, and all he knew was the chorus. The Ramones' "I Wanna Be Sedated"? He couldn't screw that up *too* badly.

The young woman finished singing. The intro to "Don't Go Breaking My Heart" came from the loudspeakers. Alison reappeared, in his face, a mic in each hand.

"We're up, Dude!" She held one mic out to him. "You were drag-assing, so I picked for you. And I'll help out!"

Wally stared at her, a chill shooting from head to toes. This wasn't happening. He wanted to impress Alison, not butcher a duet with her. The mix in his stomach gurgled, threatened to surge upward. He fought that back and set down his cup. At least he would be free of the incessant drinking for three or four minutes, even if it meant embarrassing himself. Alison's orange eyes stared up at him. Expectant. There was no way out. And he had the opening line.

He barked out the first words, voice breaking, eyes glued to the screen where his blue-shaded lyrics scrolled past, followed by Alison's pink ones. He locked all his focus on the screen, not daring to look at Alison or the crowd.

"Oooo hooo! Nobody knows it!"

His voice was steadying. They either sounded quite good together or absolutely awful. Without looking at the faces around him, there was no way to tell. Wally chanced a glance at Alison. She was watching him, grinning when he sang. That was a good. He hoped. His stomach roiled again, as if some wild animal were trying to get out. He clamped down on that, tried to focus on the monitor. Either the screen was getting blurry, or he was.

After long, agonizing minutes the music finally stopped. There was a smattering of applause. Wally chanced a look at the crowd. Most of the guests were staring at him, wide eyed, mouths open in shock. Some were still in mid cringe. A few glanced at each other, as if trying to understand what they had just seen and heard.

"Not so bad!" Alison took the mic from him. "Flat, sure, but totally not a medieval recitation."

She handed Wally another drink. He gulped a quarter of it, hoping to moisten his sand-dry mouth.

Other singers took the mic, blurring into a montage of sound pounding through Wally's head. He stayed with Alison. Laughed at whatever she said. Tried to not to be boring. Tried to quell the growing chaos in his stomach. The drinks didn't seem to be affecting him as much as they had earlier in the evening.

"Ooo! This one!" Alison said. "We're dancing!"

She threw her arms around his neck and spun them around on the deck, a quavering male voice blaring "Still the One" from the speakers. His hands were on her waist. The lights around the deck whirled, sending a fresh wave of nausea through him. Alison's face blurred, then eased back into focus. He needed to go home. Now. While he could still stand. He made a show of spinning Alison, then stepped back.

"I need to go," he said. Or tried to say.

"Damn straight!" Alison yelled to the group. "I've had enough karaoke. Let's hit Sandy Bottoms!"

Around her, heads nodded. She spun back to face Wally.

"We're headed to Sandy Bottoms for another round." She grinned up at him, face indistinct again. "You're coming, right?"

"I . . . have to work in the morning." Wally enunciated each syllable, trying to speak as clearly as he could. Trying to not sound drunk.

"It'll just be one drink. Promise. And it's on your way home, anyway."

She stepped close. The flowery scent of her hair mixed with a sweaty, earthy smell, folded around Wally. Her hand was on his arm, soft and warm. She had a point. One more drink wouldn't make tomorrow morning any worse. And Alison really wanted him to come along. His stomach gurgled, so loud Alison had to have heard it. He nodded, not trusting himself to speak.

The bike ride to Sandy Bottoms Beach Resort cleared Wally's head some, though his stomach was still rumbling. What he hoped were fireflies swirled around him. If they weren't fireflies, he was hallucinating. Otherwise, all was great. Around Alison he felt free and interesting and cool for first time he could remember. She was fun and exciting and like no one he had ever met. But he wasn't sure he could keep up the pace with the drinks. Would she see his not drinking as being rude? There had to be a way to dial the drinking back, or ease away politely before he got too drunk to speak. And he really did have to work in the morning.

At Sandy Bottoms' bar, he caught up to Alison at the outdoor bar, now talking to Cal and to Finn from Club Scuba Doo. Lee was nowhere to be seen.

"Just in time!" Alison said. "Thought I lost you."

"Not a chance," Wally said. Or hoped that was what came out of his mouth.

"Here you go." Alison slid an overflowing shot glass toward him.

"You said 'one drink' . . ."

"And here it is. Cheers!"

Alison, Cal, and Finn tossed back their shots. Wally hesitated, then drained his. He wasn't about to wimp out in front of Alison *and* Finn. Chilled sambuca coursed down his throat.

"Okay. That should do it." Wally tried to focus through watering eyes. He gripped the bar's edge to keep from swaying.

"C'mon. One more for the road."

Alison was signaling the bartender. Before Wally could respond another full shot glass was in front of him. His stomach roared, as if alive. Conversation around him stopped.

"Whoa! Steady there, Tiger!" Alison said. "You'll break the seismograph."

"I really do have to work tomorrow. Early." And he didn't want to throw up in front of Alison. Or on Alison.

Alison raised her eyebrows reproachfully. Batted her long, black lashes. Wally nodded, swallowed the shot. Then before Alison could order another, he slapped whatever money was left in his pocket onto the bar without counting it and staggered back out to his bike, hoping he could keep the roiling thing in his stomach down until he reached the empty roadway so no one would see him vomit. He wove his way up the darkened dirt road, concentrating on keeping the bike upright through the pools of light cast by the intermittent streetlights. At his apartment, he fumbled open the door and crashed face down on his bed, feeling the room spin around him.

***

A pounding on his door woke him. Sunlight streamed through the windows. Someone shouting. Vinson. Wally's head ached. His mouth felt like he had eaten half the beach. Work. Damn. He rolled out of bed, stood. Dropped back to the bed, stomach clenching. He stood again, slowly, and went to the door, a hand on the wall to steady himself. Outside Vinson was sweating, his face flushed.

"Got people waitin' on you, Wally!" He waved up the road, toward Going Under Divers. "Angela and LB're preppin' the boat, but the guests're gettin' restless, wanna see you."

"Right. Give me two seconds to get ready." The words slurred from his mouth, as if he were talking through spider webs. He couldn't remember the last time he had been this hung over.

Vinson looked doubtful. Wally waved him in, filled a glass with water, and swallowed a mouthful. It nearly came back up, but Wally kept himself from barfing. He set the glass down. One sip was enough, and at least it had wet his mouth. Sort of. He pulled on a clean STAFF t-shirt and motioned Vinson out the door.

They raced up the west coast road, Wally's bike rattling in the van's back, and dust swirling in through the stuck-open sliding door. Wally gripped the door handle and the dashboard, fighting down the urge to throw up with every bump and pothole the van hit. The inside of his mouth was a desert again.

At the dive shop, guests were pacing around the desk, wanting t-shirts, seasick pills, weather forecasts. Wally waved them away.

"Boat's 'bout to leave," he managed to croak. He waved toward the dock. "I's a flat day, no one'll get sick, and you c'n get a t-shirt after."

He shooed them from the shop, closed the door, and cranked down the air conditioning. He slumped forward in the office chair, head sideways on the desk, watching until Angela had cast off and LB had idled away from the dock. He went outside then, to the water faucet on the side of the building. He knelt, turned the handle, and let the cool water course over his head. He turned his head sideways, opened his mouth, let the water wash through it, hoping to get some moisture back in his body.

"Tried to keep up with Alison, didn't yah, now?"

Vinson stood over him, looking shorter, squatter now. Chuckling. Wally squinted up at him, wondering how Vinson knew that.

"Word does travel fast on a small island," Vinson said. "Plus, I seen that look before. Bound to happen sooner than later."

"Y'knew this'd happen?" It came out as a burble through the running water.

"Not the first one to chase Alison. Not the first one couldn't keep up, either. That Alison, she's small, but she got somethin' genetic lets her pack away the booze."

"So how d'I catch her?"

"Learn quick or die tryin'." Vinson grinned down at him. "Alison's great. Think the world of her. But she's a firecracker lit at both ends. You wanna run with that one, you got to be able to keep the pace. In every category."

Vinson walked across to the resort, head shaking and shoulders bouncing from his quiet laughter. Wally went back inside, scrabbled through the first aid kit. There was aspirin and several other painkillers. He dumped some of each in his hand, went back out to the faucet and hoped a few quick swallows to wash the pills down would stay in his stomach.

Back in the office he found the mail from the day before. He had rushed out without looking at it. Flipping through it now, he found another electric bill, an internet bill, bills for boat fuel and t-shirts and boat parts. Wally set them all on the side of the desk. He would deal with them when he had a checkbook. He locked the door, then settled into the overstuffed armchair in the corner and closed his eyes, stomach still rumbling. Head full of visions of Alison smiling, dancing, the flowery scent of the night before. 'Learn quick or die trying,' Vinson had said. That was harsh. But maybe worth it for Alison, the way she made him feel. There had to be something, some local island remedy to negate the alcohol so he could match her drink-for-drink. He would ask Vinson. When he could trust himself to enunciate.

8

Wally buried himself in Going Under Divers the next week, working with the dive guests, practicing boat handling until he could dock by himself, doing what he could to attract more divers. And staying home in the evenings to save money. And avoid drunken binges with Alison.

His battle against the rats was going well, with four dead in snap traps that week, and no signs of more. He gave up on clearing the office of spiders. They were small, didn't do any damage, and he didn't want to be constantly spraying—and breathing—insecticide in the small room.

Emails to Hank-O still went unanswered, as did his phone calls, with Hank's assistant giving multiple variations of, 'he just stepped out.' Whatever was going on, he hoped Hank, his family, were okay. Some personal crisis was the only reason Wally could think for Hank to not return repeated calls.

He had hung up from his latest Big Chicken Divers call and stepped outside to go home when Val pulled up in a white Jeep, brakes squealing, soft top off, and Chip in the passenger seat.

"Hey! We're on an island tour." She pulled her wind-swirled hair from her face. "Wanna come along?"

"Thanks, but three's a crowd," Wally said.

"Ha! It's nothing like that." Val grinned. "We're scouting shore dive sites."

"Climb on in! The more the merrier!" Chip boomed.

Minutes later they were cruising down the island's northeast coast, gravel crunching under the tires and Wally sitting sideways in the back. Dust swirled around him, and blue sky flashed intermittent through green palm fronds as they bounced down the unpaved road.

"There's some nice dives off this stretch of coast, but you also get some big seas over here." Val yelled to be heard above the sounds of tires and air rushing past. "It's rocky, too, so shore entries can be tough."

"So, the west side's where it's at," Chip said.

"Oh, you can get in over here, you just have to pick your day and entry spot. And wear booties. In the summer the seas calm down, and it's usually nice along here."

"Could you make a list of those? Or draw a map?" Wally said. "This is stuff I need to know, to have shore diving options. Just in case."

"Sure. But first I'll show you," Val said over her shoulder. "Some aren't official, marked sites. You just have to know where they are."

"There's unofficial sites?" Wally said.

"Ones without mooring balls." Val smiled in the rearview mirror. "Most of this coast's ironshore. Finding good entry and exit spots is tough."

"That's why I usually stick to boat diving," Chip said. "Unless things are ideal, going in from shore's too much work."

Wally smiled, imagining himself driving the boat down this coast, taking Chip and other divers to seldom-dived reefs. This was good, getting away from the shop and the money worries.

Val turned off the road, onto a car-wide track leading through the brush. They stopped at a sandy beach perhaps 100 yards long. Low wavelets rolled over a thin strip of reef. With the Jeep's engine off, they were surrounded with the buzz of insects in the bushes and the soft slap of waves. Val pointed to the dark shapes of coral under the turquoise water.

"This's Alligator Reef. One of the non-official sites." She grinned at Wally. "The sand makes it easy to get in and out, and the coral just offshore is super healthy because people rarely dive here. Coral arches and overhangs. Rubble with jawfish and pipe horses. Sand for rays and flounder. I almost always see an eagle ray here."

Her face took on a distant look, as if she were seeing jawfish and eagle rays now, or had gone back in time to a past dive. She spoke softly, as if speaking to herself. Her lips curled in a faint smile.

"You really love this place, don't you?" Wally said. "Underwater."

"When I'm on the reef . . . it's my Zen time, when I can just chill and not think about . . . anything."

"You make it sound religious."

"It kinda is. Depending on your definition." She laughed, high and silvery.

"Well, if you ever want company, and I wouldn't be in the way . . ." This Val was interesting. And she had a stockpile of local diving knowledge he needed to tap into.

"I'll let you know." She gave him an odd look, then started the Jeep. "Let's keep on with the survey."

They drove on down the coast, Val pointing out shore entries as they went. They passed a low, rambling collection of dark wooden buildings joined by covered walkways.

"That's Toad Hall." Val waved a hand toward the compound and the sea beyond. "If you haven't met Payne Hanover yet, you will. He throws crazy parties—famous and infamous—several times a year. You'll end up here sooner or later."

"Oh, yeah!" Chip rumbled from the passenger seat. "A Toad Hall party's not to be missed. Never sure who, or what, will show up!"

"I'll keep that in mind."

Wally had thought he was tuned in with Blacktip Island before he moved down. Then again after bar nights and karaoke. But now, almost daily, he was discovering how little he knew about his new home. Less, even, than perpetual visitor Chip.

"You enjoy running Going Under, don't you?" Val eyed him in the rear view. "Even with all the hassles."

"Some days less than others." Wally half-laughed. "Things seem to be falling into place now, though, so . . . yeah. I'm making less money than I was, but my quality of life more than makes up for that."

"You took a big chance buying that place."

"Things usually work out."

"And when they don't?"

"Doesn't happen often, but when it does, I move on."

"To here?"

"Yeah, actually. And it's starting to pay off. I think. I hope. Big expenses are manageable, and diver numbers are inching up."

"Glad you're making a go of it." She flashed a bemused smile. "There's always been such potential there."

"How could it not succeed?" Chip said. "Best dive op on the island. The boat's not crowded. The staff's laid back. Word'll get out quick. Sounds like it already is."

"That income-versus-expense thing can get dicey," Wally said. "And I have to make sure Angela and LB are covered. I'll go bankrupt before I let them down."

"Hell, you can always make money."

"For you, in finance, sure. But not when you have a boat that keeps breaking. Frankly, I'm holding my breath waiting for the next thing to blow up in my face."

"You're doing great," Val said. The wind swirled her hair around her face again. She clawed it back into place. "And I have a friend who may be able to help. A quick, question, though, if it's not too nosey. Why'd you pick Ferris Skerritt as your partner?"

"Vinson recommended him. I didn't know anyone else."

"Vinson? Suggested Ferris? Huh."

"I admit, he's a little dodgy."

"Ferris Skerritt's a little dodgy like the beach's a little sandy." Val rolled her eyes in the rearview mirror.

"You had an attorney look over that contract, right?" Chip said. "Right?"

"Of course . . . So what's the story with Vinson? And with him and Skerritt?"

Hopefully he could distract them both from asking more pointed questions about his deal with Skerritt. And the mistakes he had made.

"Ferris and Vinson?" Raised eyebrows in the rear view.

"Vinson's laid back but . . . enigmatic," Wally said. "And Skerritt is super edgy around him."

"Oh, he's enigmatic, all right. Nice use of the word!" Val paused, as if not sure what to say next. "He just has a . . . unique sense of humor some people don't always appreciate. The Noboddies and Skerritts go way back. Descended from some of Blacktip's original settlers."

"A family feud, then?"

"Sort of. Years ago, to impress his greedy father, young Ferris conned Vinson's folks out of their land and most of their money. Wiped them out. They had to move to Tiperon to get by. Vinson raised enough money to buy a worthless chunk of land on Blacktip close to nothing, moved back, and built the Inne a bit at a time. A way to thumb his nose at Ferris, I guess. Showing he wasn't beaten. Him suggesting Ferris as a partner, maybe that's an olive branch. Burying the hatchet. That, or his odd sense of humor's about to take a gnarly turn."

"Skerritt's in fight-or-flight mode when he's around." Wally thought back to the office scene with the two men.

"Vinson's good side's the preferred side to be on."

"You're the second person who's said that. I don't see it."

"Vinson just has . . . his own agenda and his own way of looking at things." Val's eyes unfocused for a moment. "But that describes most people on the island."

All three were silent.

Val slowed, waved her hand toward several rows of precisely-spaced palm trees, a broad stretch of beach beyond, and the calm, blue surface of a sheltered cove.

"This's Spider Bight. Nice place to dive, and hang out on the beach post dive. Sharky, too, so that's a plus, if you're into that kind of thing." Another smirk and rear-view glance.

A tan, oblong-shaped house loomed on the headland at the far end of the beach. As they drove past, Wally thought it looked oddly like a football.

"Why's that house shaped like that?" he said.

"All kinds of theories," Val laughed. "You want the true story, track down Cal at the next happy hour. His dad built the original, then Cal rebuilt it after it burned down. He'll tell you all about it. In detail and at length."

They passed sporadic wooden houses, most on stilts or pillars, tucked among the palm trees. Most had broad verandahs overlooking the sea.

"These places look nice," Chip said. "Any of 'em for sale?"

"Probably," Val said. "Pretty much everything on Blacktip's for sale. If you have the money. And these'd take a *lot*."

"They that fancy?"

"This's Mahogany Row. Mostly second- and third-homes for gagillionaires. You could buy four or five regular houses for what they'd want for one of these. If they'd sell."

"You in the market for a house?" Wally said.

"I'm spending enough time over here, makes sense, even if it's just a rental," Chip said. "Vinson wouldn't be too happy to lose a customer, but I'd still eat at The Spinner. And I'd save money long term."

They continued down the coast, Val pointing out breaks in the brush leading to more shore entry sites, smiling, laughing, happier than Wally had seen her. Chip kept up a steady stream of questions. Wally barely heard them, unexpectedly caught up in Val's surprising, infectious cheer. The dirt roadway narrowed. Trees on either side crowded the shoulder on either side, bright green leaves hanging over the road. The air thickened, oppressive, almost choking. Then a sharp right turn and the trees fell away and the air was lighter, fresh with a sea breeze. Wally had a glance of a low, blocky building with peeling turquoise paint and something about 'THE LAST BALLYHOO' scrawled in orange over the door.

"Popular watering hole for locals," Val said. "Out of the way, so it doesn't get many tourists. The Spinner's the place to be, though. The manager's nicer, and the clientele's better."

Chip laughed, nodded approval.

Val gave Wally another rear-view glance and smile. Yes, this was a new, different Val than Wally had come to know. Relaxed. Upbeat.

Soon they headed down a steep switchback leading to sea level. Next, they were headed back north, up the island's west coast.

"Things'll start to look familiar now," Val said.

They passed several smatterings of multi-colored cottages baking in the sun. They passed Eagle Ray Cove. Wally smiled, thinking of singing with Alison. Minutes later, he cast a wistful look at the inland track leading up to Blacktip Haven. He needed to patch things up with Elena. Eventually. If Going Under Divers lasted long enough. He pushed that negative thought from his mind. Things were falling into place now. He was on a roll.

"There any houses on the market down this way?" Chip said.

"Lots of older places along here," Val said. "They're all quirky. The salt climate takes its toll on houses. And if they're right on the coast, storm surge's probably hit them, too."

"Where's good, then?"

Val gave Chip a long, appraising look.

"I'll keep an eye out, let you know."

"You looking to buy a dive operation, too?" Wally half-laughed from the back seat.

"Don't need one." Chip chuckled. "Got you."

"And you're working miracles," Val said. "It's a bit of an inspiration to watch."

They neared the island's other road running from the west coast to its east. Just before it was a thin track running up and inland, where a pale green wooden cottage perched on stilts above the tree line.

"How 'bout that one?" Chip pointed at the cottage. "Nice view, I'll bet. It worth looking into?"

"Absolutely not." Val grinned at him. "That's where *I* live. Named 'Parrett's Landing,' after the original owner."

"Worth a try." Chip shrugged.

"Does everybody name their houses here?" Wally said.

"It's a thing," Val said. "Appropriate, I guess, since each house has its own personality. Parrett's, up on those stilts, dances in the wind like it's going to take off, but it's home."

The algae-and-bird-poop stench of the island's central booby bird preserve hit them then, making Wally's eyes water.

"Never mind any houses along here." Chip pinched his nose, shook his head.

Club Scuba Doo was a sea-side blur, then the imposing pink walls of Sandy Bottoms, and the airstrip after that. Then Diddley's Landing public pier. Soon the Tail Spinner came into view.

"I'll drop you both off at the Inne," Val yelled above the tires' rumble. "If you both want to stop by The Spinner later, we're doing a blanquette de veau special tonight," she said.

Wally smiled. He had had a surprisingly-fun afternoon with Val playing tour guide, watching her come alive showing them her island. If she was as knowledgeable under water as she was topside, he definitely needed to go diving with her.

He crossed the dirt lot to the Inne, wanting to ask Vinson about two of his late-arriving guests. Like the last time Wally had visited, the central building seemed different. Somehow changed. The paths to the satellite rooms, too, seemed to curve in odd ways. He had been in the topless Jeep for more than an hour, though, and had probably taken too much sun to his head. Wally followed the round path circling the center building, found the out-of-place door and stepped into the cool, darkened room.

He didn't see Vinson, but he heard noise—metallic clangs, a voice singing—from the kitchen. He crossed the dining room, stuck his head in the door. Vinson, his back to the door, was stirring a soup pot with a big metal spoon, singing to himself.

"Ol' Vin-son, he the only one . . . Got ev'rybody on the run . . ."

"This a private concert?" Wally said.

Vinson spun, grinning, looking more gangly than ever.

"Wally! You just in time to taste my fish-head stew!"

He held the big spoon out to Wally, its bowl filled with a green, oily liquid smelling of low tide.

"No, thanks . . . I'm . . . no." Wally kept the door between him and the spoon. "I was checking to see if the Steinhauers had checked in yet."

"Got here 'bout an hour ago. Excited about divin'" Vinson still held the spoon out, as if expecting Wally to change his mind. "Seem like good folks. Y'ought to come back later, have supper with 'em."

"I . . . No . . . I'm having dinner with Val at the Spinner."

"There you go!"

"And Chip."

"Well, that's all right, too. Less to recover from than a night with Alison."

"Yeah. Hey, Vinson, have you been moving things around over here?"

"What sorts of things?"

"Doors. Windows. Pathways, maybe?"

Vinson studied him a moment.

"Too early for you to be drinkin,'" he said. "Coconut fall on your head?"

"No, it's just . . . lately when I wander over, things seem, well . . . different." It sounded stupid as he said it. "You know what, never mind."

"Been workin' too much. Stressin' too much. Need to take a break from that."

"That's probably it." Wally had been working long days.

"Folks get turned around here all the time, though," Vinson said. "Guests go to the wrong room, forget where the dinin' room is. Normal day at the Inne."

Wally looked from Vinson, to the still-extended spoon, then nodded and left, making his way outside—taking note of where everything was—and back to the dive shop.

Inside, Wally swept the spiders off the counter with a file folder and made out the next day's dive roster, adding the Steinhauers to the list. He would drink more water, see if being dehydrated was causing his passing confusion. He would start wearing a hat, too, to keep the sun off his head. And pay more attention to the surroundings when he went to the Inne. And make the time to take a few minutes to relax, destress throughout the day.

He locked the shop and pedaled south, toward home. Odd, thinking of the grimy little shotgun apartment as home, but that's what it was now.

When he passed the Tail Spinner, the scent of something roasting wafted across the road with the onshore breeze. Onions. Celery. Coriander. Other savory spices he couldn't identify. His stomach rumbled, and he stopped to savor the smell. Val's promised 'blanquette de veau,' whatever that was, no doubt. The island tour had sidetracked him from eating lunch. He had used dinner with Chip and Val as an excuse to avoid Vinson's dubious cooking, but it seemed an obvious choice, standing here in the road and realizing how hungry he was.

He would get a quick shower, then head back to The Spinner. He hadn't had a proper, sit-down dinner since he had returned to Blacktip. Yes, things were definitely looking up.

It was dark by the time Wally returned to the Tail Spinner. He opened the door, and the rich smell of a sauce, or a stew, wrapped around him, set his mouth watering. Several small groups of locals clustered at the bar when Wally arrived, divemasters in staff shirts, construction workers in work clothes, fishermen in ragged pants, all talking in subdued tones. Nodded greetings to Wally. In the far corner of the dining room, a group of six island gentry talked together, paying no attention to anyone else. He saw Chip and Val at a table on the back deck, and crossed the dining room to join them.

"You did make it," Val said. "We weren't sure."

"Weather's nice, so we decided to sit outside." Chip waved a glass of red wine at Wally, inviting him to sit. "We started with a Burgundy, a Santenay."

Wally smiled, nodded, not sure what that meant other than 'red wine.'

Val reached in a cabinet behind her, handed Wally a wine glass.

"You can stick with this, or switch to something else with dinner."

He sipped the wine, smiled at its earthy, red-berry taste. Yes. Much better than rapid-fire tequila shots chased with beer. From his chair, he had a view of the dining room and bar through the plate glass windows.

"You really do draw a diverse crowd," he said.

"The Spinner's kind of a quiet place people can gather," Val said. "And out of the way, so people have to seek it out. That's what I was aiming for, anyway. Anyone can come in, relax, not worry about island drama or politics. I leave the big parties for the resorts and keep this place low key."

"And the food's some of the best on the island," Chip said. "Nothing against Vinson, but . . ."

Wally held up a hand to stop him.

"I have a hard time walking anywhere near the Inne's kitchen," Wally said. Then, to Val, "This place is like something from a spy movie, with all the quiet conversations and furtive glances."

"Well, I do tend to know what happens before it happens." She laughed.

"So . . . you've got the dirt on everyone." Was Val a barracuda behind her unassuming front?

"If I wanted to." Val rolled her eyes. "It's interesting to know what's going on. That's about it. And people know I'm discreet. They can come here, relax, and talk freely. Hungry?"

Val stepped away, into the dining room and to the kitchen. She returned a minute later with bowls of creamy white stew, filled with chunks of white meat, sliced carrots, celery and onion, topped with snipped chives. Wally hadn't been sure what to expect, but his stomach rumbled and his mouth watered again.

"Here's the Tail Spinner's take on blanquette de veau." She set a bowl in front of each of them. "Fancy name for veal stew."

She set three fresh wine glasses on the table, and a bottle of white wine.

"The red goes well with this, but some people like the crisper taste of a Chablis. See what you think."

Wally dug into the stew, rich with thyme, coriander, and garlic. To either side of him, Val and Chip were doing the same, tasting first the red wine, then the white with the stew. He looked around him, smiled.

"You know, this is the first real, proper, sit-down dinner I've had since I got to Blacktip," he said.

"Well, enjoy." Val raised her white wine glass to him. "The way you've been going at it with Going Under, you deserve a nice meal."

"It'll come together," Chip said. "Keep doing what you're doing. I'll see if I can send folks over, too."

"I'll take any help I can . . . Ooo! What the hell?"

Wally pointed to the base of The Pinnacle, where the wavelets were shimmering a pale neon blue where they splashed against the pillar.

"Oh! Bioluminescence!" Val said. "Some species of plankton glow when they get jostled. Dinoflagellates. It's fairly technical. But pretty. We don't see it much here."

"There's something new in the sea here every time I come over," Chip said. "You, both of you, are good luck."

"Can't take credit," Val said.

"Know what? Next time I'm over, we need to do one of those unofficial shore dives together. Just the three of us."

Val and Wally looked at each other, then back at Chip. A smile crept across Val's face.

"I have an idea," she said. "Next time you're on island, Chip, weather permitting, I know just the place."

Wally nodded agreement. A social outing not involving mass quantities of alcohol would be good. And Val was growing on him.

9

The next weeks were a blur for Wally. Income from the increasing trickle of diving guests still wasn't quite covering his expenses, and he ended up using more of his reserve money to pay bills. Then, when Ferris Skerritt took his monthly percentage, Wally moved more of his savings into his Tiperon Bank account to cover payroll. He still had heard nothing from Hank-O, despite multiple messages and phone calls. He sent his buddy Geoff a quick note, asking him to stop by Big Chicken Divers to make sure Hank, and the store, were okay.

His outings with Alison were sporadic, and he made sure they ended early in the evenings—as hooked as Wally was on the island's wild child, he had a business to run, divers to take care of every morning, and he didn't have the luxury of spending a night trying to keep up with her, or to be utterly hung over the next morning.

The bright spot for the business was Lemuel Chromis was finally flying over from Tiperon to fix the *J-Valve's* hull. Now Wally just needed to come up with the money to pay him, probably by again dipping into his savings.

He sat on the Tail Spinner deck at sunset, looking over the sea grapes surrounding the deck and across the water at The Pinnacle. A cooling breeze blew off the sea. Val set a plate with a burger and a mound of fries on the table next to his beer.

"Divers finish up this morning?" she said.

"Yep. Thanks for sending them my way." He gave her a weak smile. "Not sure what happened to my guy in Atlanta."

"Glad to help out. It's good for Vinson, too. And the island." She sat in the chair across from him. "How bad of a spot are you in, really? Money-wise?"

There was concern in her eyes, on her face. Wally chose his words carefully. All the island didn't need to know the fix he was in.

"I'm not getting the divers I thought I would." He paused, not sure how much to share. Vinson had said Val was out of the island's gossip chain. He might as well put that to the test. "There's more expense than I expected. And the boat's falling apart."

"I figured." Her face was still filled with concern. "Anything I can do to help?"

"Keep steering people my way. And not having divers for a few days gives me a chance to fly someone over to repair the *J-Valve*'s hull tomorrow."

"I have a friend who can help," Val said. "Plays with browsers and search engines for fun."

"That'd be great, but I don't really have money to pay him, or her, right now."

"No worries. I know how difficult rebuilding a business on this island can be." She raised her hands indicating the deck and dining room. "You're taking time to enjoy the island in all this, right? You didn't move down here to work eighty-hour weeks."

"I'm trying to strike a balance and still afford groceries."

Small, yellow lights flickered in the sea grapes, moving randomly. Fireflies, or something like them. Wally blinked, stared at the unexpected sight, not sure he was really seeing them.

"Ooo! The peenie wallies are back," Val said. "Local myth's they're visiting spirits. They're unusual this time of year. Seeing them's supposed to be good juju."

"I could use some of that."

"You need to destress. Blow off some steam."

"Easier said than done."

The fireflies rose from the sea grapes, circling upward in the twilight.

"Well, Chrissy down at Eagle Ray Cove's looking for people to be in the fashion show tonight." The corners of Val's lips curved up into a semi-smile.

"Fashion show? On Blacktip?"

"She does it a couple of times a year. People parade around the bar wearing whatever she's trying to sell from the resort boutique. It's a hoot. The whole island'll be there."

Fireflies drifted across the deck in the onshore breeze, swirled around Wally and Val.

"If I go, I'll watch from the bar."

"There's free booze for all the volunteer models."

"Not an inducement."

"Pretty sure Alison's modeling . . ."

Val watched his reaction.

"You don't play fair, do you?" he said.

Val grinned, said nothing.

"What time and where?"

"That's the island spirit! Be in the Eagle Ray Cove lobby at eight. I'll let Chrissy know." She gave him a warning stare. "Eat before you go."

That evening Eagle Ray Cove was throbbing with techno dance music when Wally arrived. The lobby was packed with dive staff and resort guests, all holding up shirts on hangars, shorts, skirts, sizing up how they would fit. The reception desk had been transformed into a bar, with liquor and mixers lined up across the counter and an ice chest full of green-bottled beer on the floor. A tall, beefy, freckled woman, green eyes bird-bright and red hair flying, grabbed Wally and thrust a yellow linen shirt and a pair of khaki shorts into his hands.

"You must be Wally! I'm Chrissy!" The accent was northeastern U.S., but he couldn't place exactly where. "Grab a drink and put these on. First round's in five minutes."

She spun off into the crowd.

Wally felt his nerves kicking in, fixed himself a gin and tonic, sipped it, then added more gin.

"Hey! There y'are!" Alison burst from the crowd, gazing up at him. "I heard you were coming but wasn't sure you'd be down with this sort of thing."

She wore a bright orange-and-blue sarong, with a blue bikini top, and a red hibiscus flower tucked behind one ear. She clanked her plastic glass against his.

"Break a leg, huh?"

She took a big gulp of her drink. Wally drank, too, already feeling the gin make its way into his system. He excused himself, stepped to the lobby restroom to change. When he came back, Alison was standing with a male resort guest by the double doors, waiting to lead the show. Chrissy grabbed Wally's arm, pulled him face to face with a short, pale, thickset woman with short black hair.

"Wally, this's Rhonda. Rhonda, Wally. You guys're partners tonight. I've got you bringing up the rear, so you can chill for a few minutes."

She disappeared back among the milling volunteer models.

Rhonda was an interior designer from Brooklyn and immediately began plucking and tugging at Wally's clothes.

"There. Now the shirt and shorts are hanging perfectly," she said, her words leaning against each other as she spoke. She retrieved her drink from the reception counter, twirled once in her red sarong. "I been pregaming a li'l."

The line of models in front of them shortened. A deafening blast of the outdoor speakers announced whenever a couple opened the door to start their walk. Alison and her partner were already back and changing into their second outfits. Wally and Rhonda took long pulls at their drinks.

"Rhonda! Wally! You guys're up!" Chrissy's voice blasted like a bullhorn from the double doors.

"Follow them." She pointed to Finn and a tall woman cat-walking toward the bar. "Around the bar, loop past the tables on the deck on the other side, then through the dining room and back here. Camp it up as much as you can."

She shoved them both in the back.

Wally laughed, did a fair impression of Finn's flouncing bounce-walk down the boardwalk, arm-in-arm with Rhonda. At the bar the full force of the big speakers hit them like a physical thing. Hoots and catcalls and applause came from the guests crowding the tiki bar. Val, grinning bigger than Wally had ever seen, raised her glass to them. Wally guided Rhonda around to the deck on the far side of the bar, where a central space had been cleared for the models to show off. Wally added an extra bounce to his walk. Rhonda did the same. The crowd roared, whistled as they circled the deck, then exited back toward the lobby. There, Chrissy rushed at them, pressed new outfits into their hands.

"Change! Quick! You guys're doing great!" Then she was gone.

Wally gulped more gin, dived into the restroom and came out wearing neon green-and-pink board shorts and a black hooded sweatshirt. Rhonda was dressed in a matching outfit. The second circuit was as rowdy as the first, with guests and locals alike cheering them on. The alcohol was taking effect, and Wally and Rhonda's struts became more pronounced. Rhonda dropped Wally's arm, shimmied her shoulders at the crowd, bringing cheers from the deck.

The next outfit change had Wally in linen shorts and a bright green Hawaiian shirt two sizes too large. He laughed when Rhonda had to lean on him to tug at the shirt to get it to her satisfaction.

"That sh'do it," she slurred.

Another big gulp of booze for both of them and out they went, back into the noise and lights and cheering. When they returned to the lobby, Chrissy was thundering to the gathered models, all looking more than a little drunk.

"Everyone put on your favorite outfit for the grand finale! Two minutes!"

Rhonda pulled Wally's head down to her level, eyes bright.

"We needa cross dress."

"We . . . what?" Wally's head spun, being held down at that angle.

"Swish clothes wi' me." She undid his top shirt button, began tugging the shirt over his head. "An' here, wear my s'rong from the first round."

She vanished into the restroom, with Wally's too-big shirt and a pair of shorts. Wally wrapped the red sarong around his waist, looked for a suitable shirt to wear with it. The double doors burst open and Chrissy charged in.

"Grand finale! Now! Go! Go!" she bellowed. "Rhonda! Get outta there! We're walking! We're walking!"

The restroom door flew open. Rhonda, wide-eyed, staggered out. Only the top three shirt buttons were buttoned. The green Hawaiian shirt, big on Wally, hung halfway down her thighs like a mini skirt. Wally offered his arm, and they trailed out behind the others.

This time the crowd was more raucous than before, lobbing flowers and bar coasters at the models, clapping, laughing, shouting encouragement. Val was still grinning at the edge of the crowd. When they reached the open deck, Wally leaned down to Rhonda.

"Let's give 'em a surprise!" He grabbed her hand.

She grinned back at him, squeezed his hand.

At the center of the deck, Wally raised his arm, spun her once, twice, the tails of the oversized Hawaiian monstrosity billowing out and up as she spun, flying up above her waist.

"Wheee-heee!" Rhonda yelled.

The faces around the deck froze, as if turned to stone. Jaws dropped. The music blared on, but none of the guests moved or spoke. Then the spell broke. The crowd roared, clapped, cheered louder than before. One man fell backwards in his chair, knocking over several other people and chairs in a bizarre domino effect. Some guests simply stared at Wally and Rhonda, eyes wide, mouths open.

"I guess we really impressed them," Wally shouted above the music.

"Oh! I f'rgot," Rhonda slurred. "I didn' have time to put on shorts or panties."

"You mean when the shirt swirled up . . ."

"We gave 'em a s'prise, all right!" She giggled, half-skipped back toward the lobby. "This's a blast! You guys a'ways have this much fun?"

"Rarely. I don't . . ."

"Walleee! Pick me up!" Alison barreled into him, full cup of something sloshing over her hand. Her flowery scent surrounded him.

"Do what?"

"Put me on your back. We're doing another turn." She tapped his chest with a finger. "And don't gimme any B.S. about having to work tomorrow. I know you got no guests, and I'm off, too. You been bailing too much!"

The thought of Alison on his back was intoxicating. Wally downed another swill of his drink, knelt down, and let Alison straddle his hips and wrap her arms around his neck. The crowd at the bar roared its approval when Wally and Alison rounded the corner. Alison pumped a fist in the air, sending a juniper-smelling cascade of gin and tonic water over Wally's head. Chrissy followed behind, shouting for them to stop, tugging at Wally's sarong and Alison's shirt tails, yelling for them to give the clothes back.

A guest swapped a fresh drink for Alison's empty cup. Another pressed a full cup into Wally's hand. Syrupy rum punch, sickly sweet, but it didn't matter. He downed a third of it in one swallow. He finished his tour of the deck, Alison yelling and kicking in time with the music, then mingled with the crowd, Chrissy still with a death grip on the boutique's clothes.

Wally, head spinning, grinned at the crowd, happier than he had been since he arrived on Blacktip. He hadn't wanted to be in the fashion show, but it was the most fun he had had in ages, all his dives included. He set Alison down. She grabbed his arm.

"C'mon!" She grinned up at him, eyes bright, tossed her hair to one side and set the entwined beads clattering. "I'm stoked, and we're just getting started!"

She pulled Wally free from Chrissy and into the roiling crush of people at the bar, where guests pressed them with drinks. After a quick sip, Alison pulled him into the cleared center portion of the deck, now an impromptu dance floor. The music was too loud for conversation, so Wally gyrated in time with Alison, their bare feet scraping across the wooden deck, doing his best to keep up with her. As he danced, the night's alcohol seemed to burn off, leaving him with a refreshing sense of clear-headedness. He had come to Blacktip looking to break out of the comfortable rut of his old life. Now here he was, on a tropical island, dancing maniacally with a beautiful—if half-crazy—young woman, in a sarong, as if he had no other cares in the world. He laughed, let out a whoop of joy. Alison joined him, thrashing her head from side to side, sending her long hair flying, creating a sand-hued nimbus around her head.

***

Wally woke, face down on something soft, smelling faintly of flowers, certain someone had driven a length of rebar through his skull and connected it to an electrical outlet. His tongue was glued to the roof of his mouth. He tried to push himself upright, stopped when whatever was in his stomach threatened to force its way up. He rolled onto his back, scanned his surroundings.

Light filtered through pink plastic mini blinds. He was in a bed, looking into a small kitchen area, what counter space existed was covered with dirty pans and plates. Tan linoleum tile floor. Pink sheets. And beside his head, a pair of tanned bare feet sticking out from under the sheet, soles up. His eyes scanned past the feet, up the legs, past rounded, sheet-covered buttocks, to a bare, narrow back, to faint-freckled shoulders, and up to a splay of sun-bleached hair interwoven with beads. Alison, face down and snoring softly, torso bare, with only her hips covered by the sheet. He had no memory of getting there, of anything after the dancing.

Wally inched his way out of bed, leaned on the wall to keep semi-upright, willed his stomach to calm, his head to stop throbbing. At his feet was the red sarong, gift shop tag still attached. His shirt and flip flops were strewn across the floor by the door. Alison mumbled something, rolled onto her side, but didn't wake. On the bedside table was a dark box with glowing green figures. Wally squinted, tried to decipher them. Numbers. A bedside clock. Reading '6:03.' That seemed important... but... He had to meet Lemuel at the airfield at 7!

Leaning one shoulder against the wall to keep himself upright, Wally wrapped the sarong around his waist, scraped himself around to the door, pulled on his shirt and shoes, and slipped outside as quietly as he could, hoping he recognized some landmark to tell him where he was. He stood on the deck of a stilt house, ten feet above the ground, staring down at an ocean of tree tops. A one-lane dirt road ran past the house, turned and looked like it headed downhill. That was a start. He groped his way down rickety wooden steps, pulled his bike from the bushes, hiked up his sarong, and started out.

Once he rounded the turn, sure enough, the roadway descended. At the bottom of the hill it flattened, made a sharp turn to the left, and Wally found himself on the graveled main road, rising sun behind him glinting off the bright sea beyond the roadway. He stopped, leaned against the handlebars until his nausea subsided. He was on the west coast, then. And he didn't recognize any landmarks, or the dirt track he had just traveled. That meant he was south of Eagle Ray Cove. He turned right, pedaled as hard as he dared. With luck he could get home, change into shorts and borrow Vinson's van before Lemuel landed.

Soon he passed the Eagle Ray Cove bungalows on the left. Once past the resort, he stopped, leaned over, and vomited tonic water into the ditch. He pedaled on. Past the pink and turquoise stucco cottages of Club Scuba-Doo. Another stop to vomit what liquid was left in his stomach, and he kept going. He felt slightly better now and could pedal faster past the monolithic Sandy Bottoms' Beach Resort, its room lights still dark so early in the morning.

His mouth was parched, and he was dripping sweat by the time he reached his apartment. He ducked inside long enough to splash water on his face, swap the sarong for board shorts, and grab a Going Under Divers staff shirt. He paused to swallow a glass of water. It was a mistake. No sooner had he stepped outside than he vomited a pale stream of water and bile into the bushes beside the door. Hands shaking, he pedaled north, hoping he could get the van and get back before the first plane arrived.

Vinson was sweeping the Inne's central building's porch, singing to himself, when Wally got there. He grinned when Wally half-fell off the bike, bent double over the frame until the nausea subsided.

"You want to run with that Alison, told you you better get your rest." He chuckled, crossed to greet Wally. "Haven't seen anybody yet can keep up with her."

"How'd you know . . . ?"

"Alison's a candle, and you the moth." He slapped Wally's back, sending a new wave of nausea through Wally. "You wait here. I get you somethin' for it before you go to the airfield."

Vinson disappeared into the resort, came back moments later with a glass of greenish-brown semi-liquid. He dropped two bicarbonate of soda tablets into the liquid and let it burble.

"What *is* that?" Wally eyed the swampy-looking gluck, nose wrinkled. It reminded him of Vinson's fish stew, but smelled worse.

"Private remedy." Vinson winked. "Put you right in no time, head and stomach both."

When the tablets stopped fizzing, he handed the glass to Wally.

"Bottoms up. One go." He waggled a finger at Wally.

Wally held the glass up to the sun. Whatever it was, it couldn't be worse than what he was feeling now. He closed his eyes, held his nose, and downed the concoction in three swallows, then spat out the solid remnants. It tasted of dirt and leaves and . . . rotting fish, and flowed down his throat in chilly lumps. His stomach rolled, then settled. Wally gave Vinson a nasty look, rinsed his mouth with the hose, then staggered to the Noboddie's Inne van.

At the airfield Wally squatted in the van's shadow, leaning against its front tire and watched the twin-engine Islander taxi in. Four obvious tourists deplaned, colorful shirts flapping in the breeze, each sporting white sneakers and neon-colored fanny packs. Lemuel Chromis was the final passenger. Short, slender, of an indeterminate middle age, with sun-dried skin and long black hair pulled back in a greasy, braided ponytail hanging halfway down his back. Dusty cargo shorts and a paint-splattered black t-shirt. He stepped off the Islander with a half-rolled, well-worn brown paper grocery bag under one arm and shuffled to the parking area, flip flops smacking in the dust. Wally greeted him, pointed to the Noboddie's Inne van.

"We'll throw your bags in the back once they unload them," Wally said.

"Just got the one," Lemuel said. He patted the paper bag under his arm.

"Everything you need's in there?"

"Prob'ly more'n I need." Lemuel swung himself into the van's passenger seat.

"I've got you set with a room at Nobbdie's Inne. And food."

"Oh, no," Lemuel said. "Heard about that food. Take my meals somewhere else, you don't mind."

"Fair enough." Wally stifled a laugh. "You go by Lem?"

"No, sir. I'm 'Lemuel.'" He paused. "Call me 'Lem,' you take 'you well,' out my name."

Neither man said anything more for the ride back, Wally leaning against the driver's side door.

At the dive shop, Wally showed Lemuel the *J-Valve*, on blocks next to the dock. They climbed in the boat. Wally opened the bilge covers, and Lemuel clambered down.

"Yah, mon, that stringer got to go!" he called up. He tapped on the other stringers, front to back. "Just that one. Makes the job easier."

"So how long to fix it? LB said a day. Two, max."

"Oh, be longer than that. Got to do the job right."

Wally didn't have the energy to argue. He needed to sleep. He could check on Lemuel midday.

"Tools are in the shed." Wally waved a hand toward the maintenance shack. "LB'll be here soon to help. Let me know if you need anything else."

He went to the dive shop, turned on the air conditioner, sat, and rested his forehead on the desk, letting the cool air flow over him. Whatever Vinson had given him was good stuff—his stomach was settling and his headache wasn't quite so bad. He needed to call Hank-O, but that could wait. He closed his eyes, tried to will his head to stop throbbing. Dozed off.

A pounding erupted outside, as if multiple hammers were bashing, out of rhythm, on giant drums. Someone was shouting at the top of his voice. Lemuel. Yelling in the local patois Wally didn't understand, sounding angry enough to kill someone. More shouting, just as loud. From LB, sounding just as angry. The pounding quickened. Both men were shouting now, words incomprehensible, but by the sound of it, the two had launched into a major brawl.

Wally pushed himself up from the desk, his head throbbing along with the hammering outside. He rushed out, panicked, headed to the *J-Valve*, wondering how he would break up the fight. If he should call the police. Or the island nurse. And how much blood had been spilled. He climbed onto the boat's stern and stopped. Lemuel and LB were in the boat's bilge, both swinging hammers at crowbars wedged under the damaged stringer, both shouting, and neither appeared to be listening.

"What the hell?" Wally shouted, then pounded on the hull to get their attention. "What the hell's going on?"

Both men stopped, smiled at Wally. Lemuel waved his hammer.

"Mornin', Mister Wally! Beautiful day! We workin' good!"

"But the shouting, the pounding . . . I thought there was a fight." Wally's head still throbbed. His heart still raced.

"We just encouragin' that ol' stringer to come loose from the gel coat."

"But all the noise."

"Yah, mon! We workin' good!"

Both men turned back to the boat, restarted their hammering and shouting, if possible, louder than before. Wally watched them for a minute, trying to come up with something to say to make them be quiet, then went back to the shop, defeated. He grabbed two rental wetsuits from the back closet, pressed them over his ears, lay down on a pile of dive bags and slept.

By noon, Vinson's concoction had done the trick. Wally's headache had subsided, and his stomach hinted it might be safe to try some food. He stepped out back to see how Lemuel was progressing. He found the repairman crouched in the bilge, old stringer out, sanding the fiberglass where it had been. LB was gone. A half-dozen green beer bottles littered the bilge, and another, half full, sat on top of the starboard engine.

"Beer . . . make the work go faster?" Wally said.

"O, yah, mon! Grinding and sanding's thirsty work." Lemuel waved the sander at Wally.

"You think it might go better, and quicker, if you drank water instead?"

"Water? Lord, you wanna drown me? I drink water in this heat, I just get sick."

"Yes, but, beer . . . and power tools . . ."

"It does keep my hands steady." Lemuel took a swig of beer, bent back to sanding.

Wally stared, not sure what to do next. The man shouldn't be drinking while working, and certainly not that much in one morning, but he *was* making good progress. And was doing the work for a good price. More importantly, he hadn't destroyed anything. Yet. Wally crossed to the Inne.

"Vinson, what do you know about Lemuel Chromis?"

"Does good work, what I hear. Don't know him personal."

"Does he . . . drink a bit?"

"Most folks here do."

"While he works?"

"He doin' good work? Yeah? I wouldn't worry 'bout it."

Wally went back to the dive shop, still not trusting his stomach with food. Silence from the *J-Valve*. Lemuel was breaking for lunch. Wally checked messages. There was a note from Geoff in Marietta. He had stopped by Big Chicken Divers to check on Hank-O. The shop was fine, Geoff said, and so was Hank-O, and he had promised he would call Wally when he got a chance.

'*He said it's been super busy, and it might be a few days before he can break free,*' the note said.

It was strange Hank-O was so busy he couldn't make time for a quick call. Business must have really picked up. Or he needed more staff. Wally would give him a few days and try again. He needed just that little boost in diver numbers to break even financially. Hank-O had his back, though. And once the stream of divers started coming down, they'd be so happy Big Chicken Divers would double the number of trips they made to Blacktip. That was the last puzzle piece for Going Under Divers' success.

10

Three mornings later Wally's phone rang.

"Wally, this's Peachy at the store. Thought you might wanna know your guy Lemuel's running up quite the bill. On your account."

"A bill for what? He gets his meals at the Spinner."

"Well, he gets beer and ice here. Has Linford Blenny run it out to him."

"Okay." Wally rested his head on the desk. That explained the piles of empty bottles accumulating around the *J-Valve*. The boat repair was getting more expensive every day. "I'll go talk to him. If need be, I'll take it out of his pay."

Wally went out to the *J-Valve*, found Lemuel in the bilge, humming to himself, ponytail swaying while he wiped down the installed-and-fiberglassed stringer, beer in hand and surrounded by empty bottles.

"Lemuel, you been charging beer to Going Under Divers?"

"Oh, yah, mon!" Lemuel gap-tooth grinned up at him, waved his half-full green beer bottle.

"Beer wasn't part of our deal. You need to pay for that yourself."

Lemuel looked confused. His grin faded at the edges.

"You said lodging, food, *and drinks* was included."

"Yes, but that didn't include alcohol."

"Mister Wally, you did say, *and drink*." Lemuel said it matter-of-factly, with eyebrows raised, as if stunned anyone could not understand the point. "You 'spect me to drink water?"

"No, but . . ."

Lemuel raised his eyebrows higher than Wally would have thought possible, cocked his head to one side.

"I . . . fine." Wally knew he was beaten. And Lemuel did seem to be doing good, if slow, work. Whatever it took to get the boat seaworthy. "How soon 'til you finish?"

"Jus' need to turping time it, then paint it." Lemuel nodded at the repair, giving it his approval, then squinted up at Wally. "You got any turping time?"

"Turping . . .?"

"Turping time. Wipe that 'glass good and clean 'fore I paint it." He gave Wally a look, as if he doubted Wally's intelligence.

"Turp . . . turpentine! Yes! I'll be right back."

Lemuel was already mixing paint when Wally returned with the turpentine. Lemuel poured the solvent on a rag, then pounced on the new stringer, rubbing it down as if he were polishing a pair of dress shoes.

"She be ready by lunchtime." Lemuel gave Wally another gap-tooth grin. "Get me one last burger at the Spinner, then I be on the afternoon plane back to Tiperon."

Wally sighed, relieved the work—and the beer buying—was almost done.

Wally spent the rest of the morning paying bills, scheduling divers, answering email. Cringing at how quickly his savings were dwindling. He stepped out mid-morning to see what was happening with the suspiciously-quiet boat repair. There was no sign of Lemuel, yet the stringer was painted and looked as good as new.

At noon he stopped at the Tail Spinner and found Lemuel at the bar, finishing off a burger and fries, sipping on an ever-present beer.

"That boat, she good to go," Lemuel said, spitting bits of bun across the bar top. "Make sure that bilge pump works, keep that compartment dry so the other stringers don't rot."

"Will do. I'll run you to the airfield whenever you're ready."

Lemuel nodded, gulped down the last of his burger, and chased it with the last third of his beer. Wally borrowed Vinson's van again, and ten minutes later they were barreling down the coast road, Lemuel with his paper bag carry-on on his knees.

"First time I been to Blacktip." Lemuel stared out the van's open window at the passing trees. "Good folks. Good food. Ought to come more often."

Wally stifled the urge to say if someone gave *him* free lodging, food, and booze for four days, he would love to go back, too. And maybe work slow to get as many meals and drinks as he could.

Wally stopped at the Tail Spinner on his way back to Noboddie's Inne. He found Val clearing dishes from one of the tables.

"I need to settle up Lemuel's food bill."

She crossed to the register, pulled a scrap of paper from beneath the till.

"Including today, that's three dinners . . . and four lunches." Val flashed a twisted smile.

"Oh, he milked it," Wally said. "And was done working today before ten."

"Plus $80 for his beer."

"Eighty . . . Just for beer?"

"He's a thirsty fellow."

"Don't I know it. He about filled up the Inne's parking lot with empty bottles."

Wally slid cash across the bar to Val.

"See you at happy hour?" she said. "Scuba Doo?"

"Not likely. The way I'm blowing through money today, I need to take it easy. I'm biking back to Peachy's to pay Lemuel's beer tab there. And hoping that's the only other place he got beer."

At Peachy's, Wally had a similar conversation, parted with more cash and bought humus and chips for lunch. He stepped out of the store, grocery bag in hand. The Blacktip Haven pickup truck roared past, its bed full of the morning's divers headed back to the resort for lunch. Wally stared, stunned. He recognized the divers. Knew them. Kenny and Lisa. Colette and Kelly. Several others whose names he couldn't recall. From Big Chicken Divers. He had led their group at The Haven last year. Kelly saw him and waved.

Hank-O wouldn't return Wally's calls, but he was still sending divers to The Haven? Wally pulled out his phone, dialed the Big Chicken land line.

"Hank's not here," Jenny at the cash register said. "He . . . um . . . had to step out . . ."

"No! I know he's there. Put him on the phone. NOW."

Jenny gave a startled squeak and dropped the receiver on the counter. A minute later Hank's voice came on the line.

"Wally! Buddy! Glad you finally got me! How's it going?" His voice was too high. The words came too fast.

"I'm bleeding cash, the boat's a money pit, and I have no divers."

"Ouch. Rough start, huh?" A nervous laugh.

"And you're ghosting me. Oh, and the Blacktip Haven dive truck just blew past with a bunch of Big Chicken divers in the back. Kelly what's-her-name-blonde-woman waved at me. What the hell? You're supposed to send *me* divers! Ages ago!"

"I didn't have any choice, Wally. I had to send 'em to Elena. Legally."

"Hank, you set me up! You stuck a knife between my shoulders, and now you're twisting it!" Wally tried to keep from shouting. Failed. Two shoppers leaving the store looked away, quickened their pace. "You could have told me up front!"

"I didn't know before you left. I feel awful and was trying to find a good way to tell you." Hank's voice wavered, broke. "I didn't know it was such a big deal for you. Elena's got me over a barrel, though."

"What barrel?"

"Our contract. I didn't realize. Until she called and told me. And sent a copy of page whatever, with that sub-paragraph highlighted. Apparently, you haven't been subtle about getting BCD divers. I should have read the thing closer, but it seemed like a straight, standard agreement at the time."

"I've . . . been sitting here waiting for Big Chicken divers for months! That was key to my business plan. You could have told me!"

"I know. And I'm sorry. But I can't send you divers. You know the slim margins we have at the shop. Deep-pockets Elena files a lawsuit—and she would—I'm out of business."

"You think she'd actually do that?"

"You know her as the hippy-dippy party host holding court down there, Wally. You've never dealt with her as a business person. She's ruthless. Cutthroat. And never loses."

"This is crazy. I've known Elena for years and've never seen anything remotely like that. I'll go talk to her in person and sort things out. We have a great relationship."

"She'll gut you like a fish, Bubba."

Wally snatched his bike from the rack. He would go see Elena now, talk things through. Hank-O's description of her made no sense. Other than cutting him off from The Haven's food, she had always been helpful, supportive of Wally. They would work things out in no time. Hank must have pissed her off and assumed her worst was the norm.

He found Elena in the Blacktip Haven lounge, sorting through papers at a table by the bar. Jessie flashed him a silent 'eek' face and ducked into the kitchen. Familiar Big Chicken dive guests milled in the dining room around the corner.

"Hey, Elena. You have a minute?"

Elena looked over the top of her reading glasses, stared him down, said nothing. He glanced at the chair opposite her. She didn't offer it.

"Hey, I just got off the phone with Hank at Big Chicken." Wally smiled, shifted into his friendliest, most persuasive voice. "I think there's been some sort of misunderstanding about . . ."

"The only misunderstanding was you thinking you could steal guests from me." Elena's voice was cold. "You thought you could get away with that?"

"No! I'm not trying to steal, or get away with anything. I just wanted Hank to send the occasional group my way."

"Which is stealing. We have a contract. Big Chicken divers are Blacktip Haven divers. Hank sends his groups to The Haven. *Exclusively*."

Several of the Big Chicken divers, full plates in hand, looked into the lounge, then darted away without making eye contact with Wally.

"But I'm talking about *future* groups, additional groups, not existing groups. I need them to make a go of Going Under."

"Future BCD dive groups are, by definition, legally *my* future dive groups."

"Not if I recruit them, market my operation to them."

"You're concerned about your diver numbers, Wally. That's good. And if you get the odd BCD diver or two, that's fine. But what would your reaction be if I went behind your back and . . . recruited . . . swaths of your guests to The Haven? Ignore it? Congratulate me? Invite me out for drinks and a round of "Kumbaya"?"

"That's a different . . ."

"You have a choice, Wally. You can stay away from my divers—past, present, and future—or I can add you and your little wannabe company to any and all lawsuits I file against your buddy Hank. You can go out of business together. That sound fun?"

There was silence from the dining room now, the Big Chicken guests there not wanting to miss a moment of the face off, while trying to look like they weren't eavesdropping.

"That's not reasonable. I'm barely hanging on . . ."

"*That* is not my problem. You dug that hole for yourself. After *I* warned you not to." Her voice went icy. "Frankly, you need stay away from my resort, too, unless it's business related. If you return, for *anything*, I'll have you arrested for trespassing."

"You can't do that!"

"I just did."

"What about our past, our relationship?"

"Our relationship is adversarial. Now go away. I've wasted too much time on your silliness."

Elena picked up her stack of papers and strode to her office, long gray hair streaming, letting the swinging door slap shut behind her.

In the dining room, feet shuffled and plates clanked as the divers went back to their lunch.

Wally stared at the flapping door. He had gone from friendship to banned in less than a minute. Or perceived friendship, anyway. Hank-O had been right. If Wally wasn't bringing money into Blacktip Haven, Elena had no use for him. And now, with him starting a dive operation, she saw him as an enemy. He could patch things up with her eventually, he hoped, but that wouldn't be anytime soon.

He walked out to his bike, heart racing and hands shaking. The plastic bag with its chilled humus hung from one handlebar. He would need to eat it quickly before it spoiled.

After lunch he went back to the Going Under Divers shop and stared at the latest diver counts, head in his hands. His business was going out of business faster than before. He would have to put even more of his savings into the operation, and those savings were drying up fast. But there was no other option if he was to cover payroll the next week.

Wally counted the cash in the strongbox, then turned on the computer, signed in to the Going Under Divers bank account to deposit Skerrit's percentage. The account transaction history page opened. Wally sat back, wide-eyed. There had been barely $300 in it the day before. Now it showed a balance of more than $300,000. He checked the account number, refreshed the screen to correct the total. The number didn't change. The bank had mistakenly deposited hundreds of thousands of dollars into the business account? They, or whoever the money belonged to, would notice the error. Soon. He grabbed his phone to call the bank's central branch on Tiperon, then realized it was Saturday. There would be no one there until Monday morning. In the meantime, there was a ton of someone else's money parked in that account. Only Ferris Skerritt could access it, but Wally's name was on it, too.

For a moment he imagined the money was his, the business was booming, everything on Blacktip Island was going to plan. Then the reality hit him. It was as if the Universe was toying with him, dangling hope in front of him, just within reach, only to snatch it away. No, he was trapped in a failing business, pouring more and more of his savings into it every day, hoping things would magically turn around.

This was no good, though, moping alone in the shop. Obsessing. Val was right—he needed to get out. Enjoy the good parts of island life while he could. Being around upbeat people would lift his spirits. He *would* go to the happy hour, have a beer or two, and then come home. Worst case, he could drown his sorrows for a night and tackle his finances fresh the next morning.

At sunset, Club Scuba Doo's over-the-water bar was already full, white fairy lights strung around the railings and in the surrounding hedges. Hugh and Jessie greeted him at the crowd's edge.

"How're you holding up? After . . . Elena?" There was concern in Jessie's voice. And worry in her gray eyes.

"That was . . . a body shot out of the blue," Wally said. "Not sure how she even found out."

"I . . . might have mentioned you talking about it." Jessie face scrunched into a grimace. "That first night, at happy hour. Sorry?"

"That explains it," Wally said. There truly were no secrets on the little island.

"Always a shock the first time anyone sees that side of her," Hugh said.

"Well, tonight I'm going to forget all that and enjoy the evening," Wally said. "There's too much positive going on here for me to focus on negatives."

"That's the spirit!" Val joined the group. "Boat's repaired? Set to go?"

"Again, for tonight I'm focused just on the positive."

"Ah. Gotcha." Val frowned for a second. "Well, that was a nice thing you did, paying all of Lemuel's expenses when you didn't strictly have to."

"At that point I was done," Wally laughed. "I didn't have the energy to fight it, or him, anymore."

Hugh and Jessie wandered toward the bar, leaving Wally and Val alone.

"You seem to be fitting into island life," she said.

"Trying to. It seems like . . ."

"Hey, stranger!" A thin arm wrapped around his neck. Surf-and-frangipane scent. The clatter of beaded hair. "You been dodging me?"

"Hey, Alison." He turned to face her. "I've just been busy fixing the boat."

"You bailed without saying goodbye the other morning." Her breath smelled faintly of orange juice. She glanced past him, at Val. "Hey, girl! Good to see you out again."

"I . . . need to talk to Antonio," Val said. She patted Wally's shoulder, then crossed the deck and disappeared in the crowd.

"I had to pick up . . . I had to get the hull repairer at the airstrip," Wally said. She was as exotic, as alluring, as ever. But he didn't need another booze-soaked evening with Alison, not with everything going on with Going Under Divers. He hadn't figured he would meet her so early—she usually went out later.

Her orange eyes locked on his. Her thin lips twisted into a lopsided smile.

"You can make it up to me now," she said.

"Wally! How you doin', Mate?" Lee Helm appeared beside them. He nodded at Wally's beer. "You're laggin'!"

"Damaris! Another round!" Alison yelled across the crowded bar. "And a double for Wally, here!"

"No. I'm fine. I just . . ."

Alison threw her other arm around his neck and kissed him, silencing anything else he might have said. Her lips, the press of her body against his, her ocean-and-flower scent overwhelmed him. Something inside him jumped, did a slow roll. The only place he wanted to be was here, like this, his arms full of alluring Alison. She pulled her head back to look into his eyes.

"There. That's more like it. You're goin' nowhere, boy-o." Alison handed him an icy glass. "We're gonna have fun tonight."

After a long swallow, they set their drinks on the bar, and she led him to a cleared area of the deck where others were dancing. Speakers pulsed out a syncopated something salsa-esque. Alison shuffled her feet, swung her knees, and swayed her hips in time with the syncopation. Wally stared, tried halfheartedly to follow her steps, failed miserably.

"Dude, listen to the beat," Alison said. "And dance from your hips."

She put her hands on his hips, pushed them one way, then another, mimicking the motion of her own hips. Soon Wally had the hang of it, moving to the offbeat, concentrating on Alison's swaying hair, her swaying hips, her bare feet scuffling on the bare boards. He grabbed her around the waist, spun them around, watching the multicolored lights blur overhead. His money troubles, problems with Lemuel, his faceoff with Elena, they all disappeared.

The music shifted to something hip hop. Alison stepped back from the dance area.

"I'll go get us fresh drinks," she said and disappeared into the crowd.

Wally looked around, hoping for a chair or bench or anything else to sit on. Found Antonio Fletcher staring at him, a slight smile at the corners of his mouth.

"Warren! You out mixin' and minglin' again. That's good." Antonio nodded his approval. "Startin' to act like a real Blacktipper."

"It's still Wally. And I'm just trying to survive." Wally laughed at the idea of being a local, as flattering as it was.

"Doin' better than that," Antonio said. "Still not going after the dark, though."

"Yeah, I still have no idea what that means. I should work harder to get my business in the black?"

"Sometimes the thing you're chasing, the thing you think you need, it ain't the thing you need." Antonio shook his head, as if trying to be patient with a dense child. "Need to look down deep, see what's really important. What your inside self really needs."

"Antonio, whatever it is you have to say, just say it. In plain English."

"Oh, no." Antonio grinned at him. "Got to find out yourself, or the lesson won't take."

He slapped Wally on the back, then raised his eyebrows as if he remembered something. "Hear ol' Lemuel did a good job on your boat."

"He did a good job on Peachy's beer cooler. And my bank account."

"Lemuel, he does like his beer." Antonio laughed. "I shoulda warned you 'bout that. Good soul, but he's like a child. Got to watch him like a child, make sure he stays focused. And don't drink *too* much."

"I paid off his $80 bar tab at the Spinner, too."

"That tab was only $80? You got off easy." Antonio studied Wally for a moment. "That Val, she lookin' out for you."

Alison was back then, pressing a cold drink into Wally's hand. "You setting him straight, 'Tonio?" She grinned up at him.

"He figure things out soon enough. On his own."

Antonio gave Wally a long look, then stepped away.

"Set me straight?"

"Oh, I was just making conversation." Alison gave one of her throaty laughs. "Best to just smile and nod when 'Tonio gets up a head of steam. Drink up!"

Wally sipped at his drink. His stomach was rumbling already, threatening to become unmanageable. He burped, coughed at the orange-juice taste in the back of his throat.

"How about we have a light-on-booze night so we can remember it the next day?" he said.

"Where's the adventure in that?" She shook her head in mock dismay. "You're not going all act-your-age on me, are you?"

Wally smiled and took another sip of his drink, torn between wanting to be with Alison and not being able to match her drink for drink. Between his attraction to her and his desire to not vomit in the bushes, or have a blinding hangover the next day. If he could just get her to slow down, even slightly, he might be able to survive spending time with her.

Alison was watching dancers, ignoring Wally for a moment. An empty plastic cup sat on the bar railing beside him. He glanced at Alison, then poured half his drink into the cup. If he couldn't stop the number of drinks Alison ordered, he could limit the amount of alcohol he ingested. If he did it carefully.

She turned back to him, bright eyes locked on his. He just had time to set his drink on the railing before she pulled him back onto the makeshift dance floor. Soon they were back to the syncopated rhythm she liked so much, swaying to the off-beats. Yes, this was good, dancing with a beautiful, exotic divemaster, thinking of nothing but her. And if he could keep dumping his drinks without her knowing, they might have a great evening.

Things would be different tonight. He was sure of it. He would make sure of it.

Most of the crowd was dancing now, swaying to a slower bossa nova-sounding song Wally didn't recognize. More drinks appeared from somewhere. Alison laughed, downed a quarter of hers in one swallow without missing a beat. Wally intentionally took several clumsy steps, splashed as much of his drink out of the cup as he could without making it too obvious.

The crowd moved, shifted, as if it were a living thing. Wally and Alison flowed with it, now near the bar, now by the pool. Wally made another purposeful misstep, hoping to spill more of his drink. His foot caught the foot of a dancer next to him, and he stumbled for real, bumping into another couple. They all staggered, trying to catch their balance. The bright blue of the pool lights yawed at his feet. Wally caught himself for a moment, then he fell, taking two, three others into the pool with him. He surfaced, waist deep in the cool water, to find a sea of stunned faces staring down at him and the others in the water.

Then, with a loud, "Woohoo!" Alison launched herself into the water next to him, sending water cascading across the deck with a belly-flop landing. Others followed, and soon there were a dozen people in the water, splashing each other, dunking each other. One couple at the edge of the scene began dancing again. Wally ducked down for a moment, so only his head was out of the water. Alison pounced on him from behind, legs straddling his neck.

"Chicken fiiiight!" Her yell set Wally's ears ringing.

Around them, people climbed on each other's shoulders. The woman on the shoulders of the man closest to Wally tried to grab Alison's arms. Alison laughed, twisted her hands away, grabbed the woman's forearms and pulled her into the water.

Someone slammed into Wally's back, and he and Alison crashed underwater. They surfaced near the wall closest to the bar. A portly man, with a bald head protruding through shoulder-length reddish hair, loomed above them, waving his arms over his head.

"Everybody out of the pool!" He bellowed.

People in the pool ignored him. He yelled again, to no effect.

"I'm the manager, damn it!" He tugged at the chest of his green polo shirt, emphasizing the 'Club Scuba Doo' logo stitched there. "Pool's closed! Everybody out! Now! Before someone gets hurt!"

People in the pool and on the deck laughed. He tried a different approach, bending down to confront individuals in the water.

"You get out of there NOW!" he barked at Alison, leaning out and shaking a finger in her face.

Alison laughed. Grabbed his wrist and yanked him headfirst into the pool. Wally had a glimpse of wide eyes and a gaping mouth before the man hit the water. Wally grabbed Alison's shoulders, pulled her away so others were closer to the surfacing manager.

"That's assault!" The man pointed at the nearest woman. "You pulled me in. In front of a ton of witnesses!"

People around him laughed. The woman put a hand on his head, dunked him back underwater.

Alison motioned to the bartender, and soon drinks were arriving in plastic cups. Wally drank some while Alison was watching, then poured out half of it. The manager left, stomping up the steps and off to find dry clothes.

"Think he might call the constable?" Wally said.

"Won't have to," Alison said. "He's right next to you. Out of uniform, of course. Wally, meet Island Constable Marquette. Rafe, Wally."

The man towered over Wally, shoulders nearly twice as wide as Wally's. He held out a giant hand. Wally took it.

"Welcome to Blacktip, Wally. Figures Alison's at the center of something like this."

He turned away, leaving Wally with Alison, surrounded by fairy lights that seemed to spin around him.

11

Wally dragged himself into the dive shop the next morning, head pounding, stomach churning, and an ashy taste in the back of his mouth. He had stopped at his apartment long enough to change out of his wet clothes from the night before, re-donned when he left Alison's, and hurried up the coast road. Alison was addictive, but he couldn't take many more mornings like this.

Angela and LB grinned when they saw him arrive.

"Little late gettin' back from the pool party," Angela laughed.

"Got the boat prepped and'll handle the guests," LB said. "You look like you could use some . . . office time."

Wally nodded, ducked into the office and the blessedly-cool air. He rested his head on the desk. At the sound of the door opening, he turned his head sideways to see who it was. Vinson, looking squatter and heavier, or seemed so from Wally's angle, anyway, shuffled across the room and stared down at Wally.

"You and Alison have a good time again?"

"Dunno," Wally managed to croak out. "Don't remember. Never do."

"Yeah. You lookin' pekid. That Alison's gonna be the death of you, you're not careful."

Wally waved one hand to cut him off. Vinson grinned at that.

"Got some elixir for you." He pulled his hand from behind his back, set a glass of his mysterious green-gunk hangover cure next to Wally's face. "Figured you'd need it, carryin' on that way last night."

Wally held his nose and gulped the lumpy, slimy stuff down. Shuddered at the feel of it sliding down his throat. Wiped his tongue with a paper towel.

"I'll leave you in peace." Vinson chuckled. "Or by yourself, at any rate. Why you keep doin' this to yourself..."

The office door swung shut behind him.

Wally leaned back in his chair, waited for the cure to kick in. Vinson was right—Alison was going to be the death of him. He had never met anyone like her. Or thought someone like her would ever be attracted to him. But as exciting as this adventure was, he couldn't afford to be at less than his best for the business right now. And he couldn't afford to buy that many drinks with his cash supply dwindling so rapidly. He didn't like the idea, but he would have to stop spending so much time with Alison. Or drinking so much with her. Or both. He could stay on friendly terms, then maybe start things back up once the business stabilized. If it stabilized.

The office door swung open again. This time it was Ferris Skerritt, looking paler, more cadaverous than ever.

"Ah, young Wally. How ... fortuitous to find you here this morning."

He stepped to the desk and looked down at Wally. Wally motioned to a chair.

"Oh, no. No time to chat. I just stopped by to ascertain my share of this month's earnings."

"I haven't had time to do the month-end numbers," Wally said. "I can have something by lunch though."

Wally had no idea if he could afford for Skerritt to take his month's percentage or not, with the bank balance so low. He recalled the deposit error from the day before.

"Hey, online right now the business account balance looks phenomenal, but that's because there was an erroneous deposit yesterday," he said. "Someone dropped $300,000 in the account."

"No error. No error at all." Skerritt gave Wally a thin smile. "That was put there at my behest."

"So . . . you *are* investing in the business?" That would be a game changer, with Wally not relying solely on divers for income. He wouldn't have to use his own money to pay bills and payroll.

"Absolutely not." Skerritt shot him a disgusted look. "There will be times finances will need to be . . . ah . . . redistributed from other . . . ventures. The Going Under account serves well for that."

"Why not just leave it wherever you had it?"

"Some places are better than others, at certain times. And, in future, there may be scenarios where I'm holding the funds for . . . friends and colleagues. The healthiest course of action for you would be to ignore it."

Skerritt gave Wally a thin, yellow-tooth smile.

"You're parking cash . . . but that account has my name on it!"

"We'll just keep it between us. For the sake of the business. I'll return at midday for an earnings projection."

Skerritt left.

Wally didn't exhale until he heard the big Caddie rumble off. Between Vinson's concoction and Skerritt's news, his hangover was gone. Skerritt was moving big chunks of money into the G.U.D. bank account. Moving money through it. And would keep doing so. Wally could think of no legitimate reason for him to do that. Even if it was legal in the Tiperons, Wally could still be arrested as soon as he set foot back in the U.S. if his name was associated with . . . whatever Skerritt was involved in. And Skerritt's colleagues, with lots of money, who could make people unhealthy.

His fortunes had to change. There had to be an end to all this bad luck. Wally opened the accounting program, checked the past month's totals, compared it to what he could use from his personal bank account. Yes, Skerritt would take his cut, but Wally would have to use his own money to cover payroll. Again.

A logical part of his brain said he should cut his losses, get out of Going Under Divers before he lost everything. He could sell his forty percent, go work somewhere else. As a divemaster, guiding dives, he would at least still be in the Caribbean, be getting paid instead of bleeding cash the way he was now. But who would be foolish enough to buy him out? If Skerritt would even allow the sale—there was probably a clause about that in their contract, too.

He could take what money he still had and run off, leave no word where he was going. Fake his death, maybe. Fly to South America, somewhere, find a place he could live cheap. No, in today's interconnected world it was all but impossible to disappear like that. And he wouldn't do that to Angela and LB. Or his dive clients. For a moment he saw himself slinking back to Marietta, restarting his life up there.

Anger surged up at the thought. He had come to Blacktip Island chasing a dream. Things weren't going as planned, but that didn't mean he couldn't turn things around. He was exactly where he wanted to be, doing exactly what he wanted to do. How many other people could say that? And the place being a beautiful tropical island made things even better. He would ditch his negative thoughts, make Going Under Divers the success he knew it could be. The *J-Valve*'s hull was fixed, diver numbers were inching up, and he had a good staff. That was a great combination. And if he had to throw in a bunch of his savings to succeed, so be it.

Wally needed to clear his head, go for a dive, remind himself why he had come here. Spend more time doing that and less time with Alison. He would go in from shore, at Diddley's landing, after lunch. He printed out the month's earnings, set it on the counter where Skerritt could find it.

Voices laughing outside, shuffling feet told him the divers were back early. The door swung open, and Chip Pompano's head poked through, grinning.

"With the weather so good, any chance there could be an afternoon dive?"

"With just one person, I'd lose money." Wally gave a brief laugh. "And I can't afford to lose money right now."

"Shame." Chip frowned, disappointment on his face. "I was hoping to get one more dive in before I head back to Tiperon tomorrow afternoon."

"Well . . . I tell you what. I'm thinking of going in from shore after lunch. At the public pier. You're welcome to join me."

"Yeah? Sounds great!" Chip's face brightened. "I'll see you at one? One thirty? One thirty!"

Chip disappeared out the door, whistling as he went. Wally left Skerritt's financial statement on the counter, grabbed his bike and pedaled off to the Tail Spinner. He would have lunch and be back in time to meet Chip and, hopefully, borrow Vinson's van.

The Tail Spinner was nearly empty when Wally arrived. He ordered fish tacos and thought about the upcoming dive. He hadn't dived at the Diddley's Landing since that first day, going north for the first dive, then, at Val's suggestion, due west for the second. Today he would go south, see what the reef was like in that direction. Val stepped from the kitchen, set his lunch on the bar in front of him.

"Business picking up?" She smiled at him.

"Slowly." He grimaced. "But not fast enough."

"Well, things'll turn around. I put the word out. My friend's working on more ways to promote the place."

"What'll that cost? Seriously."

"Nada. She's just playing with an idea, using G.U.D., and The Inne, as a guinea pig. And it's nothing complicated—mostly SEO stuff, pushing traffic to your site."

"I can use all the help I can get right now."

"I've heard."

Wally shot her a sharp look.

"What?" she said. "It's a small island. Plus, you don't have many divers, and you're making boat repairs. And you've been acting fairly . . . erratic."

"Well, I'm shaking that off. Focusing on the future. I'm taking Chip on a shore dive this afternoon to ditch the negative vibes."

"You up for a third?" Val studied him a moment. "I said last week I had a dive in mind for the three of us. And the weather's perfect for it. Down south. By Mango Sound. What time you leaving?"

"One thirty. If Vinson lets me borrow the van."

"I'll give him a call. Pick me up on your way."

Sure enough, back at Noboddie's Inne after lunch, Vinson was waiting for Wally, grinning.

"Going divin' with Val, huh?"

"Not like you're thinking." What had Val said to convince Vinson to loan out the van? "I'm taking Chip out from shore, and she asked if she could tag along."

"Oh, no, not suggestin' anything. You the Three Amigos. Folks're noticin'. Just remembering how I told you Val ends up involved in 'most everythin' on this island, and you rolled your eyes."

"Yeah. Yeah. And a friend of hers is doing a marketing experiment that may send business our way."

"I'd never say 'I told you so . . . the keys are in the van."

Wally piled his and Chip's dive gear into the van, then drove to the Tail Spinner. Val was waiting when they arrived. She tossed her gear in the back, then slid onto the seat behind Wally.

"Drive south 'til I tell you to stop," she said.

They rattled south down the coast road, the van sounding like it might fall apart with every pothole they hit, dust billowing behind them. The hot, humid air flowed semi-liquid through their open windows, smelling rough, woody from the trees crowding the road. They passed the public pier, then Sandy Bottoms and Club Scuba Doo on their right. The island's central bluff towered over them inland. The turnoff to Blacktip Haven flashed past on their left, then Eagle Ray Cove on their right. Vegetation, tree limbs grew closer to the road, encroaching on the asphalt with lighter traffic so far south. The road veered left, switchbacked up the bluff.

"Keep straight." Val pointed away from the climbing roadway, toward a narrow track hugging the ironshore coastline. "You want 'unofficial'? You got it."

Wally slowed, and they bounced down a two-rut pathway, passing several turn outs. The vegetation thinned, revealing the black, pockmarked ironshore and the sea lapping against it. The bluff edged closer, the gap between the cliff and the sea narrowing.

"Pull over here." Val pointed to a smooth-ish part of the ironshore. "Welcome to Pikeblenny Patchreef. One of Blacktip's least-dived, least-known dive sites. It's also one of my favorites."

Beyond the dark ironshore was a broad expanse of turquoise water, dotted with dark, irregular-shaped blobs—dark coral heads scattered thick across a sand bottom. The forearm-long gray shapes of several barracuda lurked under the surface just offshore. Wally studied the coral heads, trying to fix the pattern in his head so he wouldn't get lost. Val saw him concentrating.

"Yeah, it's like a big labyrinth, with no real pattern to the coral," she said. "I'll navigate us through it. We probably won't get deeper than thirty, thirty-five feet."

"What're we gonna see?" Chip pulled his mask and fins from his dive bag.

"Besides pikeblennies? No telling," Val said. "I see something cool every time I'm here, though. It's been a while since I've dived it."

They geared up and waded into the warm water, Val in the lead, and Wally at the back. She slipped beneath the surface, followed the sloping sand bottom toward the nearest coral head, black fins sculling lightly to not disturb the sand. She stopped shy of the coral, settled to the sand on her stomach, pointed in front of her. Wally and Chip settled, too. In front of them, thinner than a pencil, a pale, yellow head with a long, flattened snout poked out of a hole in the sand. Val pointed again, to three, four more of the creatures, so pale they were almost invisible in the sand, looking for all the world like small, yellowish eels, each peering out of their own hole at the curious divers. Wally had only seen a pikeblenny once before, and slipped a small magnifying glass from his BC pocket for a closer look.

Val reached into her pocket, too, pulled out a white cable tie. She held it, pointed end up, and wiggled it in front of the nearest pikeblenny. The fish, the length of Wally's little finger, eyed it for a moment, then charged out of its hole at the cable tie, jaws wide and dorsal fin erect to confront a possible rival. Wally and Chip laughed at the tiny fish's aggression, sending gouts of exhalation bubbles streaming toward the surface. The pikeblenny charged two, three more times, its serpentine body lashing in defiance, before it retreated to its hole, glaring at the divers.

Val inhaled deeply, rose from the sand, and kicked towards the nearest coral head, her thin legs seeming barely to move. She glided through the clear water, around the coral heads, her buoyancy as neutral as any divemaster's. She pointed to a pair of French angelfish, black with yellow speckles. A flounder in the sand, its spots bright blue. A trio of juvenile spotted drums under a ledge, no bigger than pencil erasers, their outsized black-and-white dorsal fins fluttering like long banners as they circled each other.

Wally followed happily, enjoying not leading the dive for a change. He could simply dive, look at the fish, let Val, with her knowledge of the site, show him around. And the coral here was stunning, with its purples and reds and greens. Healthier than any other reefs he had seen on Blacktip, with forests of sea fans, sea plumes, and other soft corals growing amid the stony corals of the coral heads. Clouds of blue chromis swarmed above the coral, and schools of bluestriped grunts clustered together beside the coral, the colors bright here in the thirty-feet-deep water with the white sand bottom.

Chip seemed happy, too, pointing out fish, a green eel looking out from a crevice, a spiny lobster tucked under a ledge, as if he were an excited child at the zoo. And Val seemed nearly as happy as him, pointing out everything she found. She had been right about this section of reef being a maze. They looped around one coral head after another, with no apparent pattern, and with the sand a uniform depth, Wally had no idea which direction shore was.

Val tapped her tank twice, pointed, knelt in the sand. Ahead, something big swam toward them at an angle. Wally and Chip knelt beside Val. The fish came closer, flattened head sweeping from side to side, studying them with one eye, then the other. Its pectoral fins were up, parallel to the sand, and its tail barely moved, yet it came toward them at a steady pace, longer than Wally was tall. He watched the hammerhead, transfixed, Val and Chip forgotten for the moment.

The heavy muscles in front of its dorsal fin made it look as if it were arching its back, but then Wally realized it was simply the bulkier muscles of an open-ocean shark, not the sleek lines of the reef sharks he was used to seeing. No, the shark was relaxed, unthreatened, curious, wondering what the three noisy, bubbling creatures were, what they were doing on the reef. It circled them from ten feet away, it's left eye scanning up, down, back and forth. Then a closer pass, so close Wally could have touched the tip of its pectoral fin, while the tip of its tall, thin dorsal rose higher than their heads. Then, as if bored with them, it veered away and back to its original travel direction.

They looked at each other then. Val and Chip's eyes were wide, and Wally knew his were just as big. Val was grinning around her regulator. Chip pumped his fist, gave a 'woohoo!' through his regulator.

They waited several minutes in case the shark returned, then Val motioned them to follow her and kicked toward the nearest coral outcropping. The sand became shallower, and soon they were in waist-deep water. They stood. There, on the ironshore, was the Noboddie's Inne van. Wally had no idea how Val had navigated her way back so accurately.

"You seriously have no desire to be a divemaster?" Wally said.

"Nope. I love being out here too much. That'd ruin it. And the hours at The Spinner are better." She laughed. "*And* I make more money there."

"Are you kidding me with that hammerhead?!" Chip's eyes were still wide, and his grin covered his face. "That normal?"

"Absolutely not." Val grinned back. "I've only seen five or six the whole time I've been on the island. And never that close."

"This site's phenomenal," Wally said. "Why does no one dive it?"

"It's a long boat ride down here, and there's no other sites nearby, so if the current or visibility's bad, it's a wasted trip. And a lot of people on Blacktip don't like diving from shore."

"Seems a shame, with this right out your back door," Wally said.

"If I lived here, I'd be down here all the time." Chip paused, a thoughtful expression on his face. "Makes me want to spend even more time over here."

Soon they were dried off, their gear stowed, and Wally was driving the van back up the two-rut track and onto the main dirt roadway.

"You guys up for a post-dive beer?" Val said from the back seat.

Wally and Chip glanced at each other, shrugged.

"Cool," Val said. "Turn right, up the bluff. I'll introduce you to the Ballyhoo."

Wally downshifted, and the van growled its way up the steep incline, clattering all the way. The road leveled out at the top on the bluff, and Val directed Wally to the parking lot of the low wooden building he had glimpsed on their island tour, pink and teal, with bright orange script proclaiming it to be 'The Last Ballyhoo.'

"Doesn't look like much, but it has the second-best views on Blacktip," Val said.

Inside was dimly lit, made dimmer and dingier by dark wood paneling, despite the floor-to-ceiling glass windows on the far wall. Val waved to the bartender, then led Wally and Chip through a glass door and onto a wide, covered, outdoor patio overlooking the sea. There were no other customers, and she picked a table by the iron railings at the patio's edge, where they could see a small bay with several boats 100 feet below them and the thin white lines of waves rolling across a fringing reef.

"Below us is Mango Sound, the only sheltered harbor down this way," she said. "And beyond, just past that far headland, was where we were diving."

The breeze rushing up the cliff face brought the salty scent of the sea, along with something sweeter, fruity, almost peach-smelling.

"Definitely mango trees down there," Chip said. "Makes me kinda hungry."

They ordered beer, sat watching the distant waves, Wally and Val with their feet on the railings.

Wally leaned back in his chair, relaxed, enjoying the warm sun, the cold beer and the stunning view of the island's southern tip. This had been a great idea, stopping here. And now he had visited Blacktip's northernmost and southernmost bars. Chip seemed content, too. Across the table, Val had her eyes closed, soaking up the sun.

"It doesn't bother you to spend money at your competition?" Wally said.

Val opened her eyes. Smiled.

"Not really the competition." She gave a quick, faint smile. "We're a long way away from each other and offer different vibes. This is more the rowdy divemaster-and-construction-worker hangout. The Spinner's a bit more sedate. Gentrified. And a change of scenery's nice."

"You've got that right."

Wally realized he hadn't thought about Going Under Divers, his financial woes, Elena, Alison, any of it, all afternoon. He sipped at his beer, smiled. Yes, he definitely needed to do this more often.

"You got a great dive op here." Chip stretched out his legs under the table. "I wouldn't dive with anyone else. But mixing in dive trips like this, for small groups, that'd put it over the top. You need to get you a van of your own, run afternoon shore dives."

"That's certainly an idea." Wally didn't dare tell Chip he would be paying Angela and LB from his own pocket. He was as likely to buy a van as he was to buy a unicorn. But he *did* need to figure some way to attract more divers.

A group of six newly-arrived tourists, obvious with their floral shirts, sunburned limbs, and sweat-soaked faces walked onto the deck, sat at the tables next to Wally, 'ooh'ed and 'ahh'ed about the view and ordered drinks.

"See? Now *this* is what I was talking about," one of the men said. "You don't get that view in Louisville!"

"I just wish there was more to do," one of the women said. "The rental house's nice, but we've been driving around for a while, and this island's just one big jungle. With a swamp at one end."

"Where's the shops and restaurants and . . . entertainment," said another woman. "This view's great, but what are we gonna do all week besides drive in circles and drink?"

Their drinks arrived, all variations of bright-colored punch with mini umbrellas in them.

"Well, since everything seems centered on scooby diving, I'm thinking of trying my hand at that," another man said. "Can't be that hard."

Wally sized them up. Mid-40s to mid-50s. Reasonably fit. Could it be that easy? He took a deep breath, reminded himself to pitch them low key.

"Scuba's really pretty simple." He said it nonchalantly. Smiled at the man. "We just got back from a nice relaxing dive just down there."

He pointed at the water below.

"Yeah? Whadja see?"

The man turned to face him. The others looked mildly curious.

"Oh, all kinds of fish. Lobster. An eel. And the coral . . . it's like an underwater garden."

All six tourists sat up straight, interested.

"And anybody can just put on the gear and jump in?"

"Oh, no. There's a certification process . . . for safety." Wally paused for effect. "But there's also an introductory scuba course—a quick safety chat and a practice session in the pool—that lets you do shallow dives with an instructor straight away."

All six sets of eyes were locked on Wally now, some more intent than others. Three of the tourists glanced at each other, questioning.

"Sooo . . . where do you get one of those quickie courses?" the first man said. The woman beside him coughed. He turned to her. "Honey, this could be fun. And it beats sitting around the house. Or a bar."

"Actually, I teach them," Wally said. Val stifled a laugh behind him. "We could jump in the pool first thing in the morning. Then, if you like it, you can dive with me the rest of the week."

Several of them looked suspicious.

"I'm Wally." He crossed to their table to shake hands. "Here's my card. We're Going Under Divers, up on the north end. Those classes are always a lot of fun. Think about it, call me with any questions or concerns. Or just show up in the morning. Anytime between 7:00 and 7:30's good."

"I can vouch for him," Chip said. "He and his crew're top notch!"

Wally, Val, and Chip left, leaving the group to discuss whether they would take the course.

"Subtle, Dude," Val laughed once they were out of the building.

"Hey, at this point I'll take any diver I can get, any way I can get them," Wally said. Six discover diving students, plus a few days of private guiding would cover payroll nicely.

Val and Chip both looked at him strangely.

"What? I have hull repairs to pay for."

Wally drove back north smiling, ignoring the clattering van and Chip and Val's conversation. If he could pull in divers like this, find new arrivals who didn't have diving pre-arranged, that could keep the business afloat. It would be more work, but that wasn't a problem. For the first time since his initial days as owner, he felt truly optimistic about Going Under Divers.

12

Weeks passed. Wally's newfound tactic of seeking out divers on the island was bringing in a stream of much-needed income. There weren't many, but they were enough to slow the bleeding from his personal funds.

The *J-Valve* was doing well, too. Lemuel had been slow and expensive but had done solid work. Wally and LB checked the bilge every morning, and the new stringer was holding up perfectly. Whatever else Lemuel had done, the bilge wasn't getting nearly as much water in it as before either.

Wally was in the dive shop, waiting for LB to arrive so they could do their now-standard morning bilge inspection when Angela strolled in.

"LB's not comin' today." Her tone was matter-of-fact, as if it were another way to say 'good morning.'

"Is he all right?" Wally said.

"He's fine. Just won't be in."

"Any reason why?"

"Got arrested last night."

"Arrested? For what?" Wally couldn't imagine calm, reliable LB committing robbery or fighting or driving drunk or . . . anything.

"Got caught lobsterin'." Angela shrugged. "Out of season. Happened twice before. That's why Rafe Marquette's prosecutin' this time."

"He's in jail? For how long?" Wally hoped for a quick booking and release. There were divers to take out. Wally didn't have time to drive the boat and leave the shop unattended for days, or weeks, until LB got back.

"No tellin'. Have to see what the judge says. Prob'ly a couple of months, though."

"I . . . need to be in here looking after the bills, payroll, all that. I can't be on the boat full time right now. Would you be willing to run the divers out today? By yourself?"

Angela lowered her head, raised her eyebrows, like an annoyed librarian looking over invisible glasses.

"Right," Wally said. "Okay. I'll drive and you dive. Today only."

"I maybe know somebody available. I'll give him a call."

"Please! Just until LB gets back."

Angela nodded, walked out tapping numbers into her phone.

The divers that morning were no trouble and self-sufficient in the water. Angela jumped in to keep an eye on them, but none were interested in following her. On the boat between dives they were cheerful and chatty. With everything else going on, Wally had forgotten how much he enjoyed being on the boat, in the sun, on the water, interacting with guests. He needed more of this and less office.

Back at the dive shop at midday, a familiar figure was waiting. Tall, thin, dreadlocks to his shoulders, a narrow face with a broad grin. Booger Bottoms, the Blacktip Haven boat captain. What new trouble was Wally in with Elena?

"Booger? What brings you up here?" Wally braced for a threat. An ultimatum.

"Angela, she did say you were looking for a captain."

"I . . . yes, but what does that have to do with The Haven?"

"Nothin'. I can drive your boat."

"My boat . . . you want to work here?" Booger even having this conversation with him could start fresh hostilities with Elena.

"Be better'n workin' at The Haven anymore. And I know you from way back. You're fair. You good people."

"Yes, but Elena . . . you can't just quit like that. Aren't there work permits and employment contracts and things like that?"

"Quit anytime I want. And don't need a permit. I'm Tiperene. Can work wherever I want, for whoever I want."

"You can work here, and there's nothing Elena can do about it? Except get angry?"

"Oh, she'll get angry, all right. Give us both an earful. But can't *do* anything 'bout it."

Wally looked from Booger, out the glass door, to the *J-Valve*. He needed a captain. Elena couldn't sue him for hiring her former employee. And she had banned him from Blacktip Haven—it wasn't like there was a bridge there to burn anymore.

"It'd just be until LB gets back."

"That's all right. He might be gone for a while, getting caught with twelve lobster out of season."

"Can you start in the morning?"

"Yah, man. Like a look at that boat today, though."

Wally walked Booger to the pier, gave him an introduction to the *J-Valve*'s controls, engines and equipment, as well as a rundown on the boat's peculiarities.

"There's an odd shimmy above 2,000 rpm, so we run her below that." Wally tapped the gauges for emphasis. "And the ignition's finicky—if the engines won't start, take the key out, put it back in, and jiggle it when you turn it."

Satisfied with Wally's boat tour, Booger left, promising to be there at seven the next morning. Wally went back to the dive shop to sort through bills and see how many he could pay. A quick glance at the Going Under account balance showed the $300,000 was gone. That, at least, was a relief. Though Wally was sure financial authorities could still track it and find his name attached to it.

He was still sorting through bookings when the dive shop door exploded open and Elena Havens stormed in, hair and sundress streaming behind her.

"How dare you hire Booger behind my back!" She leaned across the counter, waggled her index finger at Wally.

"Booger came to me. Out of the blue and without my asking."

"You tempted him in some way!" Her face was bright red.

"Haven't seen Booger since I stayed at The Haven. That was six months ago."

"Well, I want him back!"

"That's between you and him." Wally shrugged. "But it didn't much sound like he wanted to go back."

"This will have consequences, you . . ."

"What? You'll sue me for hiring a local? That'll play well."

"You've just ruined any relationship we had."

"Our relationship is . . . adversarial, Elena. You said so yourself. Right before you banned me from The Haven. I should probably ban you from Going Under Divers after this harassment. It's interesting, really . . ."

"Interesting?" She spat the word, leaned farther across the counter.

"I have two boat captains, and you have none. Need me to take your divers out?"

Elena stared at Wally, mouth open.

"You'll regret this!"

She spun, stormed back out the door, slammed it behind her.

Wally sat, exhaled. Smiled. Perhaps Elena's bad side was the only acceptable one to be on. Or possible *to* be on. Either way, she would think twice before trying to push him around. And he had someone to drive the boat the next day.

He opened email, checking for new bookings. Hoping for new bookings. There were two, joining a booking from the day before in what he hoped would be a trend. And a note from Hank, from his personal account, not the Big Chicken Divers account. Wally opened it.

'*Wally, I still feel horrible about how things worked out down there. You didn't get back to me, so I figured things didn't go well with Elena. Thing is, I have a family of four wants to come down and dive Blacktip next month. If you have room, I'll send them to you. Just keep it on the QT so Elena doesn't find out. Let me know. Hank-O.*'

Wally read the note twice, making sure he had read it correctly. Hank was sending divers on the sly, despite the risk. He didn't need to check the next month's schedule or ask for the dates the family wanted to come—the boat was half empty at best next month. He sent Hank a note thanking him and saying they could come down whenever they wanted and stay as long as they wanted. Then added, '*After this morning there's about zero chance Elena and I will ever talk again, and if we do, I guarantee I won't mention this.*'

He leaned back in his chair, smiled. In one afternoon, he had gotten the better of Elena *and* had a dive booking *and* had a dive group coming down from Big Chicken. And maybe more BCD divers in the future, if Hank kept feeling guilty.

Unable to sit still, Wally biked to Peachy's store to get water for the office. He stepped inside. Saw Alison. With Finn. With her arms around Finn. She laughed at something he said, then stood on her toes and quickly kissed him. Wally stood frozen, blindsided. He had wondered if, how, to politely break things off with Alison, and had avoided her for weeks, but he never expected this. Alison looked up, saw him, smiled.

"Hey! Where you been, stranger?"

"Working . . . look, do you have a minute?" Wally pointed at the glass door, toward the dirt parking lot.

"Sure!" She turned back to Finn, beads clacking. "I'll be right back."

Wally stopped just outside the door, turned to face her, torn between shock and anger. Alison put a hand on his chest, grinned up at him as if nothing were wrong.

"So what's up?"

"That's my question to you."

"About what?"

"You and Finn. In there. All over each other." Anger was building now. Finn, of all people. Probably his way to get back at Wally for yelling at him.

"Oh, that's just Finn."

"I thought *we* were together."

"We are! And how. Even when you ghost me." She put both hands on his waist, leaned close.

"So what's with Finn?"

"We're together, too." A confused look crossed her face. "Don't go all heavy on me. We talked about this."

"When?"

"That first night at my place. You said you didn't care."

"The night I was so hammered I don't remember anything? I thought we were a couple."

"Exactly! We are!"

"But . . . you . . . and him . . ."

"I'm monogamous. With each of you. Call it 'binogamous.'"

"You're . . .? That's not a thing." Confusion pushed his anger aside.

"Dude. Don't give me that butthurt, Whore-of-Babylon look. I'm not shagging everybody on the island. I like him. Then I met you, and I like you, too. You're different. Exotic. Not the standard dive dude. That's it."

"I'm not okay with this whole threesome . . ."

"Who said 'threesome?' Dude, that's perverted. When I'm with you, I'm with you. Period. Totally and completely. What's the problem?"

Wally stared at her. He had wanted an exotic, romantic adventure with someone totally different, and here he was over his head in exactly that.

"I'm . . . not sure I'm okay with that," he heard himself say.

"For real? Wally, I was right up front with this."

"There's 'dating' and there's *dating*. We're . . . *dating*."

"I'm not sure about that. Right now, I'm not so stoked on you." She wrinkled her nose at him. "I never thought you'd be so . . . Presbyterian."

Alison walked back into the store, leaving Wally standing alone in the dirt lot.

He took his time pedaling back to the dive shop, thoughts and emotions swirling. He had been distancing himself from Alison, yes, and avoiding her, but there was still an attraction there. He had wanted to be the one who walked away from her. And the fact she had been . . . seeing . . . Finn the whole time she and Wally were together was still sinking in. She hadn't lied, and it obviously hadn't been a secret, but he wouldn't have pursued her so hard, or at all, if he had been conscious of it.

Wally was still sorting through his emotions in the dive shop when Chip stuck his head in the door.

"Hey! I'm grabbing a drink at The Spinner in a bit. You in? That dive from shore the other day got me thinking, and I been picking Val's brain. She's a local diving encyclopedia."

"Umm . . . sure." He liked Chip, and talking with him and Val would get his mind off Alison and onto something happier.

"I was hoping you'd say that!" Chip grinned. "We're meeting at six-ish."

The sun was setting when Wally arrived at the Tail Spinner. Val and Chip greeted him as soon as he walked into the dining room.

"Right on time. That's unheard of on this island," Val said. "Glad you came."

"Well, Vinson *does* call us the Three Amigos," Wally said.

"It always this empty?" Chip did a slow turn, taking in all the vacant tables.

"This time of day, yeah," Val said. "Midday it's busy, and things'll pick up in an hour or so, but for now it's quiet. And the sunsets are great."

She pulled three beers from behind the bar and led Wally and Chip out of the dining room and onto the wooden deck overlooking The Pinnacle, backlit with the setting sun. Val set the bottles on a table, and the three of them sat, facing the sea. Fireflies flickered in the sea grapes, drifted across the deck.

"Welcome to sunset at the top of the island," Val said.

"Thanks for letting me pester you with my questions," Chip said. "You know more about diving here than anybody else I've run into."

"No problem," Val said. "People get so locked in to diving just where the dive boats always go, they miss out on some nice stretches of reef. Not that that's a bad thing. More divers mean more coral damage. It's nice to have some unspoiled, less-dived places."

"I just gotta get this guy to take us to 'em." Chip jabbed his thumb at Wally.

"Why don't we keep them as our little secrets, and just the three of us dive them?" Val said.

"You make it sound like a conspiracy," Wally laughed.

"It is. Kind of." Val smiled at him.

"I need to get over here more often, then," Chip said. "Tiperon doesn't have reefs this healthy. Or traffic this light. Not by a long shot."

"If you like Blacktip, but not Tiperon, you probably never want to go back to the States," Wally said.

Chip stared at Wally for several seconds, gauging a response, then chuckled to himself.

"It wouldn't be a good life choice for me to go anywhere near the continental U.S. anytime soon," he said.

Wally waited, not sure how to respond.

"A while back, rules were broken, money was mishandled, warrants were issued, and I moved to the Tiperons."

Wally and Val looked at each other, eyes wide, then back at Chip.

"All parties could afford it, I did it to them to keep them from doing it to me, and no one was hurt . . ."

"I'm not sure I want to know any more," Wally said. Cheerful, laughing Chip was a crook?

"Suffice to say that was a one-off. I'm semi-retired and enjoying life on this little island. Life's too short not to."

Wally raised his beer in agreement, and Chip and Val both clanked their bottles against it in a silent toast.

"Hey, I almost forgot," Val said. "My friend says you should be getting some dive bookings."

"That's where the uptick's from!" Wally said. "Whatever your buddy's doing, it's working. And couldn't come at a better time."

"Money that tight?" Chip said.

"There's been some . . . unexpected expenses lately," Wally said.

"Well, lemme know what I can do. I want your operation to succeed. You go away, I'm stuck diving with one of those big, cattle-boat outfits."

"Just keep diving with us." Wally said. "And bring friends."

Wally stared at The Pinnacle, mind wandering over all he had been through that day, losing LB and Alison, gaining Booger.

"You're quiet all of a sudden," Val said.

"It's been an odd day," Wally said.

"Because of . . .?"

"How well do you know Alison?" He might as well brace it head on.

"In terms of . . .?"

"Finn."

A slow smile spread across Val's face.

"I was wondering how long that would take. Alison has a heart of gold, but she's definitely a free spirit."

"I found out how free just this afternoon. Pretty sure I blew up . . . whatever it was."

"Ouch. Sorry. I figured you knew and were okay with it." Val half laughed. "Welcome to the Blacktip Island dating scene: your odds are good, but the goods are odd."

A group of four guests filed into the indoor dining area, and Val excused herself to help them. Wally and Chip finished their drinks and headed out. He took his time pedaling home, relaxed for the first time in recent weeks. The split with Alison wasn't necessarily a bad thing. It had just been a shock. Skerritt's dodgy money was out of the Going Under Divers account, more divers were booking thanks to Val's friend, the *J-Valve* was in good shape, and he was developing a decent friendship with Val and Chip. He had finally turned the corner financially with the business, and with life on Blacktip. There was more hard work to be done, but he was no longer drowning in debt.

The next morning Wally arrived early, checked his email. Two more bookings had come in overnight. He needed to do something to thank Val's mysterious friend and her 'software experiment.' He signed in to the company bank account. Then froze.

The balance was more than $400,000. Wally would be lucky if he didn't get dragged down in whatever that was part of. And not knowing what that was was worse than knowing the money was being parked in the account. He left the dive shop, crossed to Inne's main building and found Vinson in the kitchen, with guests milling around the coffee dispenser in the dining room.

"Vinson, do you know what kind of . . . activities Ferris Skerritt is mixed up in?"

"Besides Going Under Divers, you mean?"

"Including Going Under Divers."

"That Ferris, he *is* into a little bit of everything." Vinson gave Wally a thin smile, watched him through narrowed eyes. "Ask him 'how much is enough,' he'll say 'just a little bit more.' You got any specific . . . activity in mind?"

Wally hesitated, unsure how much to tell Vinson. If telling Vinson would end badly for both of them. But he needed to know.

"What reason would he have to . . . put money—a lot of money—in the G.U.D. bank account, then take it out a few days later?"

"Oh, all kinds of reasons he'd do that." Vinson was grinning now. "And you worried you'll get swept up with whatever it is?"

"If it's illegal, yeah. Either by the cops or . . . his associates."

"That Ferris, he's crooked as a dog's hind leg. But Tiperon police, and law, don't care about offshore money passin' through. They get their cut. For his associates . . . depends on the associate."

"So, there's no way to know exactly what I'm dealing with."

"Not unless Ferris decides to tell you." Vinson grinned again. "Best thing is turn a blind eye and don't get involved. Or worry too much about it. It'll sort itself out, in the end."

"Hopefully it's not *my* end."

Wally ran a hand through his hair, started back toward the dive shop. He knew as little as he had before he talked to Vinson, though Vinson didn't seem surprised, or concerned, about the money. Wally would try not to think of where the money was coming from. Or going to. His cheerfulness of the night before dimmed. Illegal cash randomly moving through the business's bank account was a sword hanging over his head. He had no choice but to cross his fingers, hope no off-island authorities found out about it. At least business was picking up, and the boat was in good shape.

Booger met him walking across the dirt parking lot.

"Mr. Wally, I need you to look at something, tell me if it's normal."

"Normal in terms of . . ."

"With the boat."

Wally followed Booger down to the dock, a sense of dread building. What could Booger possibly think was abnormal about the *J-Valve*? He stepped onto the boat. The smell of diesel fuel hit him immediately.

"There normally that much diesel in the bilge?" Booger pointed to the engine compartment. "Like this when I raised the hatch this morning."

A yellow slick of diesel covered what little water was in the bilge, and coated the fiberglass higher up, from the boat rocking overnight. Wally had never seen, or smelled, anything like this before.

"That's completely new," he said. "Can you tell where it's coming from?"

"Checked the fuel filter and lines. They're all good," Booger said.

"Where's that leave us?"

"Starboard fuel tank leakin'."

"How do we tell where, and how do we fix it?"

"Could be anywhere. Prob'ly down low where the bilge water splashes against it. 'Luminum rots quick on Blacktip," Booger said. "Only way to find it, fix it, is to pull that tank out."

"Pull the tank . . .?"

Wally glanced toward the Inne, where the first guests were starting to shuffle their way toward the dock. He stared at the aluminum fuel tank, fiberglass deck above it, and the engine blocking it from the side.

"How do we do that?"

"Engine got to come out." Booger's voice was matter-of-fact. "Or tear up the deck."

Wally's stomach tightened. His optimism of that morning completely evaporated. Neither option sounded cheap. Or quick. The first of the guests had reached the dock.

"So what do we do for now?" Wally said.

"Close the hatch so folks don't smell it so much. Squirt dish soap down there to break it down. Hope Marine Parks don't notice when the bilge pump throws diesel oil into the sea." Booger lowered the engine cover, motioned the divers aboard. "Not a big leak, mind you. Just a messy one."

"How long will it take to remove the tank, repair it, and reinstall it?"

"No telling. Pull that engine'd be the easiest, if you have the right pulley." Booger was silent for a moment. "I got a friend on Tiperon could do it. Name's Lemuel . . ."

"No!"

It was out before Wally realized it. Booger gave him a shocked look.

"What I mean is . . . Lemuel's a great worker, I love Lemuel, but I'd prefer someone who . . . works a little faster."

"He does take his time." Booger laughed. "But he does good work."

"I'll see if I can find someone else."

All the guests were aboard, followed by Angela. Wally pulled in the dock lines and watched the *J-Valve* idle toward the cut. Liquid poured out of a fitting midship near the waterline for a few seconds—the central bilge pump spewing a smelly mix of water, diesel and dish soap in a multi-colored slick across the lagoon's still surface. Wally wasn't sure what the fine was for dumping fuel in the sea, but was certain he couldn't afford it.

At the dive shop Antonio was getting out of a rusty, once-white hardtop Jeep. The hinges screamed in protest when he leaned his considerable weight against the door to close it.

"Warren, you just the person I come to see!" he stepped toward Wally, hand extended, flip-flops kicking up dust.

"It's still 'Wally,' Antonio." He didn't know what Antonio wanted but didn't feel up to his double talk.

"Look like you got the weight of the world on your shoulders." Antonio studied him. "Don't realize things are looking up?"

"You're a day late, Antonio."

"No, no. Just the beginnin'. You finally after the dark. Came to let you know I *Seen* it, tell you you're on the right track." His eyes took on an unfocused look.

"Antonio, the only thing I'm after right now is getting a boat engine removed and an aluminum fuel tank repaired."

Wally headed for the dive shop and its air conditioning. Antonio's eyes snapped back into focus.

"You be needin' Shedrick, then," he said.

"Shedrick?" Wally stopped, faced Antonio, not sure who, or what, Shedrick was. And hoped it didn't involve sacrificing chickens.

"Shedrick Graysby, down at Public Works. Does jobs on the side. Got a big chain hoist. Swapped out boat engines before. Welds 'luminum, too."

"Yes! Thank you, Antonio! How do I reach him, and what does he charge?"

"Dunno what he charges, but I give you his number, you and he can sort things out." He slapped Wally on the shoulder. "See, Warren? You double lucky I came by today!"

Shedrick Graysby was a short, wide man, with a poker-tournament face badly in need of a shave, dark eyes, skin like weathered leather and oily, thinning black hair. He came by that afternoon, cigarette between his lips, a faded green, oil-stained shirt tucked into his jeans. He inspected the *J-Valve*'s engine compartment, tapping on the deck and bilge with a small Teflon hammer and kneeling down to squint at seams while Wally looked on.

"Pop that engine out, yeah, be quicker than tearing up the deck then patching it again." He spat over the side. "Tear that tank out. Haul it off to find that leak and seal it up."

"How long will that take?" Wally said.

"Two, maybe three days, I get help."

"Booger can help. And we don't have guests for a few days next week. Could you start Wednesday?"

"Yah, mon. Not doing much next week."

"And the cost?"

Shedrick squinted at Wally. Stared for five, six, seven seconds. Lit a cigarette off the butt of the one he was finishing.

"$7,000," he said.

"To weld a fuel tank?"

Wally didn't have even close to that much money in the bank. And payroll was coming up.

"Touchy work, welding 'luminum," Shedrick said. "Only me on island knows how. Or you can send that tank to Tiperon, if you got the time."

"But that's a lot of money." Apparently the age of piracy was still alive.

Shedrick shrugged.

"Could we work out a payment plan where I pay you in installments?"

"Uh huh. Can pay in one installment soon's the job's done."

Wally stared. The man had him over a barrel. Shedrick was his only option, unless he waited who-knew-how-long to get the tank to Tiperon, repaired, and back again. He couldn't close the business for that long. He did a quick calculation in his head. If he used the last of his own funds, he might be able to pay Shedrick's price. Barely. He wiped a stream of sweat from his eye. What choice did he have?

"Shedrick, Booger and I'll be here first thing Wednesday morning to help you pull that engine."

Shedrick nodded, still expressionless. Lit another cigarette off the butt end of the last, and walked back to his truck.

Wally retreated to the air-conditioned dive shop. Double-checked his finances. Yes, he had enough to cover the repair and payroll. Once this week's divers cashed out. And the repair had to be done, whether it took the last of his money or not. He glanced at the upcoming diver counts. There would be more money coming in the days and weeks immediately after the repairs to offset that. If he could get to the end of the month still solvent, he would be fine.

13

True to his word, Shedrick, with Booger's help and Wally's supervision, had the engine hoisted out of the *J-Valve* in a few hours. The men worked in silence, a far cry from LB and Lemuel's shout fest while removing the stringer.

Wally gritted his teeth watching them disconnect the propeller shaft, unbolt the engine mounts, and hoist the engine out of the hold, heavy chain clattering through thick pulleys suspended high on a rusty steel-frame boom arm. The aluminum fuel tank was soon muscled out of the compartment and lifted onto Shedrick's flatbed truck.

"I clean her up, then seal her." Shedrick picked his fingernail at clumps of salt crust on the tank's seam. "Get her back quick as I can."

He drove off, leaving an oily cloud of blue smoke drifting across the parking area.

"Be good to have that boat ship-shape again," Booger said.

"Be good to take in more money than I spend."

Wally said it under his breath, but Booger gave him a quick, sharp look.

Wally left Booger working on regulators, and Angela sorting out the latest bookings, went off in search of potential divers he could recruit for when the *J-Valve* was running again.

Two days later Shedrick had the repaired fuel tank reinstalled. Wally and Vinson watched him and Booger lower the engine into place. The job was expensive, but at least Going Under Divers would be operational again. Things were back on track.

"Getting' her back in workin' order just in time," Vinson said. "Bunch of folks gettin' in this afternoon. She be in the water tomorrow?"

"Shedrick says he'll give both engines a sea trial this afternoon."

"Things looking up, then. For both of us. Told you it'd work out."

Wally said nothing. He would need every diver he could get for the next two weeks if he was going to cover the month-end bills.

The next morning, a dozen sleepy divers shuffled down to the waiting *J-Valve*. Among them was a familiar face. Chip Pompano brought up the rear, dive bag slung over his shoulder and an underwater camera in both hands.

"Working for yourself gives you plenty of time off," Wally said, hoping it sounded lighthearted after Chip's admission of fraud the previous week.

"Never did like regular hours." Chip grinned, glanced at the crowd of divers. "I didn't make a reservation. You got room for me?"

"Always, if you're okay with the crowd."

Wally went on the boat with Booger that morning, leaving Angela to watch the dive shop. If there was trouble with the reinstalled engine, he wouldn't be much help, but he was too nervous about it to stay on shore.

Guests briefed and gear secured, Booger idled through the reef, then gradually brought the engines up to speed. The starboard engine coughed smoke for a few moments, sending Wally's pulse racing and stomach curling, then ran as if there had never been a problem with it. Booger smiled at Wally.

"She purrin' just fine," he said. "I'll take it easy, but she's all right. Shedrick took his time, made sure that prop shaft was lined up perfect."

"For what he charged, he should have gold plated it."

Booger laughed. They motored down the normally-rough east side of the island, where moorings were scarce. Booger stopped the boat at a faded, algae-covered mooring ball out of sight of the other moorings, and nearer to the dark ironshore than most. Wally tied off then gave Booger a questioning look.

"Prob'ly haven't dived this one," the captain said. "Gondolin Reef. Most folks overlook it. You dive. I'll give that engine a once-over."

With the guests around him, Booger described the site.

"This's a bit of a maze," he said, his Tiperon accent turning the word into *meeze*. "Coral tops beneath us are at thirty feet, with sandy canyons between 'em starting at about forty. That sand gets deeper as you swim toward the wall."

He waved his hand at the open sea, where the water changed from green to deep blue in a sharp line 100 feet from the boat.

"Slopes drop off into the deep-deep at about eighty feet. Out on the wall, go either way you like . . ." A glance at Wally. ". . . but seems like there's more fish if you turn left. Pick a canyon to come back up, make your way through the maze and find the boat."

Wally nodded, mentally following the directions. Booger's repeated use of 'maze' was concerning, but Wally refused to let it show. He helped the divers gear up, then followed them into the water.

The reef was as Booger had described—a jumble of long coral ridges, with no regular pattern, lay perpendicular to shore, separated by thin sand channels. Several divers were already in the channel directly beneath the boat, kicking toward the wall, stirring silt with their fins as they went. Wally signaled to the other divers, then followed the first two divers down the channel.

The walls of coral to either side were riddled with holes, and in places, the tops spread to form ledges over the canyon. In one of the holes, a green moray eel watched the divers pass, jaws pumping to feed water through its gills, unconcerned by the flash of Chip's camera strobes. The sand channel led them deeper. Wally pointed out a nurse shark sleeping under a ledge. The camera strobes woke it, and the shark swam up, over the group, and back to the shallows. He pointed to more sea life as he went: a feathery gray crinoid on a purple sea fan; a flamingo-tongue snail, looking like a fingerprint-sized giraffe skin; a pair of pale-green, thumb-sized lettuce sea slugs, looking like a cross between a ruffled tuxedo shirt and a glob of snot.

The sand sloped down still. A lighter patch of water loomed ahead. The sand beneath him dropped in a sheer cliff, and Wally burst out into the open water off the wall, with nothing but dark blue water in front of him and below him. Wally turned, watched the divers coming out of the canyon behind him. When they were all through, he turned left, keeping an eye on the two divers ahead of him, and led them along the wall.

The wall's craggy vertical face was studded with clusters of brain coral and pale pink sea plumes waving willow-like in the slight current. Car-sized barrel sponges grew horizontally from the wall, as if the vertical surface was the seabed. A pair of French angelfish, black with dozens of small yellow crescents on their sides, matched the divers' pace and course, but twenty feet deeper down the wall. A hawksbill turtle rose from the depths, front flippers pulling it shallower. It eyed the divers as it passed, unconcerned.

Ten minutes later Wally caught up with the buddy team in front of him, led all the divers up to the top of the wall and inland to shallower water. He zig-zagged across the coral fingers, weaving his way back toward the boat. Elkhorn coral, nearly gone on other sites, was reasserting itself here, and hundreds of silvery mahogany snappers with dark red tail margins sheltered under and around its spreading, leaflike arms.

He checked his depth gauge, made sure they were getting shallower. He had started to wonder if he had misjudged the boat's position, then heard the thud of the boarding ladder bouncing against the stern, and saw the dark shape of the *J-Valve* thirty feet above him. He signaled he was going up and left the guests to finish the dive beneath the boat.

Wally surfaced, found the engine hatch up and Booger hunched over the starboard engine. He straightened when he heard Wally climb aboard.

"She's leakin' a little oil, but I got that tightened up," Booger said. "No fuel leakin', though, so that's done."

"Finally!" Wally grinned at Booger. "I knew this run of bad luck couldn't keep up."

Divers were surfacing then. Wally and Booger helped them aboard, then motored to the next site.

Wally stayed on the boat for the second dive while Booger led the guests. He sat at the helm in the shade, watching the divers' pale exhalation bubbles rising through the turquoise water before breaking the surface in a dozen white boils, as if the sea were a gigantic jacuzzi. An offshore breeze sent ripples across the surface, scattering the reflected sun like sequins. On shore palm fronds rustled, fluttered. He watched the bubbles move away from the boat, circle around the darker coral heads behind the stern, where Booger was leading the divers around the reef. The occasional flash of light showed where Chip was taking photos.

Wally soaked it all in, relishing it. After all the problems, all the bad breaks, he deserved a day like this. The boat was solid and diver numbers were inching up. He even had enough money to cover payroll at the end of the week. Barely, but he had it. His days in Marietta seemed so distant, as if it could have been someone else's life.

He was still smiling when Booger surfaced, and he chatted with the guests when they climbed up the boarding ladder. He took a turn at the helm on the way back to the dock for lunch, enjoying the feel of the wheel and throttles in his hands, the deck's vibration under his feet, the wind on his face. Yes, this was why he had moved to Blacktip Island.

Vinson was on the dock when they got back, grinning bigger than ever.

"Things lookin' up, guest-wise," he said. "Inne's about full next week."

"Things are definitely looking up," Wally said. "And everyone enjoyed the dives this morning. Right, folks?"

The divers cheered, clapped, hooted their approval. They piled off the boat, made their way up the dock, headed for the Inne's main building, bulging mesh dive bags slung, dripping, over their shoulders. Vinson followed them, ready to serve lunch.

Val stepped out of the dive shop, spoke with Chip for a few moments, then continued down to the dock.

"You have happy campers today." She glanced back at the divers chattering by the gear rinse tanks. "I just talked to Angela. She says your bookings are picking up."

"Slowly. Thank your friend again when you get a chance. That has to be where these reservations are coming from. It's shaping up to be a good summer season. If we can last that long."

"Still that touch-and-go, eh?"

"If things stop breaking, I'll gain some ground." Wally chuckled. "At this point I'd have been ahead financially if I'd just bought a new boat. I'm slowly getting the feeling I've been had."

"Well, at least you can laugh about it." She smiled. "I never—no one really, except Vinson—thought you'd make it this long."

"Great. So I'm beating the odds."

"Yep." She laughed. "Keep fighting the good fight!"

She walked with Wally back to the dive shop, then climbed in her Jeep and drove away with a wave. Inside, Wally found Angela biting her lip, staring at her phone, frowning, brows furrowed.

"Problem? Val said we've had more bookings."

"Oh, bookings're fine." She turned to face him. "It's LB's not. Judge sentenced him to three months. Woulda been a week if he coulda payed the fine."

"Crap. Nothing we can do to shorten that? Pay his fine?" It couldn't be much for a few lobsters.

"You got $3,000 sitting around? Yeah, me neither."

Wally sat. He wouldn't have even $50 to spare after payroll in two days.

"Maybe we could take up a collection . . ."

"Too late," Angela said. "Judge already sentenced him. Can't un-sentence."

"I'll let Booger know." At least he had someone to drive, and fix, the boat. "He doesn't like to poach lobster, too, does he?"

"Booger's vegetarian." Angela laughed. "And salad's legal to take right now."

Wally sighed, relieved. That was one less thing to worry about.

"Oh, Mister Skerritt stopped by," Angela said. "Looked in the computer and said something about his money."

Wally pulled up the Going Under Divers bank account. Sure enough, Skerritt had moved his cash out of the account again. Out of habit he slid the desk drawer open, checked the metal cash box, flipped through the notes there. A chill shot through him. There was several hundred dollars missing. He looked at Angela. No. She wouldn't make such an obvious theft.

"Angela, when Mr. Skerritt was here, did he open the desk?"

"He looked at everything." Angela shrugged. "Didn't like me pesterin' him."

Wally sat, exhaled slowly. Skerritt must have inadvertently taken the money. Otherwise he would have told Angela, or left a note. He tapped Skerritt's contact on his phone.

"Ah . . . Wally. To what do I owe the pleasure?" Skerritt's spectral voice hissed in Wally's ear.

"Ferris, I noticed you moved your money out of the account this morning."

"That was the . . . ah, timely thing to do, yes. And I know having strange sums in the account gives you certain apprehensions."

"Yes, well, might you also have moved some actual cash, from our petty cash box, without realizing it?"

"Absolutely not." A tea kettle could have been speaking. "I was quite cognizant of taking it. Very perceptive of you, though."

"But that's Going Under Divers money."

"That's my share of the profits."

"There are no profits. And I need that money to pay Angela and Booger."

"My share of gross income, as stated in our contract, is due today."

"It's not the end of the month. I'll get you your cut then. I need that money now."

"I . . . ah . . . saved you the trouble of transferring funds by simply taking the cash directly. Easier for both of us, and one less thing on your plate. And what needs to be done eventually is best done immediately."

Wally counted the petty cash again, did quick mental math.

"Wait. You took *more* than your percentage of what we made."

"I am due my remittance. And my remittance is whatever I say it is."

"That's not right!"

"You should probably file suit. Take me to court. Oh, yes, but you have a certain paucity of funds at the moment."

"How'm I supposed to meet payroll?"

"That, young Wally, would be *your* problem."

Skerrit hung up. Wally stared at his phone. Then realized Angela was still sitting beside him. Staring at him, eyes wide.

"Angela, you and Booger will get paid. In full and on time. I have some emergency cash at my place. And this is exactly why I do."

Angela's face went from shock to skepticism.

"Look. Here's *my* bank balance." He showed her his account on the computer screen. "I'm not short by much, and I have enough cash to make up the difference. And when this week's guests cash out, we'll be flush."

Angela's expression didn't change.

"Payday's in two days, right?" Wally said. "I'll bump it up to tomorrow and have your pay—in full—ready when you get here in the morning. Deal?" He couldn't afford to have the only staff available walk out.

Angela, still looking skeptical, nodded once. She handed the legal pad with bookings scribbled on it to him.

"Bunch of new bookin's, all in the system." She patted the stack of yellow legal pads. "Work here's done. See you in the mornin'."

She left the shop without looking back.

Wally studied his bank balance on the screen, did a quick pen-and-paper calculation to see how much of his own money he would have to use to cover payroll. And how much income this week's divers would bring to cover end-of-the-month bills. He crossed his fingers nothing catastrophic happened before the current divers cashed out.

The bigger problem, though, was Skerritt was now snatching whatever amount he wanted from Going Under Divers' till, whenever he wanted, and there was nothing Wally could do to stop him. He had to have cash on hand to make change. Maybe he could find somewhere to hide the petty cash but still have it easily available. He had zero control over the company's finances and had used almost all of his personal money to cover expenses. He loved the island, the boat, the diving, the guests, the nights out with other locals, but he wouldn't be able to do this much longer unless something changed. Drastically.

He flipped through the scheduling sheets. Diver numbers *were* up. He had some control over that. Sort of. Via Val's friend. If he could keep divers coming to Going Under, if he could keep increasing those numbers, Skerritt taking his self-appointed cut wouldn't hurt so much. He could still make a go of the operation. Vinson seemed to be doing well with the increased bookings. But he didn't have a greedy partner taking a cut of what he made. Maybe, with business doing so well, Vinson would be able to buy out Skerritt's shares, become Wally's Tiperon partner.

Wally wandered outside, found Vinson talking with Chip, who was rinsing his camera with the dive shop hose.

"Hey, thanks again for the great dives today," Chip said. "If you want my job, I want *yours!*"

"Be careful what you ask for," Wally said. "But yeah, it beats eight-plus hours in an office."

Chip crossed to the Inne and his room, leaving Wally alone with Vinson.

"Vinson, with the uptick in business lately, would it be possible to revisit you being Going Under's Tiperon partner?"

Vinson gave him a long look.

"Ol' Ferris pullin' his shenanigans? Figured he would." Vinson chuckled. "One day Ferris'll go to Hell, and feel right at home."

"So why'd you send me to him if you knew all that about him?" It hit Wally, again, like a punch to the gut. Was the entire island conspiring against him, trying to ruin him?

"Only person on island that'd go in on something like this."

"Something like *this*? You knew this place was a money pit and . . ." Wally couldn't go on, his mind was so busy processing everything. Were Vinson and Skerritt working together? No. The two clearly didn't like each other. Was Vinson the local crime boss, running everything from the shadows? Running the Inne as cover and making sure his lieutenants got their cut? Was that why Skerritt seemed so tense around him?

"Things'll work out fine. You'll see." Vinson chuckled again, setting his belly jumping. "Ferris, he ain't so all-powerful as he likes to think."

"Is this some kind of hobby of yours? Ruining people's lives?"

"Your life looks pretty good to me." Vinson grinned. "Better than the one you had."

"I'm having to use most of my remaining cash to cover this week's payroll."

"And that speaks to your character. Meantime, you got all this," Vinson spread his arms wide, did a quarter turn, indicating scenery around them, "and friends and happy guests."

"I can't pay staff with scenery," Wally said.

"Can't buy friends or happiness, either." He slapped Wally's shoulder. "Business's good, but not so good I can invest in a dive shop. Things'll turn 'round, though. You'll see."

He walked back to the Inne, leaving Wally staring after him, open mouthed.

Vinson had to be up to something. There was no way he could be such a Pollyanna, believing things would magically work out. Even Wally wasn't that naïve. But it made no sense for Vinson to be so cavalier about Wally's success. Noboddie's Inn was doing well now solely because of Going Under Divers. If the dive operation failed, so would the Inne. Wally was missing something but had no clue what. Maybe Vinson *was* that naïve. Maybe that was why his hotel had been failing. Maybe that was why Val said no one but Vinson thought Going Under Divers would be successful. Great. Wally had taken advice on buying a business from the person with the worst business sense on the island.

Wally grabbed his bike, pedaled toward the Tail Spinner. He needed food, a drink, and time to think, to sort out this constantly-evolving mess he was in. He would bring what cash he had left to work in the morning, make sure Angela and Booger were paid, but for now he needed to sit, let his brain work while he relaxed for an hour or so.

The restaurant was nearly empty. Wally took a table on the deck, where he could gaze at The Pinnacle and the surrounding sea, remind himself again why he was on Blacktip, why it was still worth all the aggravation.

"Penny for 'em." Val stood by the table, order pad in hand.

"Sorry. I didn't hear you walk up."

"Obviously. You looked like you were out on the ocean, far from here."

Wally ordered a burger and a beer, went back to staring out to sea. Was startled when Val thunked a full beer mug on the table.

"You're awfully quiet today."

"Yeah. Business is booming, but I'm bleeding cash." He took a deep breath. Val didn't need to know how desperate his position was after Skerritt's withdrawls. "You ever have a dream, some great thing you wanted to do or accomplish, just beyond your grasp, but you could never quite grab it?"

Val studied him, obsidian eyes scanning his face for several seconds. Then she pulled out a chair, sat next to him.

"Once upon a time I was set to leave Blacktip and sail around the world." Her eyes were locked on his. "My boyfriend and I, we had it all planned out. Pooled our money, bought a beautiful Bristol 40, over on Tiperon. *The Stormy Petrel.* Masthead rig. Lovely lines. Counter stern. Big cabin that gave us plenty of space. We were all set to start our new life. He quit his job at Sandy Bottoms. I quit mine at Marine Parks. My last day there he flew over to Tiperon to provision the boat and sail it back over here to pick me up. That's the last I saw of him."

Val paused, eyes not quite focused, gazing at Wally's sweating beer mug.

"What happened to him?" A hard knot formed in Wally's stomach. This matched what Vinson had told him, but the pain, the resignation in Val's voice was difficult to hear.

"We called the authorities. Started a search . . . Turns out he set sail that same day, headed off to who knows where. We had it planned, in detail, how we'd sail through the Windwards, then down to Brazil, and on to Africa, so that's probably where he went. Me? I stayed on Blacktip with no job and no savings, and the world kind of went gray for a bit."

"So . . . The Tail Spinner."

"The Tail Spinner. It was a project but gave steady income, since the Marine Parks job was already filled. With tips, I make more here, anyway. And it lets me talk to people, make the world a little less gray. Watching your dive company succeed helps with that, too. Nothing like a scrappy underdog succeeding to brighten things up. So, yeah. I know about ungraspable dreams."

"You handled that better than a lot of people would have."

"Just like you're handling Going Under Divers. Keep at it. It's your dream job, yeah? So keep at it. Things'll turn around."

14

Wally sat in the dive shop, looking over the roster of the day's divers. A full boat, finally. The first of the big bookings. An eight-person dive club, and other individual divers packing the boat, and Noboddie's Inne. He smiled. His luck had turned. This would bring in the cash to move him, the company, forward. With so many divers, after paying all the bills, and whatever Skerrit took, he should still be in the black. If he could avoid another catastrophe.

Wally paused in the dive shop doorway, dive roster in hand, watching his new guests shuffle across the gravel lot toward the dive shop. Two women looked familiar. One with straight black hair, the other with lighter, curlier hair. They grinned when they saw him, and he recognized them. Mari. And Wendy. From Marietta. Puzzled, he looked at the roster. No 'Wendy' or 'Mari' listed.

"What are you two doing here?" Wally stepped out to meet them.

"That's our welcome?" Wendy said.

"No . . . It's great to see you and all . . . but I had no idea you were coming . . ."

"We decided to zip down and see what you were up to," Wendy said. "And to bug you for a week."

"And if you knew we were coming, it wouldn't have been as fun," Mari said. "For us, anyway. We booked with bogus names so you'd be surprised. We're 'Boris' and 'Natasha.' Angela's really nice on the phone."

"Well, this is it." Wally spread his arms indicating the dive shop and the surrounding grounds and the docked *J-Valve*.

They gazed for a moment at the beach and palm trees, the teal water of the sound, the turquoise water outside the fringing reef, and the cotton-ball clouds in the bright blue sky, then back at Wally.

"Wally! You've got it made!" Mari said. "And you obviously don't need to worry about a haircut."

"It's a lot of work." Wally waved a hand at the shop, then at the boat. "And as soon as I solve one problem, another one pops up."

"That's why it's called *work*, not *fun*." Wendy said. "But you have this view! And your 'work' is what other people wait and save all year to do."

"Really. You *want* to be back in that office, dealing with dead fish and prairie dogs?" Mari said.

"Kit foxes."

"Whatever. You're living the dream here. I'd love to do something like this. You need an assistant? A partner?"

"Careful what you ask for. Do this a week, you wouldn't say that."

"World's smallest violin's playing for you, Bud. Good thing you got your midlife crisis out of the way early!"

"Yeah, well, something about the devil and details," Wally said. "You wouldn't say that if you saw my bank account. I'll see you on the boat."

"Yeah. Show us how rough this new life of yours is." Wendy laughed.

Wally led the first dive, at Crackerbox Wall, Mari and Wendy beside him, other divers trailing behind. Below, pale sand stretched to the wall's edge, where it dropped in several broad chutes between jagged coral outcroppings.

He took the divers to the wall's edge, then over it, dropping through a blue cloud of creole wrasse. A brown-and-tan banded

Nassau grouper, curious, swam beside Wally, then passed along the line of divers, as if greeting each one. Wendy and Mari both smiled around their regulators. Back in the shallows he found a long-limbed channel crab under a ledge, looking like a giant spider, a glitter-eyed burrfish trying to act invisible in a coral nook. A gray stingray glided across the sand in front of them.

Wally hovered, pointed to the ray, twisted sideways to follow its progress along the line of divers. Adrenalin jolted through him. A man was kneeling in the sand, oblivious to the ray, both hands clamped on his regulator, eyes as big as saucers. His head snapped back, staring at the surface. He pushed off from the sand, fins churning up a silty cloud. His hands clawed above his head, as if he were climbing an invisible wall. Wally kicked hard, grabbed him as the man's fins kicked free of the bottom and started to rocket him toward the surface. Wally flared his fins wide, creating drag to slow them both. The man kicked harder, pulled with both arms, spit out his regulator.

Cursing mentally, Wally pulled free his own alternate regulator, shoved the mouthpiece in the man's mouth, purged it of water and held the regulator in place so the man could breathe and not spit it out. He pulled the regulator to his left and down, angling the man's head so Wally could see his gray eyes, still enormous, seeming to fill his entire mask. Wally concentrated on the diver, their shared regulator, ignoring the froth of bubbles rising around them, trying to slow their upward rush by creating as much drag as possible. His computer's fast-ascent alarm went off, near-deafening squeals next to his ear. A moment later the man's computer screamed at their ascent rate, too. Wally watched the diver's eyes, hoped for the best.

They were on the surface then, breaking into the air chest-high before sinking back to shoulder level. Wally squeezed the inflator button on the man's BC until the vest was full, then shoved him away. The diver flailed his arms and legs, afraid of sinking. He ripped off his blue mask and flung it behind him.

His eyes were smaller now, though, more relaxed now he was on the surface. Wally floated far enough away the man couldn't lunge and grab him, signaled to Booger on the boat they were okay.

"What was that about?" It came out harsher than Wally meant it, but the adrenaline was still coursing through him.

"It... felt like... my reg... wasn't working." The man's words came out in ragged gasps.

"So you spit it out?"

"It wasn't working right."

"But it's the only way for you to breathe down there."

"Well... something felt wrong."

"Right. Let's get you back to the boat and have a look at it."

"No. I'm fine. I wanna go back down, finish the dive."

"You just said there's a problem with your regulator." Wally grabbed the man's tank valve, towed him on his back toward the *J-Valve*. "We need to get on the boat and see what the problem is."

Once on board, Wally dried himself, then inspected the man's regulator, purged it several times. Everything seemed fine.

"Take a breath or two from it," he said.

The man took a tentative breath, then a deeper one.

"Huh. Seems okay now."

"Yeah, well, if it happens again, get our attention. Shooting for the surface was the worst thing you could do. Next to spitting out your regulator."

Two heads popped up behind the boat. Mari and Wendy, looking puzzled.

"We wondered where you went," Wendy said.

"You were there one minute, then POOF you were gone," Mari said. "Then we looked up and saw you on the surface and a mask sinking."

She held up the man's blue mask.

"There were... some equipment issues that needed attention," Wally said.

"The guy freaked out, didn't he?" Mari whispered when she was back on the boat. "He was thrashing like crazy on the surface."

Wally said nothing, helped them off with their gear.

"What would have happened if you hadn't grabbed him? If you hadn't been there?" Wendy muttered it so low only Wally heard her.

Wally looked into her green eyes, said nothing. A chill shot down his back. He and the diver had both been lucky.

"So . . . not all fun in the sun, after all." She held his gaze for a moment, then went to find her towel.

Booger led the second dive. Wally watched the divers' bubbles, alert for any sign of trouble. Shivering as the adrenaline leeched out of his system. The dive went without incident, and soon he was speeding the *J-Valve* back to the dock, showing off for Wendy and Mari who were watching over his shoulder.

Outside the cut a shrill, deafening shriek screamed from somewhere. Everywhere. Wally winced, gritted his teeth, glanced around looking for the noise's source.

"Engine temp alarm." Booger tapped the temperature gauge for the port engine, its needle well above 200 degrees, resting on the peg. "Probably got seaweed, or a plastic bag, in the intake."

Wally nodded, as if he knew what that meant, then pulled the port throttle back to idle and turned off the engine. The shrieking alarm stopped. He idled across the lagoon on one engine, and managed to dock the boat without rattling too many cylinders on the dock.

After they had helped the guests off the boat, Booger slipped on his mask and fins, then jumped in to 'check the intake.'

"All in a day's work." Wally smiled at Wendy and Mari. "Tell you what, relax while I finish up a few things. When I'm done, we'll run up to the Tail Spinner for lunch."

Booger popped up a few minutes later.

"Don't see nothing on, or in, the intake. Prob'ly fell off when we slowed down, whatever it was." He grinned at Wally. "She'll run fine in the morning, I s'pect."

Wally filed that day's roster, printed out the next day's, then went to find Wendy and Mari.

They borrowed rusty bikes from the Inne and five minutes later were sitting on the Tail Spinner's deck, watching the scudding clouds send shadows across the sea. Val, looking surprised, came out to take drink orders.

"You have friends today." Val gave Wally one of her half-smile, half-smirks. "Where'd you find friends?"

"Hey, it can happen." Wally acted shocked. "Val, meet Wendy . . . and Mari. Friends from the States down to check out the island and soak up some sun."

"And get you away from that dive shop for a few minutes," Val said. "Congratulations, ladies. You've performed a public service."

Val took their drink orders and went back to the bar.

Mari raised an eyebrow at Wally.

"Anything going on there?" she said.

"With Val? And me? Nada." Then he added, "We go diving occasionally."

"She seemed interested," Wendy said.

"Yeah, there was some definite eye contact there." Mari laughed. "You're doing that thing you always do—thinking, 'oh, she's nice and was really friendly,' then three days later you realize she was being a lot more than friendly. And by then it's too late."

"Like I said, we go diving occasionally."

Wendy and Mari exchanged glances but said nothing.

The next morning, Wally answered the overnight emails while Booger did the engine checks and Angela went to the Inne kitchen to grab boat snacks for the diving guests. He had just finished the last response when Booger stepped into the doorway.

"Mister Wally? There's trouble with that port engine."

"What kind of problem?"

"Looks like oil in the coolant."

Wally followed Booger to the dock, climbed aboard the *J-Valve*. Booger pointed to the coolant reservoir, usually filled with reddish coolant, now filled with a lumpy, gelatinous purple goo. Wally felt like he had the same goo in is stomach.

"Oil mixed all in that coolant," Booger said. "That's why she overheated yesterday."

"But ... the cooling system and the oil are completely separate ... How could that happen?" Had someone inadvertently put oil in there? Or was someone—Elena, maybe—sabotaging him? Was this her getting back at him for hiring Booger?

"Likely a cracked cylinder. Oil pressure pushed it into the coolant circulating 'round the cylinders."

Wally nodded. That sounded more rational than Elena getting revenge.

"So how do we fix it?" Wally had zero money for boat repairs. Hopefully a small crack could be welded somehow, quickly, easily, and for not much money. "This a job for duct tape? Quick-set epoxy?"

"That engine block's cast metal." Booger shook his head. "Can't fix it. Need a new engine."

The lumpy goo in Wally's stomach threatened to surge up and out his mouth. This was the final straw. The thing that finally killed his Going Under Divers misadventure. He leaned against a stanchion, tried to will his stomach to settle. Failed. Here he was, with the boat filled for the next month, about to finally start making money, and this happened.

"Okay," he heard himself say. "I'll let all the guests know ... And refund their money."

Booger gave him a confused look.

"Mister Wally, flat seas like this, we can run this boat just fine on one engine."

"That's possible?" It was a life ring, glowing, flying through the air toward him.

"Can't go fast, or far, but we can do it. Still take folks divin'."

"Yes. Booger, thank you. You're a genius. Can you and Angela take the divers out today? I need to price new engines ... since there's *really* no way to repair this one ... ?"

Booger pursed his lips, shook his head.

"Me and Angela'll take 'em."

Wally said goodbye to Wendy and Mari, cast off the *J-Valve*'s dock lines, then headed back to the dive shop. A quick internet search showed multiple marine engine dealers in south Florida. Wally called them, one after the other, pricing a replacement for the *J-Valve*'s make and model engines. All were more than $70,000. No, the dealers knew of no used engines. Wally was welcome to call marine salvage yards, each one said, but the chances of finding the exact engine he needed were slim.

He called salvage yards but met with no luck. Wally rested his forehead on the desk. It didn't matter, really. Even if he magically found a used engine, he still couldn't afford it. And he had no way to borrow that kind of money. He would have to run the boat on one engine indefinitely. Until the other engine broke. Then he would be officially out of business. How long could he hold out, with just the one engine? Long enough to raise money for a new one? He had to. There was no other choice.

The dive shop door clattered open. Wally raised his head. Ferris Skerritt, hunch-shouldered in a black polo shirt two sizes too big, was coming toward him, face looking like the man had just sucked dry a lemon.

"Ahh . . . Salutations, young Wally." Skerritt stopped beside the desk, skeletal fingers picking at non-existent lint on his sleeve. "There seems to be some . . . ahh . . . inconsistencies with the company bank account today."

"What sort of inconsistencies?" The new topic blindsided Wally, coming so abruptly and unexpected on the heels of his engine worries. Had Skerritt moved more money into the account? Was some of it missing? At least Skerritt couldn't get at the petty cash with Wally there.

"In perusing the balance, I was struck by the fact there's not enough . . . ah . . . capitol there for me to take my share."

"Yeah, it's slim right now, but I have a ton of divers this week. As soon as they settle up, end of the week, we should be flush."

"But I'm prepared to take my earnings today." Skerritt's black eyes bored into Wally's. "Our agreement was based on a certain . . . ah . . . reciprocity, young Wally. If the funds are not in the account, I'll accept cash."

"If I don't have it, I can't give it to you. And you taking extra . . . exacerbates that."

"That contract isn't some fanciful list of suggestions," Skerritt hissed. "Money is owed. Money must be paid. I would prefer to settle this without resorting to penalties or legal proceedings concerning breach of contract."

"What're you gonna do? Repossess the shop? Good luck selling it, even for parts." Wally ran a hand through his mop of hair. "Look, I'll have money Saturday when these divers finish up and pay their bills. Until then, I'm eating noodles breakfast, lunch, and dinner."

Wally pushed the booking sheets across the desk. Skerrit's eyes scanned them, finger tapping on the desktop. Then the eyes shifted back to Wally's.

"I will give you 'til the end of the day Sunday to deliver this month's proceeds. Most people in my . . . ahh . . . position would not, but I'm a kind and understanding man."

Skerritt leaned forward, looming over Wally, threatening despite his frailty. The dive shop door swung open again, and Vinson stepped in.

"How you doin' this morning, Wally?"

He looked taller, broader today, a Richmond Spiders t-shirt grubby with breakfast remains.

Skerritt straightened, jumped back as if he had been stung, eyes locked on Vinson.

"Mornin' to you, too, Ferris. You're out and about early today."

"Wally and I were discussing some . . . ahh . . . business details." Skerritt sidled toward the door, maintaining the distance between him and Vinson.

"He does go at it hard," Vinson said. "Mornin', noon, and night."

He turned as Skerrit inched toward the door, always facing him, smiling ear to ear.

"Yes. Well. I'll check back at week's end, then, Wally."

Skerritt stepped out the door and was gone. Tires spun in the sand parking area.

"Vinson, I don't know what power you have over Ferris, but I wish I had even a little bit of it."

"Ol' Ferris, he's just a flighty type, is all." Vinson chuckled. "Just stopped by to see what he was up to. Or into. Didn't realize you stayed in today."

"Thanks, Vinson. For stopping by *and* keeping an eye out."

Vinson grinned, then ambled back across the sand lot to the Inne.

Wally leaned back in the chair, mind on Skerritt's ultimatum. He was beat. But what could he do? Money from this week's divers would go to cover payroll—for Angela, Booger, *and* LB. He would make sure of that. Skerritt would have to wait. And do his worst. There was no way he would ever be able to make enough money to satisfy Skerritt, anyway.

But what to do? He couldn't just crawl back to the U.S. with his tail between his legs. Sink the boat for what little it was insured for? Fake his own death and run off with whatever meager funds he could scrape together? Neither was workable. But he had to do something. And he couldn't run the boat with just one engine forever. But he could see no way out of, or around, this predicament. And waiting for the inevitable wasn't a plan.

***

Three days later guests confronted Wally on the dock before the boat left.

"We ever gonna go to dive sites out of sight of the dive shop?" Larry, a rotund, retired civil engineer from Cincinnati, bald head boiled-lobster red from four days in the sun.

"With just the one engine, that's the only way to get your dives in and still get back in time for lunch," Wally said.

"Yeah, but we've done Wahoo Reef three times this week. Don't think I didn't pick up on that 'Wahoo Reef North' and 'Wahoo Reef South' malarkey. We wanna go somewhere different."

Divers around him murmured in agreement. Wendy and Mari stayed at the back of the group, half-smiling encouragement at him.

"I'll see if Vinson'll serve lunch later, and we can go a little farther out."

"We made dive reservations based on being able to dive the whole island. Cutting back on that, that's kinda bait-and-switch."

"This is due to an event beyond our control," Wally said. "And we continue to apologize for that. We can do some anchor drops if you like, find some new sites nearby."

"You mean not go to an actual dive site? That's even worse. All the dive books say Hammerhead Hole's a top dive here. We wanna go there."

"Well, Hammerhead Hole's most of the way down the east coast," Wally said. "We can certainly go there, but it'd be an all-day trip. We'll get you to the best sites we possibly can."

"We'll be getting some of our money back, too."

Larry scowled at Wally. Wally went in search of Vinson to talk about lunch timing.

"If they're okay with a late lunch, I'm game," Vinson said. "Gives me time to get some chores done."

"It may be this way for the foreseeable future," Wally said. "Having just one engine's dictating our schedule. At least Val's friend's coming through for us. In a big way. The boat may be limping along, but our bookings are finally full."

Vinson studied Wally, mouth flirting with a smile.

"You know Val's friend is Val, right?"

Wally stared at him, not understanding.

"That 'friend' goin' online, tweakin' your website, rustlin' up divers? That's been Val. From the get go." Vinson gave a full-on belly laugh. "She's been in your corner a while. Told you she's good luck. And you bein' so upbeat in the face of everything, that's pulled her out of her funk. You doin' with Going Under what she did with The Spinner."

Wally sat, stunned. All the clues had been there, but he had been blind to them. Of course, it had been Val. For whatever reason. And those divers were the only thing keeping him even close to afloat. He would go thank her. Hopefully her work wouldn't be in vain.

After Booger and Angela left with the divers, he pedaled to the Tail Spinner, found Val polishing glasses behind the bar. She smiled when she saw him.

"I owe you a huge, belated 'thanks,'" Wally said. "Vinson just spilled the beans about your 'friend'."

Val's smile turned into a grin.

"I wondered how long it'd take you to catch on."

"That's a lot of work to not take credit for."

"Not really. I played with the website a bit to make it super visible. Sent a few emails. Same sort of stuff I did with this place. And it made me smile seeing you making the place work."

"All out of the goodness of your heart?"

"Cheering for the underdog. Remember? Helping you, Going Under Divers, helped me. So did seeing your eternally-upbeat attitude when anyone else would've quit. And besides, it brings me more customers."

"It's that or go crazy."

"Good choice. You have time for breakfast?"

"I need to run, but . . . is there anything I can do to pay you back? Figuratively—I don't have two quarters to rub together right now."

"Just keep getting up when you get knocked down." She grinned again. "There's a new betting pool on how long you last."

"And you picked . . .?"

"I have ten dollars on you succeeding. So you better."

"Thanks for the vote of confidence, but that's not smart money." The ruined engine was the last nail in G.U.D.'s coffin.

"You'll make it." She gave him a worried look.

Wendy and Mari were waiting for him at his apartment that afternoon.

"We were exploring the island and thought we'd check out your place," Mari said.

"Also, get cleaned up." Wendy said. "We're taking you to dinner, since you won't let us pay for diving."

Thirty minutes later they were seated on the Sandy Bottoms' Beach Resort polished limestone pool deck, drinks and appetizers on the table in front of them.

"Thanks for letting us dive for free. We know that's a big deal right now," Mari said.

"Not a worry," Wally said. "If you can't do nice things for friends, what's the point?"

"Yeah, but . . . look, we talked to Val this afternoon. We didn't realize what kind of jam you're in, money-wise."

"She told you about it?" Wally was stunned Val would do that.

"Not directly, but it's pretty clear on the boat, and there were all kinds of stuff she *didn't* say. That really stood out."

"I'm . . . at the end of my rope, frankly." Why try to hide it at this point. "Financially and mentally. Cranky guests take their toll, too . . ."

"But you still love it, right?" Wendy said.

"'Love' is strong . . ."

"Oh, your face lights up down here like it never did in the States. Even when divers are riding your ass."

It was true. He loved it here. And he had zero desire to slink back to Marietta. But every day brought some new catastrophe. Soon he would have no choice but to go back. Or somewhere.

"Worst case, I can probably hire on as a divemaster with one of the other resorts." He waved a hand around at the Sandy Bottoms' resort. "Forget the stress of managing a dying business. Be happy."

"That's the spirit!" Wendy said. "You find something you like this much, grab it with both hands. You know how many people would love to do whatever they wanted, whether it's successful or not?"

"And if you love it, you'll find a way to make it work," Mari said. "Don't you dare give up on this."

Wally sipped his old fashioned, nodded. He was stuck in this until the last cent was gone. It *could* still work. It had to work. He would make it work.

15

Wally dropped Wendy and Mari at the airport the next morning. They promised to come back soon, with friends. Wally silently hoped he would still be in business when they did. With the bookings he had, he should be okay financially through the next pay period, but the cost of a new engine was still a major obstacle.

Ferris Skerritt's car was in the dive shop lot when Wally returned, looking paler than ever. Wally ground his teeth. Skerritt had changed his mind about waiting until Sunday for his money, and Wally hadn't billed out that week's divers yet. He stepped into the shop, found Skerritt standing, hunched over the computer.

"Look, Ferris, we agreed on the end of the week. I'm at blood-from-a-stone stage, and if you could cut me some slack, that would be huge, for both of us."

He waited for the inevitable quotation of contract sections and subsections.

"Yes . . . well, young Wally, I . . . ahh . . . find myself in somewhat of a predicament. That is to say, I won't be seeking any funds today. Or this week. I have certain other . . . pressing . . . issues to address that need my complete attention."

"I can set the money aside, earmark it for later, that's fine," Wally said. "I just need a little breathing room right now."

"You'll have that, and then some." It sounded like steam escaping a vent. "I'm withdrawing my backing of your little venture. There's an inequity in the... ahh... amount of accounting time necessary versus the pittance you bring me."

"You're pulling the plug on the Going Under Divers? Just like that? If you don't have time to mess with the accounting, I can do it. Or just set aside cash for you every month."

Wally's heart raced. Going Under Divers, Blacktip Island was all he had. If that went away, what would he do? He had been steeling himself for the business to fail, but at some uncertain date in the future. This, out of the blue, was like a sucker punch.

"My attention is needed elsewhere," Skerritt said. His voice shook for a second.

"But our contract..."

"As ever, you're welcome to pursue legal action." Skerritt gave Wally a knowing look. "My advice to you would be to leave the island post-haste. The business is no more. If you're short of funds, I could certainly purchase an off-island ticket on your behalf."

Something didn't make sense. Why would Skerritt give up a steady, if minor, income stream out of the blue? And why did he seem so... sickly? Rattled? And offering to buy Wally an airline ticket?

"If this is your way of haggling for a larger percentage..."

"I am no longer in the diving business, young Wally. And neither are you. You would be well served leaving as soon as is practicable."

Skerritt shuffled out the door, leaving a stunned Wally staring after him. If something needed to happen eventually... Was this the Universe telling him he had lost? An unmistakable sign his adventure was over, his new life done?

He could sell his share of the dive shop to... someone. But who would buy it? Sell the boat, maybe, to someone who didn't know its history. Or just buy a plane ticket with his credit card, go back to Marietta, somewhere, start over. Working at a Blacktip Island resort wouldn't work, would be a constant reminder of his failure.

Wally called up the Going Under Divers bank account. There was more than $600,000 there, so Skerritt hadn't pulled out his cash yet. That was a good sign, he supposed. From his own account, he would pay Angela and Booger that day. He would break the news to them when they got back at midday.

The door swung open.

"Hey! I thought we could . . . woah. What's wrong?" Val stopped a few feet inside the dive shop.

Wally hesitated. He didn't need to dump all this on someone else. Especially Val, after all her help. But here she was, looking concerned. And after all the work she had done for the business, she deserved to know, first, from him. Wally took a deep breath.

"Ferris Skerritt just pulled his funding. Without a Tiperene partner, Going Under Divers is officially tits-up."

"He can't . . . *Why?*"

"Say's it's not worth his time for the little he makes here. Hasn't cleaned out the account, though."

"Can he just do that? Legally?" Val walked around the desk, sat next to Wally.

"Doesn't matter. I've got no money for a lawyer. Or time for a trial or . . . whatever." Wally shrugged. "This fever dream of a business's been snake bit from the start."

"No! It had, *has*, potential. You're doing great things here. You shouldn't lose it all on a rich man's whim. On something beyond your control."

"Happens all the time. Just happened to me this go-round."

"What are your options? There's always options."

"Not unless you know a Tiperon citizen who wants to throw a ton of money at a failing business."

Val winced at that. She had a lot of herself invested in this, too.

"Look, I gave it a good run," Wally said. "I can't say I didn't give it everything I had."

"So . . . what's next?"

"No clue. Back to the real world, I guess, but no idea beyond that. Things've always worked out for me. This is . . . bizarre. Skerritt even offered to buy me the plane ticket."

"Ferris Skerritt offered to do you a *favor*?"

"Right? First time for everything."

"That's . . . odd." Val's eyes took on a far-away look, as if she were working on a puzzle in her head.

Tires crunched on the gravel outside. Wally looked up, expecting Skerritt coming back. Had he thought better about supporting the business, was he back to say he had been wrong? Elena Havens stepped through the door, blue tie-dyed sundress swirling around her ankles. A toss of her head set her graying mane flowing.

"Wally! I wasn't sure you'd be in!" She smiled, too broadly. "I just heard the news and imagined you'd already be winging your way back to the States, tail between your legs."

"Hey, Elena," Wally said. "Congrats. You're the first to come gloat."

"Oh, I'm not gloating. I'm appreciating." She crossed her arms. Her smile turned into a smirk. A dismissive glance at Val. "Especially after our last conversation, about Booger."

"Fine. You have the last word. You win." The words came out through gritted teeth.

"I don't want to win. I warned you not to do this. I warned you away from The Haven. I warned you every step of the way. And you threw it back in my face. Insulted me. It's not the win I want. It's you gone. Humiliated."

"Mission accomplished. Now, if you'll excuse me . . ."

"I won't. And more than that, I've called Immigration. Told them you no longer have a Tiperon partner. Immigration takes these things quite seriously. They'll send officers to deport you. And there's no telling what the U.S. authorities will do with you after I call them."

"You'll do no such thing!" Val stepped around the desk, faced Elena. "And you haven't called Tiperon Immigration, so you won't do that, either. You really have nothing better to do than bully people first thing in the morning?"

"I don't. And the thought of you *both* in tears makes the sun shine a little brighter."

"You're a sad little person, Elena." Val stepped closer, glared up at her. "You need an audience? Now you have one. *You'll* be in tears if you do anything to make this worse for this company *or* to Wally. Or do you want Immigration looking into staffing at *your* operation, too? Go hold court back at The Haven and leave us alone."

Elena blinked, said nothing for a moment.

"My staffing is no one's business but mine," she finally said, her voice lower. "You want to hang this albatross around your neck, be my guest."

She spun, swept out of the dive shop.

Wally stared at Val, eyebrows raised and mouth open.

"Where did *that* come from?" he managed to say.

"Elena's a bully. She only respects bullies."

"And . . . her staff?"

"She's been hiring people off-permit for years." Val waved a hand, as if swatting away a fly. "Probably a third of the staff at The Haven are illegal. Or have had their wages garnished for whatever bogus reason Elena can come up with. Why'd you think Booger was so eager to work here?"

"Booger. Right. I need to tell him and Angela what's happened as soon as they get back."

"Ouch. I don't envy you." She flashed a half-hearted smile, eyes fixed on his. "I really thought you'd make a success of it. You fit here, despite all the setbacks."

Val started to say more but turned to leave. She paused in the doorway.

"Swing by The Spinner for lunch, if you want."

Wally stared after her, wishing she would stay. He had grown accustomed to her, to her perpetual optimism. He liked her, he realized, as more than a friend. He should have been spending time with her, getting to know her, instead of chasing wild-child Alison around the island. Now it was too late. For the business and for Val.

He needed to call his friends in the U.S., let them know he was coming back. Eventually. He didn't have the words, or the heart, to call them now, tell them . . . something. Later. Tomorrow. Maybe.

Guests filed past the dive shop, headed for lunch and the Inne. The boat was back from the morning dives. A few minutes later Angela came into the shop. Booger followed a moment later.

"Booger. Angela. Have a seat," Wally said.

Wally motioned to the chairs by the desk. The two divemasters exchanged looks, then sat, each looking worried.

"Okay . . . I'm just gonna say it. Ferris Skerritt stopped by this morning. He's pulling out all his money, he's no longer a partner, and Going Under Divers is finished. I'll figure out . . . some way to pay you through today."

"Heard something about that," Booger said. "But we still got divers."

"How could you hear about this?" He had just found out, and they had been on the boat all morning.

"It's Blacktip." Booger shrugged. Beside him, Angela nodded.

"Yeah, so I'll finish up this week's guests by myself. I can't ask either of you to work without pay."

"You can't run that boat alone, Mister Wally."

"I will for a few days, whether I can or not. And find alternatives for next week's guests."

"It's not right," Angela said. "Something'll work out. Always does."

"If you have any ideas, I'm all ears. Meanwhile, I'll pay you in cash from what I have left."

Wally stared from one to the other. Both shook their heads.

"We'll think on it," Angela said. "Brainstorm. See what we can come up with and get back to you."

"Thank you." Wally fought to keep his voice steady. "It wasn't supposed to end like this."

"Not over yet, y'know," Booger said.

Wally smiled, nodded, but he knew it was. At lunch he pedaled to the Tail Spinner for maybe his last meal there.

"How'd Angela and Booger take the news?" Val said.

"They said they'd brainstorm a solution." Wally tried to roll his eyes as he said it.

"Well, I don't have a solution, but how do you feel about drinks at Eagle Ray Cove this evening?"

"I've got nothing else to do," he said. Then he chuckled. "At least I don't have to sweat whether to keep Booger or LB. Or deal with angry guests."

"Graveyard humor. That's the spirit." Val set a burger and a beer in front of him. "How much time before you leave? For good? Usually they give you two weeks, unless you get fired."

"No idea. I don't have anything lined up yet, but it's probably better to leave the Tiperons sooner than later. Maybe disappear."

Val's eyes locked on his, questioning. How much should he tell her? Could he tell her? He was leaving soon, so it didn't matter, but still . . .

"This can't go beyond just you and me, okay?"

"Ah! The Blacktip coconut telegraph motto." Val raised her eyebrows, nodded.

"Ferris Skerritt was moving some kind of dodgy money through the Going Under Divers bank account." His stomach knotted more, as if saying it out loud made it more real. "It still has about $600,000 sitting in it. And my name's on the account."

Val's mouth formed a silent 'O.'

"Why would he just leave it there?"

"No clue. He's had plenty of time. I'm thinking maybe he can't, for whatever reason." The idea had been gnawing at Wally all morning.

"Sooo . . . leave the country quick as you can, no forwarding address and keep a low profile."

"Something like that."

"You don't know that for sure, though. That could be just paranoia."

"Easy to say when it's not you."

"I'll see you at six tonight." Val laughed. "I'll ask around, but my guess is you're fine."

That evening, Wally found Val talking to Alison at Eagle Ray Cove's outdoor bar. They both smiled when he approached. Alison got up, hugged him.

"I just heard the bad news. I'm so bummed."

"Thanks," Wally managed to say. He hadn't talked with Alison since that day at the store.

"Hey, I'm sorry things didn't work out," she said. "With us. I was hoping we'd end up circling back around to hang out with each other. But now, I guess not."

"Unlikely. I'd have liked that, though."

"One for the road?" She grinned up at him, signaled to the bar for drinks. "Sounds like you and Val've been chillin'."

Wally winced, glanced at Val. She was watching him, a faint smile playing across her face. Yes, he should have done something about that earlier. Idiot.

"My timing's been impeccable ever since I set foot on Blacktip," he said.

Alison smiled at Val.

"Too bad, you guys'd've rocked together."

Wally and Val looked at each other, flashed weak smiles.

Lee joined them, took a beer from Alison.

"Sorry to hear about your company, Mate." He clinked his beer mug against Wally's. "It's not fair, Skerritt just pulling his money out like that."

"It's not really an issue of 'fair' . . ."

"It is. Absolutely. You can't just go around ruining people's lives like that."

"It was Ferris' money. He can do what he wants with it. Whenever he wants. Just wish he'd done something else. Or given me a warning."

"Someone should do something about it. About him."

"Like what?" Val said. "He's a Skerritt. They own most of the island. Including this resort."

"Well, for him, the money that can change someone's life is a drop in the bucket. It's not fair."

"No. I took the bet," Wally said. "That's on me. A hundred percent. I appreciate the sentiment, but I didn't do my research and put myself in a bad position."

Lee wandered away, muttering about things not being fair.

"What was that about?" Wally said.

"Oh, Lee's always looking for something to bitch about." Alison laughed. "If he doesn't have anything to winge about personally, he'll winge about somebody else's life."

"Well, he may be one of the few people on Blacktip I don't think I'll miss."

Val and Alison both laughed.

"You're not the first to say that," Val said.

Jessie and Hugh wandered up.

"Whatever you said to Elena this morning, you really kicked the hornets' nest." Jessie glanced from Wally to Val, then back again.

"She threatened to have me deported." Wally gave Val a quick smile. "That didn't go so well."

"No kidding. She's been shouting, terrorizing The Haven staff all day. Gimme a warning next time you pull something like that."

"Won't be a next time. Unless she comes here tonight."

Wally smiled, turning from face to face. He didn't know them well, but he had grown attached to this odd group of misfits in his short time on the island.

Cal and Marina joined the group.

"Sucks about your dive op," Cal said.

"Does everyone on the island know about this?" Wally said.

"It's Blacktip," Marina said. "You sneeze at The Ballyhoo, someone'll say 'bless you' at The Spinner."

"And I *may* have spread the word you'd be here this evening." Val smiled at him. "You deserve a bit of a sendoff."

Angela joined the group. Then, a few minutes later, Booger, who bought Wally a beer, despite Wally's objection.

"You need to put your money towards a new life," Booger said.

"Buying my own beer won't break me."

"Uh huh. I seen you going over those accounts. Got money for a plane ticket?"

"Got a credit card."

Wally laughed, in spite of the situation. His business was a failure, and his money was gone. This was probably his last night out in this tropical lifestyle he had tried to build for himself. One of the last nights he would see Val. He had failed, but he had failed in style. Not getting to know Val may have been his biggest failure.

A hairy arm plopped across his shoulders.

"Warren! How you doin' tonight?"

"I'm all right, Antonio. Except for that leaving the island thing."

"Didn't *See* it. Still don't."

"We're right in the middle of it. Look under 'Wally.'"

"No. Don't feel so." He stared at Wally, searching his face, eyes unfocused. "Time to time, folks stumble 'cross someplace feels like home, even if they never been there. Find themselves in a foreign spot, with folks they don't know, but they feel like they was born there. You one of them, y'know. On Blacktip, you found you a home. Belong here. I still don't *See* it. Won't believe it 'til I do. You didn't give up, and th' island accepted you. You b'long."

"Thanks, Antonio." It was no use arguing with the man. "Thanks all of you. Really. I didn't get to know any of you as well as I wanted, but I'm still gonna miss you. And . . . this."

Wally spread his arms wide, including everyone in the group. Feeling silly, but not caring. The people he had met here were the best part of the island.

"You can still come visit anytime," Jessie said. "I'd avoid The Haven, though."

"Once I leave, I won't be back. That'd just be salt in my wounds."

Everyone in the group looked at the deck, the bar, the tiki torches, anywhere but at Wally. Val stepped up, hugged him, then stepped away from the group. Something tightened inside Wally.

"We, me and Angela, still looking for ways you can stay," Booger said.

No one reacted. Antonio watched Val, walking away across the deck.

"That Val, she can make magic happen, y'know," he said.

"We're fresh out of miracles, Antonio. But I've loved my time on this little rock."

"Still don't *See* you goin', but the *Sight* does have its blind spots time to time."

Wally stood, excused himself. He needed quiet, time to think by himself. He wandered down the wooden pier, let the bar's sounds fade away. What was his next move? He hadn't started looking for a job. Or even a place to go. He needed to leave the Tiperons to avoid Skerritt's associates. But he also needed to finish these next two days with his current dive guests. He had made a commitment to them. But while there was $600,000 in the Going Under Divers bank account, with his name attached to it, he might be better off running anywhere to avoid jail or a mob hit here.

"Penny for 'em."

Val had followed him. She sat beside him.

"Sorting through those pesky options. Do I finish up my commitments here, or bolt the country before I wind up in the hoosegow? Or sleeping with the fish?"

"You don't know if there's any action been taken, just that Skerritt has . . . suspicious money in the account. You may be worried about nothing."

"No. Ferris was rattled in the shop. Something happened to trigger all this."

"He left the money there, so he may just not have gotten to it. You're adding two and two and getting twenty-two."

"Those are big dice to roll."

"Just offering input."

"Yeah. Thanks. I . . . Ooo! Look!"

The moonless night sky, crowded with stars, was filled with bright streaks of light, all coursing from right to left, seeming to arch over them like silent fireworks.

"Meteors!" Val said. "I didn't know there were any expected. Or that there'd be so many."

They sat on the dock, feet dangling, watching the light show in silence. After a few minutes, the shooting stars lessened, one falling every thirty seconds.

"Look, I'm sorry we didn't spend more time together, get to know each other," Wally said.

"You were busy." Val smirked. "With work *and* with Alison."

"I was an idiot."

"Well don't be one now. Enjoy what little time you have left here, take care of your existing guests, and let Skerritt worry about his money."

"Yeah. A couple more days on the boat would be good. Give me a chance to sort out where to disappear to. And make alternative arrangements for my divers who've already booked. And I still need to see if Angela or Booger come up with any options."

Yes. He would end this misadventure on as happy a note as he could find.

16

Wally couldn't sleep that night. He finally gave up, biked to Going Under Divers and spent much of it on the dock, watching the stars, the meteors. Thinking of everything he would miss about Blacktip Island, and everything that had gone wrong. He was groggy when his eight divers arrived, but he didn't mention the business was in its final days.

"Folks, Booger and Angela both had something come up, so it'll just be me with you on the boat today," he said. "I'll be staying onboard and letting y'all do self-guided dives, if that's okay."

A few of them looked nervous, but most grinned, nodded agreement.

Once they were all aboard, Wally started the starboard engine and cast off the dock lines. He ran at half speed to the Hole in the Wall mooring ball, and Wally had the nervous divers team with the more experienced buddy pairs.

"Who wants to know the double-secret divemaster rule of navigation?" he said at the end of his site briefing.

Eight sets of eyes locked on his, expectant.

"Don't go far from the boat," Wally said.

Divers laughed.

"Seriously. Use it as a center point and so you won't get lost."

Once the divers were in the water, he sat at the helm, relaxed, gazed around at the turquoise water, the darker coral heads, the sea's sharp change to deep blue where the wall dropped off, and the white boil of the divers' exhaled bubbles where the two blues met. On shore, palm fronds fluttered in the barely-moving air. High, cirrus clouds shaded the sky to the east. A change in weather the next day or so, then. This was one of the last times he would be able to do this, sit on his own boat and soak up the island's beauty in peace. Yes, he would miss it.

For the second dive he moored at The Anchors. A guest favorite, and the first site Wally had dived on Blacktip as a guest. Once the divers were in the water, he tried to think of someone, anyone, who might be willing to part with even a little money for Going Under Divers. Even if it was just enough for his air fare, and maybe a month's expenses until he could settle in . . . wherever he ended up. He needed to follow up with Booger, with Angela, find out if either of them had found a potential partner, or even a cents-on-the-dollar buyer.

After all the divers were back onboard, Wally ran the *J-Valve* back to the cut in the reef with his lone engine at full throttle, enjoying the feeling of the boat slicing through the calm seas, feeling the air rush past him, making his eyes water, even behind his sunglasses. When he had docked, with minimal contact, and helped the divers off the boat, he smiled to see Booger walk down to the pier. With good news, Wally hoped.

"Mister Wally, I did talk to my cousin about partnering with you," Booger said. "Not interested. Said there's maybe legal trouble, with Ferris Skerritt and his finances. Don't want to be any way associated with that."

Wally's heart raced. His face and hands went numb. If Ferris and the Going Under finances were in legal trouble, so was he.

"What legal trouble? How does he, you, know this?"

"Something about U.S. and U.K. folks looking at all his financial dealin's." Booger shrugged. "But nobody knows for sure."

Wally sat on the gunwale, tried to breathe. Tried not to vomit. If international authorities were digging into Skerritt's financial dealings, that would explain why he had broken things off so abruptly, why the money was still in the G.U.D. account—the account had probably been frozen. With Wally's name on it. He should have run sooner. Now, the police could be, would be here any time. He could claim ignorance, show he wasn't a signatory, had never had any control over the account. Somehow, he didn't think that would help him.

Even if he was able to avoid being arrested, with all the island knowing what was happening, of course people wouldn't be lining up to be his partner. He needed to get what he could for the company, for the pieces of it, and get out. Or maybe get out and have someone else, Vinson, maybe, sell whatever there was of value.

Angela wandered down, face unreadable.

"Got bad news, Mister Wally."

"You picked the right day," Wally stood, squared his shoulders. "Constable on his way?"

Angela gave him an odd look.

"Don't know anything about that. Came to say nobody on island'll have anything to do with Going Under Divers. Folks know what rough shape the *J-Valve*'s in, and there's talk now the place's jinxed."

Wally let that sink in for several moments.

"Well, they may be right, the way things keep going from bad to worse," he finally said. "So the boat's no good even for parts?"

Angela shook her head.

"Folks've heard too much about her. They know all her parts're old and worn."

Wally sat. Looked from Angela to Booger.

"Thanks, both of you, for asking around. Sometimes 'no' can be a good answer—at least I know what I'm dealing with. Or don't have to deal with anymore. I'll . . . head back to the States as soon as I can. If the police let me."

He threw the U.S. out, as a red herring, as if it were the obvious, only choice. After the authorities questioned Angela and

Booger, they would focus their search there, not whatever random country Wally ended up running to. The reality of his situation settled around him then, like a thick fog, choking. As if saying it out loud made it more real. With Angela and Booger's leads falling through, his time on Blacktip Island was definitely over. Unless he went to jail here. There was nothing left to magically fall into place.

Angela gave him an awkward smile.

"Sorry we couldn't do anything, Mister Wally," Booger said. "Gonna miss working for you. With you."

The two left together, leaving Wally on the dock.

Back in the dive shop, he phoned the airfield to find out when the next off-island flight was, when the next flight from Tiperon to anywhere-not-the-U-S was. No answer. The midday lunch break, he remembered. No one would be there until 3:00, 2:30 if he was lucky. He should get lunch, but wasn't hungry.

Wally stared at the stacks of Going Under Divers t-shirts and caps and coffee mugs. He could sell those online. Call them 'collector's items.' He didn't have much else to take with him.

The shop door swung open. Wally tensed, expecting Constable Marquette. Instead, it was Vinson, grinning bigger than ever.

"At least someone has something to be happy about," Wally said. "Should I ask what?"

"No reason not to be happy. Beautiful day. Birds singin'. Guests're smilin'. And ol' Ferris finally got his comeuppance, moving around money he shouldn't've had. Got caught at fraud and legal malpractice, too."

"Yeah. I heard, but not in detail. Doesn't make me smile, though."

"After what he put you through?"

"My name, my business's name, are on that account. I'm an accessory. I'll be sitting in the cell next to him."

Vinson stared at Wally a moment, then burst out laughing

in a low rumble, setting his belly straining against his t-shirt.

"You worried 'bout nothin', Wally!" He took a deep breath. His laughter eased. "Your name been off that account from the get-go."

"No. It still says 'Going Under Divers' when I sign in."

"But it says nothin' 'bout *you*." Vinson started to laugh again, checked himself. "Smackie Bottoms gave me the account info and password before he left. And ol' I'm-smarter-than-everybody Ferris never bothered to change any of it. Your name was never on it. Kept an eye on the balance, too. Seein' what Ferris was up to."

"So . . . You knew Skerritt was dodgy, set me up in business with him . . . then made sure the stink didn't stick to me?"

"You, this business, are good things for the island. Always had your best interests at heart. Good to see Val out more. Upbeat again. Good for her, too."

"That's a lot of trouble to go to just to . . ." Wally's question trailed off as a new idea swept through his head. If Vinson purposely kept Wally's name off the Going Under Divers account, for Wally's best interest, that meant he knew something like this could, or would happen from the start. The tension between Vinson and Skerritt. How Skerritt was so jumpy around Vinson. It all snapped into place.

"Vinson, you used Going Under Divers to set up Ferris to take a fall."

Vinson smiled.

"Oh, wouldn't know nothin' 'bout that. Or how to even do it. I'm just a simple innkeeper . . ."

"You used *me*. Did you have anything to do with his accounts being frozen, too?"

"Wouldn't know where to start doin' that sort of thing." Vinson fought back a smile. "Ferris did put his own foot in that bear trap," Vinson chuckled. "Knew it was a matter of time before he got greedy and cocky and slipped up. Going Under

Divers was his tippin' point, the bait he couldn't pass up. That's all."

"Well, him slipping up and you settling . . . whatever it is between you, has forced *me* to lose my business, all my money, and to leave the island. And Val. So that part of your plan failed."

"Something'll pop up, I s'pect."

"If I'm not gonna be arrested, I'll take out the divers through this week. Then I have to leave, whether I want to or not."

Vinson opened his mouth to reply. The door swung open again, and Val stepped into the shop, a worried look on her face. She looked at Wally, gave Vinson a questioning glance, then turned back to Wally.

"I need to go check on lunch," Vinson said, and stepped outside.

"Why are you still here?" Val's voice was tense. "All Skerritt's accounts are frozen, and there's talk they're investigating him for malpractice and bribery . . . and fraud! Your name's mixed up in all that. Why are you still on Blacktip?"

"I have 'til the end of next week." Wally smiled at Val's shocked look. "Stand down. Apparently, Vinson, with help from Smackie Bottoms, made sure the account was solely in Skerritt's name. Technically, I was just a 'partner' on paper, so minimal legal exposure."

"That's illegal. The partnership set up like that, I mean."

"Skerritt's problem. And Vinson's. I'm guessing he'll be . . ."

Tires skidded to a stop on the gravel outside. A car door slammed. Engine still running.

"You did this." Skeritt's voice hissed from beyond the door. "I don't know how, but this is your doing!"

"Don't know what you're on about, Ferris." Vinson's voice, from the parking lot, was the essence of reasonableness. "If I did something to anger you, I'm truly sorry."

"You know damn well what you did." Skerritt's voice rose louder, yet thinner. "Your little prank might cost me my law license! I'm looking at jail time! And some *very* unpleasant people will come looking for their money that's locked in that account. Shall I send them to you?"

"Ferris, I see you in some kind of trouble, and I am sorry 'bout that. Happy to talk to anybody you want me to."

"I may save them the trouble of finding you, you fraud. I may take care of you myself. I'd enjoy that. One knife in the back deserves a literal one in return, I think. Or in the front, in your case—I want to see your face when I do it!"

Vinson's low rumble of a laugh sounded then.

"Oh, you ain't doin' nothin' like that, Ferris. 'Specially after you threaten it in front of witnesses."

"Witnesses? Where? This dirt lot's deserted. As usual."

"Wally? Val? You finish your talk in there?"

Wally and Val stepped outside. Skerritt's potato face went paler than Wally had thought possible. His eyes darted from them, to Vinson.

"That was hyperbole," he finally spat. "Not to be taken literally. And hearsay, since they didn't *see* me when I spoke. And *misheard* me through the walls."

"No doubt. Prob'ly right." Vinson nodded, as if convinced by Skerritt's points. "Prob'ly best to let the police sort it out, though. Just to make sure we're not ridin' roughshod over the law."

Skerritt shook a pale finger at Vinson, yellow teeth clenched in a snarl and face turning red, unable to speak. He climbed back in his still-running Cadillac, stomped on the gas, and turned the wheel, sending sand and gravel spraying across their feet and legs.

"Ol' Ferris, he does get himself worked up." Vinson chuckled. "Won't need you two as witnesses. He'll calm down, see reason. Or not. Either way, I got a kitchen to clean."

He walked back to the Inne, a bounce in his step Wally had never seen.

"Ol' Vinson never on the run . . ." his off-key singing trailed behind him.

"That's what reviving Going Under Divers was all about." Wally's stomach rolled as he said it, as the reality hit him. "Vinson settling his grudge with Ferris. And didn't care if he sunk me, the business, *his* business to do it."

"I . . . have thoughts," Val said. "We'll talk later. The Spinner? After the dinner rush?"

Val drove away. Wally closed the dive shop and pedaled home.

Business was slow at the Tail Spinner that evening, and cleared out earlier than Wally had expected. He found himself again sitting on the back deck with Val. There was no meteor shower tonight, only the stars reflected in the calm sea and the peenie wallies mirroring them, flashing in the sea grapes. One drifted across their table, its abdomen flashing a deep yellow. Wally upturned an empty water glass and set it down over the firefly. It circled the glass, looking for a way out. After several moments Wally scowled, lifted the glass, freeing the beetle.

"Didn't want that as a table-top candle?" Val said.

"No. It was pretty, but I know what it's like to feel trapped."

"It was beyond your control," Val said. "Skerritt backing out."

"The business was going under even before that," Wally said. "And he didn't back out. Vinson took everyone down. And is pleased with himself about that."

"The Skerritt – Noboddie feud goes way back. Unfortunately, you got caught in the crossfire. For what it's worth, I don't think that was intentional. That's not Vinson's style."

"Right. It just feels that way."

"You were incidental. Ferris wanted the Going Under bank account to route money through. Vinson made sure Ferris had enough rope to hang himself. That's it."

"Then kicked the stool out from under him," Wally said. "And ruined my life, and finances, in the process."

"Give it overnight. See what happens tomorrow. Vinson usually does the right thing, just in his own roundabout way."

"It's a sign. This whole adventure was doomed from the start. Maybe even before that."

Val said nothing. Wally sipped his beer, stared out to sea, tried to put himself in Vinson's place, in the mindset to wait years, craft the perfect scenario to destroy a rival, even if he killed his own business in the process. He couldn't.

"Where was their land?" he finally said. "Vinson's family."

"About halfway down the west coast." Val paused, as if lining up the right words in the right way. "You've been there. Skerritt's brother Rich built Eagle Ray Cove resort on it."

"Oof. So that's why he never goes there."

They both stared at the stars, neither speaking. Wally glanced at Val. Her face was tilted up, dark hair falling down her back, dark eyes bright with reflected starlight.

"I wish I'd spent more evenings like this," he said. "I was an idiot focused on the wrong things."

"You have this, now. Enjoy it. And don't give up on Vinson. He always believed in you."

At the dive shop the next morning Wally ground his teeth at the sight of Vinson, across the dirt lot, laughing, joking with the Inne's guests. The man had destroyed Wally financially yet seemed oblivious of that. Could laugh like nothing had happened. He wanted, needed to tear into Vinson, but would wait until he wasn't with guests. The business may be dead, but he would still act professionally. Enjoy the morning on the boat. Then catch Vinson alone that afternoon.

The divers began straggling down to the dock. Wally smiled to see Chip among them, unscheduled as ever. That, at least, was a bright spot.

"Got room for me today?" Chip said when he reached Wally.

"Always. A surprise and a pleasure."

Chip studied him, concerned.

"You all right?" he finally said. "You look rode hard and stabled wet."

Wally took a deep breath. Where to start.

"You'll find out soon, and I'd rather you heard it from me—Going Under Divers is . . . going under. I have no more money to bleed. Angela and Booger are already gone, and these are the last few days I'm running. I'll find someone suitable you can dive with after I'm gone."

Wally shuffled to the dock, got the divers situated, and cast off. Chip was quiet on the ride out. Wally hadn't meant to blindside him, but blunt was best, he had always found. He couldn't tell if Chip was shocked or angry or sad. Or all three.

Wally stayed on the boat for both dives that morning. He relaxed while the guests dived, enjoyed the blue water, the sound of wavelets slapping against the boat's hull, the salt tang in the air. The occasional flashes of Chip's camera strobes underwater.

Chip was quiet during the surface interval, too. Eyes stabbing into Wally. And on the ride back after the second dive. Wally's announcement must have him seriously upset. Almost as if he blamed Wally for the business' failure. After the boat was docked and the other divers gone, Chip pulled Wally to one side.

"You know how much this place means to me, right? The operation, you, the staff, you and Val, everything?"

Wally nodded, braced for an explosion. Expecting the merciless Chip who swindled his colleagues then ran off to the Caribbean without a backwards glance.

"You gave me a lot to think about this morning." Chip's voice was a low, even growl. Harsher than Wally had ever heard him speak. "I'll be back tomorrow. We'll talk then."

Wally watched him stomp his way up to the Inne, then went to the dive shop. He filled out the last of the rosters, answered what emails there were, started a rough draft of the letter he would send to all his booked guests, explaining why he wouldn't be able to take them diving, promising to book them with other operations.

He would need to contact the other dive ops, see who had room, and when. Given his feud with Elena, Blacktip Haven was not an option except as a last resort. He would check with Eagle Ray Cove first, then talk to Finn at Club Scuba Doo if necessary. Anger, resentment, surged up as he typed. This, all this, for one man's need to settle a score. All the time and money wasted.

Across the lot guests were wandering down to the beach and its shaded hammocks. Lunch was over, then. Vinson would be free and the Inne mostly deserted. Wally saved his draft letter, crossed the dirt lot. He found Vinson behind the kitchen hosing out soup pots.

"Vinson. You have a minute?" he said.

Vinson straightened, smiled.

"Wally! Hopin' I'd see you today!"

"Tell me this whole Going Under Divers goat rope wasn't just your way of getting revenge on Ferris Skerritt." He tried to keep the anger out of his voice, keep his tone even.

"No, but that's a nice by-product."

"You used me to settle a score. And wiped me out in the process. I threw away a career to come down here. Now I'm literally broke. Because of you. And you're standing there smiling? Laughing?" He stepped closer to Vinson, forced his hands not to ball up into fists.

"Wally, you doin' fine. Learnin' to be independent." Vinson's smile eased, but not by much. "Already a bigger person than when you got here."

"There's nothing 'fine' about this. I have to go . . . somewhere, only I don't have the money to do that." The anger was rising now, barely in check. "Was it worth it? Destroying two businesses, two lives, to get even? You cut your own throat to spite your face. When Going Under dies, so does the Inne."

Vinson stared at Wally, a confused look on his face.

"Wally, Ferris's the only one going down on that ship. Sure, you was part of the plan, and yeah, Going Under and The Inne're locked at the hip, but both of us, we gonna be fine."

Wally held up his hands, took a deep breath. The last thing he needed now was more of Vinson's naïve daydreams.

"How does me being broke, and having to leave Blacktip, make this a win? Be specific. As specific as possible. I'm ruined, and you need to make this right!"

"Well, to start, you ain't broke. Knew this day'd come eventually, so I been setting aside money in a rainy-day fund, a Wally Fund, for when it did. No way to get to Ferris without you, but I still looked out for you. 'Specially seeing's how you never take any meals here . . ."

It took a moment for the words to sink in.

"You're saying you put aside cash for me?" Wally said. "This was the plan from the start?"

"Not right, you goin' through all this and not being compensated."

"Enough for airfare off island?"

"Enough for you to *stay on* the island. Keep Goin' Under goin'. Keep The Inne goin'."

"You . . . I . . . This blue-skies, Pollyanna attitude is pathological! What about a Tiperene partner? And why would I trust you after you used me like this. You, the Inne, can jump off the end of that dock!"

Wally stormed back to the dive shop, too angry to continue trying to reason with bat-shit Vinson. He grabbed his bike, pedaled away as fast as he could, hoping to burn the anger, the sense of betrayal, out of himself. He passed the Tail Spinner, too angry to talk to Val, past Sandy Bottoms and Club Scuba Doo. At the island's central crossover road, he turned left, skirted the southern end of the booby pond. He stopped on a rise, breathing hard, where he could see the red-footed boobies circling above, and the black-and-white stilts and other wading birds in the water.

Vinson was crazy. And focused only on himself. Wally had been stupid to expect rationality from him. Or to have bought a company associated with him. He should have seen this coming months ago, realized he would be trampled underfoot. But he had been concentrating so much on the diving, the socializing, he had been blind to it. Vinson had been the agent, but Wally had only himself to blame. His stomach grumbled. He needed food. He would go home, grab something at Peachy's, sort out what his next move would be. What third-world country he would run to.

In his apartment, on the rickety Formica table was a lime-green plastic dry box he had never seen before. A note, on a yellow legal pad sheet, was beside it, scribbled in a spidery hand.

Wally, this here's the money I set aside for you. A ten percent Keep The Inne Going kitty for the past months, plus the value of the food you didn't eat. Fair's fair, and right's right. Spend it how you want, but I'd love to see you back on that J-Valve.
-Vinson

Not an apology, but more than Wally had expected. And Vinson had been serious about the money. Wally thumbed through the cash. Enough for a plane ticket, and a startup somewhere else. At least Vinson had done that. And hadn't completely thrown Wally to the wolves. This, at least was working out. If only he could trust Vinson enough, and could find a willing partner, to keep Going Under Divers operating.

He would run his dive charters the rest of the week. Honor those commitments. Find other resorts for his future bookings to dive. And he still had an uncomfortable talk to have with Chip in the morning.

17

Wally biked in slowly in the morning, thoughts on the day ahead at Going Under. His anger at Vinson had softened overnight. Setting Wally up at the dive operation, then knocking him down, had been a low blow, but he *had* thought enough of Wally to hold money aside when he didn't have to. And Vinson couldn't have known about, and had nothing to do with, the boat's problems. Wally's immediate thought had been to return the money, have nothing more to do with Vinson or The Inne. But this morning he was thinking more clearly. Without that cash, Wally would be stuck on Blacktip Island. Until the authorities deported him. The betrayal still stung, but he had options now. And would be able to look at Vinson without exploding.

There was no sign of Vinson when Wally arrived at the shop, which was probably for the best. Guests were milling around The Inne, and Wally prepped the boat with water, ice, and snacks, depressed it was one of the last times he would do this. By the time the guests straggled down in twos and threes, he had rallied himself and was as cheerful and upbeat as ever. The last diver to arrive was Chip, tight-lipped. He nodded a greeting to Wally but said nothing when he stepped on the boat.

Wally ran at half speed to The Pinnacle, briefed the site, with special emphasis on being careful about depth, and helped the divers into the water. Chip stayed seated on the port-side bench, with no move to get into his scuba gear, watching Wally work.

"You're not going in?" Wally said when all the other divers were in the water.

"I thought we'd talk, just the two of us." His voice was low, noncommittal.

Wally sat across from him on the starboard bench, waited for Chip to speak.

"If you'd told me what straits you were in all along, I could've helped," Chip finally said. "This operation is, was, one of the best things about Blacktip. I could've made sure you stayed afloat."

Wally nodded. Not sure how to respond, how to tell Chip he had wanted to make a success on his own. And he hadn't been in a hurry to borrow money from an admitted thief, however white Chip's collar was.

"I kept thinking I could pull things out," Wally said, not wanting to go into detail. "I was going pay period-to-pay period, but I was making it work. Then everything blew up in my face."

"You know I don't want to dive with somebody else, on one of those cattle boats, right?"

Wally nodded.

"I get you wanting to revive the place through your own hard work, but not looping me in, well, this feels like a slap in the face."

"No! It wasn't supposed to be that." Wally knew that feeling of betrayal, had wallowed in it the last few days. "It's just . . . everything was fine until suddenly, out-of-the-blue, it wasn't. It blindsided me as much as it did you. I guess I was still raw from that when I told to you. I should have eased into it."

"I get that. And thank you. It just feels personal. Of all the good things that've happened since I came to the Tiperons—exploring the Big Island, getting citizenship here, discovering Blacktip—diving with you, with you and Val, that's been the best."

"I've loved that, too . . ." Wally stopped, blindsided for the second time in three days. "Wait. You're a Tiperon citizen?"

"Paid top dollar for it and had to jump through a bunch of hoops, but yeah. I can stay here as long as I like. And can't be deported."

"No. What I mean is . . . The only reason Going Under's folding is my Tiperon partner backed out. And no one else'll touch the company. But if *you* became the local partner, Going Under'd be back in business."

Chip stared at him for several seconds, then burst out laughing.

"This's what I meant by keeping me looped in. This whole conversation, and all the lost sleep and teeth grinding, could have been avoided if you'd just led with that."

"I had no clue it was an option. You never mentioned citizenship."

"Not a common topic for conversation," Chip said. "Now, I'll need to have a look at the financials, see what shape you're in there, but that could work."

"Yeah, full disclosure, there's some significant expenses coming up." Wally gestured at the deck by Chip's feet, above the port engine.

"Let me think on it."

Wally watched for divers, left Chip in peace. Would a new engine be a deal breaker? Would sixty percent of the profits be enough? Could he trust Chip not to rip him off like he had his former partners? He laughed silently at that. He didn't have anything worth stealing, by Chip or anyone else. And Chip would be several steps up from Skerritt.

But did he want to get mixed up with Vinson again? The man had proved he couldn't be trusted. Seemed to enjoy not being trustworthy. But what choice did he have if he wanted to stay on Blacktip?

Divers were coming up then, and Wally scrambled to help them aboard and get their gear situated. He idled back toward The Inne, tied off at Hammerhead Hole, usually a guest favorite.

"So we're gonna see a hammerhead here?" said one guest after the briefing.

"I've never heard of *anyone* seeing a hammerhead here." Wally laughed. "One of the great ironies of dive site names. You rarely see the things they're named after."

It was good being able to laugh with the guests again. Going Under Divers' fate was still uncertain, but Wally felt like some of the weight had lifted from his shoulders. Chip stayed up for the second dive, too. Wally watched him for any hint about what he was thinking.

"How much money're you short?" Chip said.

Wally stared, stunned, not expecting that question.

"Month-end bills and payroll's close to $5,000," Wally stammered. "When this group settles up Saturday, I'll have most of that. The last partner took a flat sixty percent of the gross, and I could . . ."

"I can write you a check for five grand," Chip said. "I don't care about the profit. I care about diving. I'm not diving with anybody else, so keeping you in business's my goal."

"The biggest issue's the cost of a new engine."

Chip studied him.

"Why not get two? If one engine's broken, the other's on its last leg."

Wally nodded, afraid to speak, to breathe too loud and interrupt whatever was happening. Though Chip was putting words to one of Wally's biggest worries.

"I'll take a look at your books on shore, but I don't see why we can't go ahead and swap out two new engines and work out a payment plan for you that won't break the bank."

"But legally, the partnership . . ."

"We'll put whatever we need to on paper, then'll split expenses going forward 'til you turn a profit, then we'll split that, too. You run the operation, I'll float the cash and go diving whenever. And get you some divers—I know some people."

Wally hesitated. His pitch had been too easy. Things were falling into place too well. There would be details to derail it.

There were always derailing details on Blacktip. Skerritt's double-dealing and high-handedness was still fresh in his mind. And something about frying pans and fires. He didn't think Chip would cheat him, but he hadn't thought Skerritt would, either. He knew Chip, had gotten to know him. He didn't trust Vinson. But it was work with them or leave Blacktip.

"If you're sure, I'll show you my bank records and spreadsheets when we get back to The Inne, make sure you know what you're getting into."

On shore, Wally signed into his bank account, let Chip look through that, such as it was, past financial spreadsheets and the stack of bills. Across the parking area, Vinson was sweeping The Inne's entrance steps, singing to himself. Wally excused himself, crossed to The Inne. Vinson grinned when he saw him approaching.

"Wally! You feelin' better 'bout things today?"

"No thanks to you, but yeah. Going Under Divers may not be dead just yet."

"That's the spirit! Never give up."

"Chip's thinking about being the new Tiperon partner. If he does, I'm good with that. But, if I'm being honest, I still have serious issues about working with you."

Vinson nodded, eyed Wally as if reading his thoughts.

"Wally, you in a better place now than any time you been on Blacktip." Vinson threw a gangly arm across Wally's shoulders. "You had a bumpy ride, sure, but look where it got you. And if I'd a told you what was up, you'd've spilled the beans. You got no vault. You can't keep a secret. But now it's all's well that ends well."

"There's still the issue of trust. You lied to me."

"Never told you a single lie . . ."

"You weren't honest with me. We can't just go back to being friends."

"Have to be allies, then." Vinson grinned. "Good for both of us. I fill your boat, you fill my rooms. And once that boat's gussied up, you'll have fewer money worries."

"How do I know you won't pull some scam like that again?"

"No need to. You know Ferris was anglin' to grab The Inne, right? Soon's he bled you dry, his sights were on runnin' me bankrupt, and him makin' the kill. It was me or him. Now, with Ferris neutered, I can go back to live and let live."

Vinson gave one of his big belly laughs, shaking Wally with every breath. Wally tried to pull away. He had seen Vinson's live-and-let-live in action. Vinson gripped him tighter.

"You want a good laugh, Wally, think about Ferris' face 'bout now when he finds out your name's not on that account, only his. He's swingin' in the wind, with no fall guy to pin things on."

Wally stopped struggling, stared at Vinson.

"Why you think he wanted you to run so bad?" Vinson stopped laughing. "And offered to buy you a plane ticket? With you on the lam, he could send the bad guys after you, walk away clean. He's a slippery one, Ol' Ferris. Or was."

Wally went cold at that. It explained a lot. If he had run off to Central America, Skerritt's associates would have been right on his tail, with Skerritt having told them where he had flown to. He still didn't trust Vinson, but the man wasn't his enemy. And Wally did need the guests from The Inne to make Going Under Divers work.

"Thanks, Vinson," he managed to say.

Wally broke free from Vinson's arm, walked back to the dive shop. Chip was shuffling through the bills on the desk.

"If you can stop that boat from breaking, and fill it with divers, you've got a viable operation here," Chip said.

"Payroll's high right now because I'm keeping LB on until he's out of jail next month," Wally said. "Then I'll figure out whether to keep him or Booger."

"Why not keep 'em both? You'll be able to give folks regular days off."

Wally nodded. He had never thought about keeping both, hadn't foreseen having the income to pay both for more than a few months. But if Chip was willing to pay them, and could attract more divers, that worked great.

"So, partners?" Wally said.

"Don't see why not," Chip said. "I'll get with Jack Cobia, have him draw up an agreement that'll pass the government's sniff test. We'll keep our handshake agreement between us. That work?"

Wally nodded again. The handshake wasn't enforceable, but, worst case, he would go back to the arrangement he had had with Skerritt. And he would read that contract more closely this time.

"Here's a spare office key," he said. "Now I need to call Angela and Booger, let them know they're employed again."

That afternoon, *J-Valve* washed and tied up, Wally pedaled to the Tail Spinner to tell Val about everything that had happened that morning.

She was wiping down the bar when he walked in and smiled more broadly than he had ever seen her smile.

"So Going Under's a going concern again! Congrats!"

"How'd you know? Only me, Chip, and Vinson know, and only for the last couple of hours."

"Seriously?" Val raised an eyebrow at him.

"Right. It's Blacktip."

"Have time for a celebratory drink?"

Minutes later they were on the deck, sweating beer bottles in front of them.

"See? All that worry was for nothing," she said.

"Maybe not. It got me focused enough to realize Chip could be a partner. And it forced me to think about what's really important on the island, in my life here."

"Always a plus, recognizing priorities."

"One of those, a big one of those, is you," he said. "I should have spent more time with you. Getting to know you."

"So now you can."

"I was an idiot chasing Alison around when you were right in front of me all the time, bird in the hand."

Val studied him for a moment.

"Not the best analogy."

"Well, but you know what I mean. You. And me. Us."

"Yeah. Thing is, I'm not ready to be an 'us' just yet. With anyone. I'm enjoying being 'me.' I'm not in a hurry. Or back in high school."

"I . . . Okay . . . I just thought . . . the way we were talking . . ."

"As friends. Friends are good right now. And we're good at that."

"I . . . guess I can do that."

"See how it goes. Call it 'friends with potential?'"

"'Three Amigos' territory?"

"There you go."

Wally and Val sipped their drinks in silence, watching the sun drop.

Wally slept better that night than he had since he had moved to Blacktip. He took his time biking to the dive shop the next morning, enjoying the green of the mangroves, the thick scent of mud around their air roots, the twitters of birds in the foliage. He smiled to see Booger and Angela already at the shop, prepping the *J-Valve* for the morning's divers. He greeted them both, then stepped into the shop to update the day's dive roster. He had barely sat down when Booger stepped into the shop, face worried.

"Mister Wally, I hate to be the bearer . . . but there's a problem with the boat."

"Of course there is," Wally half-laughed.

"Don't know why we can't get out of this stretch of bad luck."

"It's not bad luck, Booger," Wally said. "It's just business as usual. Let's go take a look at the boat."

It's hard for books to get noticed these days. If you enjoyed *On Wahoo Reef,* (or even if you didn't), please consider writing a review on Amazon, Goodreads or wherever you hang out online. I read every review, and they're a huge help in making subsequent books even better.

For more about Blacktip Island and its quirky residents, check out *The Blacktip Times*, a weekly blog-fiction post in the form of the island's newspaper: https://blacktipisland.com/

To sign up for email alerts, go to:
http://www.timwjackson.com/contact.html

And if you haven't yet, check out *Blacktip Island* and *The Secret of Rosilita Flats*—*On Wahoo Reef*'s older siblings.

Cheers,

Tim

Printed in the USA
CPSIA information can be obtained
at www.ICGtesting.com
LVHW091025250724
786346LV00009B/780

9 781735 113654